MESSAGES

by

Mark West

ISBN 978-1-930322-29-5

MinRef Press

This book is dedicated to
Shau Ying...
for putting up with me for 40 years
and my
Children, *Sara and Sean*
and
a Special Recognition to
Michael
for going well above and beyond
to make this book the best it could be

Messages

Cast of Main Characters (in order of appearance):

Marsha Ford, Reporter, WMSG TV News
Danny Dunbar, Religious Speaker and Author
David Cranston, High School Senior
General Harris "Hope" Smithson, U.S. Air Force
Mary Hiddleston, Ph.D. NASA scientist
Ted Lang, Ph.D. Astrophysicist
Kylie Janeway, High School Sophomore
Ishmael Hadad, Middle School Student
Rylee Janeway, U.S. Navy Pilot, Astronaut
Troy Dickson, President of the United States

Prologue:

Somewhere, out in the far reaches of the solar system, gravity called to it. The rock had been among the home of frozen comets, beyond the darkness, beyond the tiny traveling caravan of Sol and its twirling planets. It mingled with the forgotten far distant remnants of system initiation.

A comet in the Oort cloud bumped it, nudging it to the edge, and also imparting velocity. It fell in and began the long, lonely journey down, down, toward the bottom of the gravity well, pulled in gently by the incessant need of Sol.

But there was an impediment, between the rock and the mighty star that called it. A dinosaur looked up and watched the rock die a burning death. The twirling planet shuddered at the impact, then, itself became part of the burning death.

Sixty-six million years later, another species looked up...

Ford: ~Two Weeks before Flyby

The Black woman tapped her lapel mike and got a thumbs up from her technician. She smiled and looked into the phone's camera that was mounted on a tripod. A second phone, on its own tripod, was pointed in the opposite direction. Bright LED light banks were also mounted on the tripods, illuminating the speakers. An older man with sparse red hair and thick glasses gazed at the second phone.

"This is WMSG News correspondent Marsha Ford. I'm reporting to you today from NASA's Planetary Defense Coordination Office in Washington D.C. I'm speaking with Dr. Gerald Spitzer, PDCO's Executive Director. Dr. Spitzer, thank you for agreeing to speak with me today."

"You're very welcome, Marsha."

"Dr. Spitzer, NASA has recently confirmed reports that in approximately two weeks from now, an extremely massive asteroid will either impact the Earth or pass very close to us. Can you comment on the accuracy of those reports?"

Spitzer smiled into the camera that was pointed at him. He was short and stocky. His eyes were a brilliant blue, and he exuded an air of calm and confidence. "Well, Marsha, you're certainly half right. We have identified a very large asteroid headed our way. Its closest approach to our planet will be approximately14 days from now."

Ford interrupted. "Some are classifying the asteroid as a dinosaur-killer-sized rock. Is that accurate?"

"Actually," Spitzer replied, "it's probably even bigger than the so-called Chicxulub asteroid that may have ended the reign of dinosaurs. My experts have assured me, however, that this asteroid will miss the Earth, despite its close approach."

"Exactly how close is close?"

"It's going to be very close," Spitzer said slowly, leaning forward. "It's expected to pass well within Earth's exosphere, or the most distant portion of our atmosphere."

"That sounds scary. Wouldn't Earth's gravity field capture

an object of that size, and that close, and pull it in?"

Spitzer chuckled briefly. "Conventional wisdom would support that hypothesis. However, in reality, this particular asteroid is traveling much too fast relative to Earth for that to happen. Gravity will cause the object to curve around the Earth very slightly as it passes, but its velocity is such that it cannot be captured by the Earth. So there is absolutely no danger of an impact."

Ford looked down at her notes, then back at Spitzer. "Some independent researchers dispute that assessment, Doctor, stating that even the smallest error in calculation could mean the end of life on this planet. Do you have any response to those researchers?"

"When the asteroid was first detected two years ago, and its orbit identified as a possible threat several months ago, we assembled a distinguished panel of scientists, astronomers, military officers, and even FEMA experts to assess all the observations and calculations. We observed the object, studied it, measured it, and in the final analysis, our findings were unanimously confirmed. Look, even if our calculations are off slightly, and the object enters Earth's thermosphere, it will still be traveling fast enough to carry it past the Earth and back out into space, like skipping a rock on water. I can assure you and your viewers, Ms. Ford, that we are in absolutely no danger, despite what irresponsible conspiracy theorists might claim."

"Given your assurances, what can we expect to see in two weeks?" Ford asked.

Spitzer chuckled again. "If you're fortunate enough to live somewhere in the middle portion of the Western Hemisphere, and the sky is relatively clear, what you see will be nothing short of Biblical. However, you'll have to look quickly, as the rock will be moving at forty to fifty thousand miles per hour relative to Earth. Imagine a shooting star, only about ten thousand times bigger, with a brief flare almost as bright as the sun."

Ford looked into the cell phone camera. "You're right, it's hard to imagine such a sight. So, in about two weeks we will know everything. Until then, as new information becomes available, we will provide special reports as needed. Thank you for your time, Dr. Spitzer. I'm sure we'll be speaking with you again as the asteroid gets closer to the Earth."

"My pleasure, Marsha."

"This is Marsha Ford reporting from NASA's PDCO. Back to you, David."

Ford stared at the camera for a second or two, then drew a finger across her throat and took a deep breath. "Thanks, Jack. Get that uploaded to the studio. We need to edit the back-and-forth and add in some graphics before this posts or airs."

"Got it, Marsha. I'll have the whole thing ready in two hours. I'm outta here." Jack detached the two speakers' lapel mikes, flipped his laptop closed, grabbed the tripods, and headed for his network van.

"How'd I do?" Marsha asked Dr. Spitzer.

Spitzer looked up from his computer. He seemed somewhat distracted. "Oh, yes. It was fine, thank you. Just fine..." his voice trailed off as his eyes returned to the computer screen.

"Is there, possibly, something you want to tell me?"

He looked back up. "Uh, no...nothing. Not right now, at least."

"Oh? Are you sure? You look a bit worried."

Spitzer sighed and sat back, giving his whole attention to the woman. "We're getting preliminary reports that some Earth stations are receiving anomalous radio signals..."

Ford looked alert. "Anomalous? What does that mean, exactly?"

Spitzer shrugged. "Strange, unidentified, unexpected.

Really, the word's definition is not difficult." Impatience had crept into his voice. He glanced again at his computer.

"Can you pinpoint the origin? Any possibility these signals have something to do with the asteroid?"

"Absolutely not. Well, probably not. Right now, the reports are unverified. We need to do more checking."

"But are you saying that these undetermined radio signals aren't originating from Earth? Is that an accurate assessment?"

"I'm sorry. For the moment, I'm really not at liberty to discuss that. The reports have just come in, and we need confirmation and verification. Our people are working on that aspect as we speak."

"But you're not denying it, either." She looked at him intently.

Spitzer did not respond, but when his eyes shifted away, Ford knew the answer, and her eyebrows rose.

"And this is happening at virtually the same time that an asteroid is going to hit the Earth?"

"As I told you before, it's not going to hit the Earth. We've been over that already."

"Yeah, but I'm a reporter. It's my job to not believe what people tell me, especially when they work for the government."

"I'm sure," he replied, his public smile fading. "I'm afraid I'll have to cut our conversion short for now. I've got some important meetings coming up."

Ford stood and swung her purse over her shoulder. "Thank you, Doctor. We'll be speaking again, soon, I'm sure." But Spitzer's eyes were already back on his computer screen.

Ford exited the Director's office. She checked her watch. She had some free time to kill before lunch, so she hung around the NASA facility a while longer, keeping her visitor badge prominently displayed. She took care to loiter near some of the other offices. While waiting, she used the time to arrange for an Uber later that afternoon, to pick her up, with stops to get her kids, then home. When she'd finished that task, she held the phone in front of her, trying to look busy, but in reality listening. Sometimes idle loitering resulted in snippets of conversation that could prove interesting.

That radio signal was tingling her intuition. She needed some expert advice. She pulled up her large collection of contacts and began searching through the hundreds of people who knew something about something. There had to be someone she knew who could clue her in about strange radio signals, possibly from space.

Ford was an up-and-coming reporter for the D.C. media. Within the past six months, she had scooped other reporters on three major stories, one of which had a Senator contemplating resignation. Her intelligence, determination, and ability to dig into the underlying facts were assets few others had. And she wasn't afraid to make people squirm.

Physically, however, Ford was rather unimpressive, with tightly-curled close-cropped black hair and a dark complexion. She was also rather short and very thin, and she wore glasses. Her diminutive stature certainly did not look intimidating, which she considered an asset. Ford also had the ability to hang a stupid expression on her attractive face, a technique that worked especially well with certain men. This sometimes resulted in the man explaining things in small words, revealing information, and saying stuff he would not otherwise have mentioned, convinced that the cute but ignorant little Black girl wouldn't understand. In such cases, she smiled, looked dumb, listened carefully, and soaked it all in like a sponge.

Her intuition was normally a reliable indicator. Today, that intuition pointed her toward those mysterious radio signals. While the big story on everyone's mind was the upcoming asteroid approach, Ford couldn't help but dwell on Spitzer's reluctance to talk about the signals. If there was nothing to it, he would have said so. Mystery drove ratings, and ratings elevated her career.

Her phone rang. "Ford," She said.

"It's Tito. Marsha, I want you to do a quick run over to National Harbor."

"Whatever for?"

"There's a speaker there. I want you to get his take on the asteroid. You need to hurry, though. He's packing up for his next gig in Boston."

"Name?"

"Danny Dunbar."

"Tito, I've heard of him. He's some kind of religious nutcase. I've got better things to do with my time."

"Listen to me. He's a popular speaker and he has half-a-million followers on his YouTube channel."

"So what? He's still a…"

"He's written three bestselling books."

Marsha sighed.

Tito said softly, "He's good for ratings. I've already made the arrangements. I really want you to do this."

"Oh, hell. Okay. I'm on my way. Damn you!"

Tito laughed. There went lunch.

When she arrived, Ford met Danny Dunbar in the hotel lobby. He was seated in one of the plush chairs with a cup of coffee on the table and a tablet in his hands. "Mr. Dunbar? I'm Marsha Ford, WMSG TV news. I was told you would be expecting me."

"Oh, yes." He stood and shook her hand. "This will have to be quick. I'm afraid I only have a few minutes before we head off to Boston. So what can I do for you?"

"I'd like to do a quick interview regarding the asteroid approach."

Dunbar looked around. "So where's your camera crew?"

Ford laughed. "I'll be doing this one solo, I'm afraid." She set up her phone on a mini-tripod she pulled from her purse. The light was barely okay. The setup stunk, but it would do.

"Ready?" Dunbar asked.

"Ready." A short pause. "Pastor Dunbar, can you give us your opinion of the giant asteroid that's approaching Earth."

"Certainly, Marsha."

"A lot of people believe it's going to hit the Earth. What do you think?"

Dunbar shook his head. "I really don't think so. An impact would cause immeasurable destruction, perhaps even extinction of the human race, and I don't believe God would let that happen."

"Do you see a spiritual aspect regarding this asteroid appearing at this time?"

Dunbar chuckled. "Scientists tell us that 66-million years ago, a similar asteroid burned up Earth's atmosphere to the extent that it caused the extinction of dinosaurs, along with many other species. While I don't completely agree with the chronology, dinosaurs were never meant to exist on Earth. So God removed them."

"I'm afraid I don't understand."

"Dinosaurs were never created by God, Ms. Marsh. Someone else had a hand in that."

"Someone else? That long ago?"

"I would invite you to attend my talk in Boston on Tuesday, Marsha. While I won't be addressing the asteroid, *per se*, my topics will make it clear why God won't allow this asteroid to impact our planet. If God sent this asteroid, He did it to send us a message. God protects His people, and there is a very good reason for that. But sometimes, He needs to get our attention."

"And that reason He needs that attention is...?"

"You'll have to come to my talk. I'm afraid I can't tell you any more at this time."

"I see. And if you're wrong?"

Dunbar smiled. "I place my trust in God. And in scientists, Marsha. Both convince me we will be fine, just fine."

"Thank you, Pastor Dunbar. This is Marsha Ford reporting from National Harbor."

"So...we're done?"

"Yes, Mr. Dunbar. Thank you for your time."

"My pleasure."

Marsha packed up her things and quickly exited the hotel. "I gave up my lunch, for this?" She thought, shaking her head. She rescheduled her Uber to pick her up here. The sooner she was away from that creepy preacher, the better she'd feel. Tito was going to pay for this!

She stepped off the curb as her ride drove up. She got in, sat back, and relaxed, putting Dunbar out of her mind and thinking of whom she might contact regarding radio astronomy.

A short time later, her phone rang. "Ford," she said.

"Tito here. That was a good story you did on the asteroid. We'll run it tonight. I'd like you to talk to Spitzer again in a couple of days. I want more depth." Tito paused. "And look, Marsha, if you find out that thing's going to hit us, we need to know about it, like immediately. You know that, right?"

"Of course," she replied. "He was pretty insistent that it would miss. I didn't get any vibes that he was lying. But I'll stay on it. These scientists could just simply be wrong, but if they are, I'll know about it. Then everybody will know. Then we'll all die."

"Yeah, there is that." Tito paused and she heard a sigh. Tito always seemed to have more on his mind than he was willing to share. It was a trait Marsha wanted to emulate.

"Uh, how did the meeting with Dunbar go?"

"It stunk, Tito. He's wacko."

"But you did get some usable footage, didn't you?"

"I'll send it to you. It's your decision. I think it was a waste of my time."

"Making contacts is never a waste. You'll see. Keep up the good work," he said, and hung up.

She didn't tell her boss about the radio signals. Not just yet, as she didn't have a story to go with her intuition. There was one out there; she was sure about that. She just had to dig it up.

The vehicle interrupted her thoughts when it pulled up to the daycare. Her daughter, Ana, waved and ran to the car.

Cranston: ~Two weeks before Flyby

"*Garbage!*" Seventeen-year-old David Cranston shook his head, but otherwise ignored his mother's shout.

"David, you listen to me, damn it!" she yelled from the living room.

"Mom, I'm doing my homework!" David replied from the kitchen. "I've got school today, you know."

Janet Cranston appeared at the kitchen door. "Your 'homework' right now, young man, is to get that freaking garbage out to the curb. The truck will be here in a few minutes. Now do it! And stop yelling. If we wake Biff up, neither one of us is gonna be happy."

She stepped into the kitchen, wearing a robe, with a bottle in one hand and an amber-filled glass in the other. Janet Cranston was a middle-aged woman, a bit overweight and certainly out-of-shape. She drank a lot and did not work. She lived frugally on the remnants of her dead husband's life insurance and the generosity of a string of loser boy friends. She had, in David's opinion, aged beyond the ability to attract non-losers.

David sighed and stood. His mom emptied the glass and poured another one as he brushed past. It was still a few minutes before 8 a.m. He had to leave for school in twenty minutes, and he still had homework to finish. David was disgusted.

His mother's latest beau was still in bed, sleeping off the previous night's binge. Bernard "Biff" Boyd was middle-aged, overweight, and he usually smelled bad. He was a minimally-employed auto mechanic who cut corners and cheated people. David hated the slob, and the feeling was mutual. This latest loser had been bunking with his mom for two months now. It was not a record, but he'd lasted longer than most.

Thankfully, it would all be over soon for David. He had to endure another three months before he graduated high school and could leave this dump. After that, he'd be free and looking forward to his university studies. He'd be on his own, and he couldn't wait.

David Cranston was tall and thin. He played varsity basketball and was pretty good at it. His eyes and hair were light brown, his skin held a light Winter tan. He was able to fully relax only around his good friends, but became intense when working on a math problem, shooting hoops, or some other task that interested him. He was a straight-A student in most of his classes, and he was one of the geeks everyone came to when they had technical problems with their electronics. His skill with various computer games was legendary among his high school peers. At one time, he had seriously considered a career designing such games but found the field was bloated with high-quality talent.

He was in contention for several scholarships, and had recently applied to a half-dozen universities, using all of his meager savings for the application fees. He'd mowed a lot of lawns for that money. Once he heard back, he would decide which institute of higher learning would be his new home, his avenue of escape. He was confident that his grades would allow him to choose the university rather than the other way around.

He was tempted to pick the school farthest from St. Louis and away from the influence of his mother.

Paradoxically, Cranston's earliest memories were happy ones. Back then, his parents were loving and close, and as a small only child, he was the center of their lives. Then alcohol, affairs, and arguments had changed everything. Fights, anger, and throwing stuff had replaced joy and fun. His life had become intolerable before his father died five years ago. He didn't think it could possibly get worse with just his mom, but he soon discovered that two terrible parents often canceled each other. When they were fighting, they left him alone. With Dad gone, Mom had only David to fight with, and she made the most of it.

He hurried outside with no jacket and pushed the large green container to the curb just as the truck turned the corner from Spring Avenue and began working its way up Russell Boulevard.

Shivering, he rushed back into the house, sat down, and tried to concentrate on his calculus homework. He was determined to finish his senior year by graduating with honors.

"So," his mom said from the doorway, "our brilliant student *can* manage to do some real work even if it only takes two minutes." Her voice was thick with drink and sarcasm.

David muttered under his breath. She just wouldn't let it go. Pick, pick, pick.

"What was that? What did you say?"

He calmly looked up at his mother. "Just as soon as I get accepted to a good school, I am so out of here. Then you'll have to take out your own damn garbage, or get that lazy bum in your bed to do it."

She leaned across the table and made blubbering noises at him. Then she smiled. "I've got a surprise for you, genius. I wasn't going to tell you until later, but maybe this will shut your yap up."

"I doubt it. And I'm not interested in your surprise."

"Oh, Sonny Boy, you should be." She snickered.

"Okay then, tell me."

"Surprise. You ain't goin' to no college." She said it slow and nasty.

"And why not? You can't stop me!"

She giggled. "Oh, yes, my darling baby boy. I *can* stop you. I already did stop you. Because I pulled all your envelopes out of the mailbox before the postman showed up. I ran all those silly applications through the shredder, then I added up all them checks and used that money to buy something worthwhile." She held up a half-full bottle and shook it. "Surprise, surprise."

David sat back, his eyes wide in disbelief. "You're not serious...you can't be..."

"Totally serious, Sonny Boy, I shredded and ripped and had a great 'ol time. Then, just to make sure, Biff and I burned everything. You ain't goin' to no college, hear me?" She took another drink and laughed. "Nope, not you. You're gonna stay stupid, just like your worthless father. You better learn to flip burgers, my boy."

He slammed his laptop closed and jumped to his feet, breathing hard. "If that's true..."

"What? You gonna do something? You gonna hurt me?"

"That was *my* money, Mom! I earned every dime. You had no right!"

"You live in *my* house, you eat *my* food Sonny Boy. So whatever money you earn while you're in this house goes to pay your rent."

"You tore up the checks, but how did you get access to my account?"

"Oh! Did my baby boy forget? That's right, you were only ten when we opened that account...that joint account."

"You *bitch!* You stinking mother..."

"Watch your mouth, boy. You better just watch it. Homelessness might be in your future, if you ain't careful."

"At least it would be an improvement," he shouted.

He heard a noise from the upper stairway. "What's going on down there?"

"No problem, Honey," Janet said, her voice suddenly sweet. "Just talking with my worthless son."

"Yeah, Bernard," David said sarcastically, "it's none of your business."

"We'll see whose business it is, boy," Boyd said from the stairs. "It's about time you learned some respect." The stairs creaked as the big man lumbered down.

"From you? That's a laugh." David shook his head again. He was angry enough to do something he'd later regret. And he was closer to tears than he wanted to admit. He started for his room in the basement, then decided that wouldn't do. If he stayed, he'd have to keep himself from confronting them both. That would only cause more trouble.

He grabbed his jacket and his laptop and slammed out the front door. He sat in his car for a few minutes, breathing hard. When the front door opened and a bare belly appeared, followed by an attached half-bald, half-dressed moron, his mother trying to hold him back, he knew it was time to be somewhere else. David turned the key, praying the old clunker would start. The engine protested, blowing smoke, but came to life, and David drove off.

He went to the coffee shop nearest the high school and tried to study. It didn't work. He'd pinned so much hope on getting into a good college or university...but now? He could re-mail the forms, of course. They were all on his laptop. But where could he get money for the fees?

His phone rang. It was Dwight James, his closest friend.

"How's it goin' Dude? You ready for this bright and terrific Tuesday morning?"

"No. It hasn't started so good, Dwight. I don't even know how to tell you how crappy it is."

"Must be somethin' bad. Real bad."

"Even worse than that, my friend."

He took a few minutes to relate the past hour to Dwight.

"Not believable. Must be some mistake. You're White, dude. Stuff like that don't happen to White dudes."

"Yeah, well. There's exceptions to every rule."

"So where you at?"

David was about to answer when his phone began clicking. There was a click and a pause, three more clicks, a pause, three more clicks, a pause, and another click. It didn't sound like static. He opened his mouth, "Did you hear that?"

Before James could reply, there came two clicks then two more, a short pause then three slow clicks.

"What are you talkin' about?"

"You didn't hear that?"

"Hear what, exactly? The only thing I heard was your frightfully frustrated breathing."

"Quiet. Here it goes again."

The sequence of clicks repeated.

"I did hear something that time," Dwight said slowly. "Very faint clicks."

"Not faint on my side," David said. "Cell phones don't usually pick up static, most of it's filtered out..."

"You're at that coffee shop, right? Maybe somebody's trying to hack into your phone."

"Possible. Wait, here it is again. The same pattern of clicks."

"Weird," Dwight said. "Good thing you got no money in your bank account to hack. Come to think of it, you ain't even got a piggy bank."

That hurt, but Cranston said nothing. Sometimes, Dwight could be a tad direct.

As David continued listening to the clicks, it started making a pattern in his head. He pulled out a pen and opened his notebook. "Look, gotta go. Call you soon."

"Yeah. We'll do something. Take your mind off you-know-who and you-know-who-else."

Dwight ended the call, but David kept his phone on. Even though the call disconnected, the pattern of clicks continued. Listening carefully, he was able to distinguish the length of pauses between clicks. He wrote the data down in a line across the top of his notebook. He ended up with a series of dots, dashes, and spaces, 55 of them to be exact. He thought about it for a moment. Were they just random clicks, caused by something nearby creating an interference pattern? Or? It wasn't likely, but...could it be a message of some kind? If so, what kind of message? And from where?

Smithson: ~Two Weeks before Flyby

General Harris "Hope" Smithson had joined the United States Air Force twenty years ago as an enlistee. Four years later he secured an appointment to the U.S. Air Force Academy in Colorado Springs. Following his graduation, he attended advanced pilot training at Vance Air Force Base in Oklahoma. He flew F-117 stealth fighters for two years then became a flight instructor. He was a decisive and competent leader, and moved up the ranks quickly. Smithson was promoted to Brigadier General in 2015, Major General in 2018, and Lieutenant General in 2020. He was named commander of Air Force Global Strike Command (AFGSC) shortly thereafter. In mid-2021, AFGSC was given primary responsibility for the development, deployment, and tracking of strategic space-based weapon systems at Barksdale Air Force Base in Louisiana.

This was not a command that General Smithson enjoyed. He did not really believe that space-based weapons would ever become viable threats or useful assets in a global confrontation. But here he was, in charge of a bunch of radar geeks and astronomers, as well as a gaggle of gung-ho wannabe Space Rangers. And he totally hated Louisiana.

Absolutely worst of the geeks was Colonel Roger Meyer. The T.O. labeled him as a chief research specialist. What he was...was Smithson's liaison in charge of nonsense. It was a good fit. Meyer considered himself a scientist first and an Air Force Colonel somewhere else on the list. He barely managed to conceal his contempt for the military, which irked Smithson to no end. Meyer's observance of proper military protocol was haphazard at best. And he seemed to have an almost inexhaustible supply of nonsense, which tended to keep him out of Smithson's hair much of the time, thankfully. But, not today.

"We've got something unusual happening, Hope," he said, bursting into Smithson's office without so much as a "by-your-leave."

Harris looked up from his computer screen and glared at the Colonel. Nobody came into his office without being announced, but Meyer kept forgetting about that courtesy. Smithson continued to stare. Was Meyer really that thick-headed?

The Colonel hesitated, looked confused, then the light came on, and he straightened himself and saluted. Smithson returned the salute but continued to stare.

"General..."

"Where is your service cap, Colonel?"

"Sir? I believe it's on my desk. Why? Sir?"

"Correct me if I'm wrong, but isn't your office across the quad?"

"Why, yes Sir. What..?"

"Did you walk here?"

"Well, of course."

"I'm sure you are aware that regulations require that you wear your cap if you are out of doors. Next time you come in here, I want to see that cap on your head or at your side. Understand me?"

Meyer turned red. "General, I have some very important information..."

"I asked you a question, Colonel."

Meyer sighed. "Yes, Sir. Thank you, Sir. I will wear my service cap next time. Now..."

"Good. And I would appreciate it if you would stop at the front desk and allow my receptionist to announce you. If that's not too much trouble."

"No, Sir. No trouble. I just...I needed to speak with you right away. I thought..."

"I understand, Colonel. But there are reasons for the way we do things in the Air Force. I'm sure you understand. Now, Colonel Meyer, what is the information so important that you felt it was necessary to neglect proper military protocol?"

It took a moment or two for Meyer to process his superior's words. When he found his voice, the excitement had returned. "We've picked up some anomalous radio signals, General..."

"From who?"

"That's just it, Sir. The signals appear to be coming from space, from somewhere beyond the range of our satellites."

"Have you fallen off the deep end, Colonel? There's nothing out there that can send radio signals."

Colonel Meyer hesitated. "Of course you're right, Sir. That's what makes this so exciting and important. The only possible sources for such signals are either a satellite or spacecraft in an orbit significantly beyond the Moon. Either somebody launched something we don't know anything about, or..."

"Or what, Colonel?"

"We have to consider the possibility that It might... be...uh, well, alien."

Smithson sat back in his chair. He didn't laugh, quite. "You mean bug-eyed monsters?"

"Sir, unless you can come up with a third alternative, yes. Aliens. Very near to Earth. Relatively speaking, of course."

"What kind of radio signals?"

"Uh, it's a repeating pattern of 55 dots and dashes and some spaces, along the lines of Morse code, but a little more sophisticated. The signal frequency is just at the lower end of the Water Hole."

"The Water what?"

Meyer waved his hand in frustration. "It's a range of radio frequencies that are relatively devoid of background noise. Between 1.42 and 1.67 gigahertz. We call it the Water Hole."

"I see. Have you detected a message of some kind in those dots and dashes?" Smithson asked slowly.

"Some of our team think there is, but so far we haven't made any sense of it. The, uh, 55 dots and dashes are received, then repeat a little over a minute later. This has been ongoing for over two hours so far. We think it has something to do with mathematics, General, as 55 can be factored into 5 and 11, which are both prime numbers. We've made a grid 11 wide and 5 down and plotted it, but it's still gibberish. John Harvey was working on the reverse when I left. We'll see if that has any significance."

"Colonel Meyer, what are the chances that this radio signal is nothing more than a hoax? Radio signals bounced off the Moon or something else floating around out there that we've forgotten about? And there's a lot of junk orbiting Earth these days, you know. Every once in a while a satellite may come back to life and start spewing out radio signals, coherent or otherwise. Hoax? Or resurrected satellite?"

"Uh, well, we're not sure. But we've checked with several radio telescopes around the globe, and those that can align with our coordinates are also receiving the signals. Whoever is sending this stuff, they aren't trying to hide it."

"That's what concerns me, Colonel. Makes it much more likely to be a hoax of some kind."

Meyer's phone began ringing. He glanced at it. "It's from Harvey, Sir. He may have more information. Excuse me for a moment," he turned away and bent over, speaking softly.

Dunbar: ~Two Weeks before Flyby

Danny Dunbar didn't consider himself a pastor or a priest. He was not the leader of a particular church nor was he affiliated with any recognized denomination. He had no flock of his own. He suspected that when it came right down to it, he did not even really believe in God. But he was a good public speaker, and he had a great imagination. That made him a popular guest speaker at churches all over North America and parts of Europe. Although he seldom spoke on Sundays, he packed in large crowds. And no matter what day of the week it was, large crowds gave donations. They also bought his books and subscribed to his YouTube channel. All which translated into income. A nice, fat, comfortable income.

Dunbar was 60 years old, but his hair, with a little help, was still mostly brown, and he had quite a bit of it. He wore shoes that elevated his five-nine height to five-eleven. It not only made him a bit taller, but he looked thinner as well. He was energetic and tended to pace while he talked.

He specialized in "alternate ideas" about the Bible and religion. For believers who had been fed "same ole, same ole" all their spiritual lives, he was a breath of fresh air. He never claimed to know the ultimate truth; he never pushed his findings or his beliefs on anyone. He made his case and let the listener make up their own minds. He had, however, written three best-selling books expanding on his rather unorthodox views of the Bible and religion. As long as the money kept rolling in, he would keep coming up with unusual things to say about God.

Today, he stood before a congregation of about three-hundred Christians, eager to hear his ideas. He'd just finished research on a brand new talk, one guaranteed to raise eyebrows. This was to be the first performance of his new material. The title? "Science and the World of Satan." His research had taken him months, and now it was ready. No doubts he was going to give them a message today! He liked preaching in Boston. The turnout was good and the dollars were great, but the crowd often tough to reach.

He gazed out over his audience. The majority of them were fundamentalist Christians, and they were wary of new ideas. Before he was finished, he suspected that many of them would be angry at him. A few would get up and walk out. Some would shout their dismay at him. Those who stayed, and listened, however, they'd give bigger donations. They'd buy all three of his books. They'd subscribe to his online channel. Cha-ching.

It always worked that way. Don't sugar-coat it. Don't water it down. He could give a rat's hairy hiney about those who couldn't take it. Whether or not he believed what he was preaching, himself, didn't enter into it. It just had to be logical and unique. He planned to buy himself a nice yacht, and this sermon would seal the down payment.

Along those lines, there were two young women in the second row. Super-model types. He smiled at them and they smiled back. He tried a quick wink, and the girls giggled and leaned toward each other, whispering. Maybe they'd ask for his autograph after the talk. If things worked out just right, he might invite them to visit his private jet. There was something about powerful preaching that caused particular reactions in some young women. He was not averse to taking advantage of those reactions.

He smiled and continued looking at his audience, eyes moving row upon row. The few people who had been speaking stopped. The shuffling of feet became quiet. Several latecomers found seats. A cough echoed. Now he was ready. His first rule: Always begin with a question.

"Who's in charge of this world?" he said, his voice fairly reverberated throughout the hall. Whenever possible, he had the A/V tech set the PA volume higher than normal for his first question. It got their attention and set the tone.

Silence was the reply. They suspected it was a trick question. Which, of course, it was.

"God," someone shouted, "the creator."

"Jesus!" another added.

Dunbar shook his head. "Wrong," he said. "In reality, the ruler of this world is Lucifer, Satan, the Devil." He let that sink in.

He heard murmurs of dissent from the audience.

"Let me explain," he said. "The Bible," he held his book up, "is a tall tale of an all-powerful creator God, the Devil that opposes Him, and the squishy, soft, and rather pathetic creations sandwiched in between. Predictably, the soft squishy things don't fare so well." The voices were quiet again. They were still suspicious, but he'd tossed out the worm. All he needed now was a nibble.

"People who don't believe in the creator God dismiss the whole Biblical thing as a fantasy or a myth. A good percentage of those who do believe in the creator God blame Him for all of the bad things that happen on this blighted world, based on the belief that Man is a sinful creature beyond redemption and must be punished. Except, of course, for the intervention of a Messiah.

Lucifer, on the other hand, gets pretty much a free ride. Dismissed from memory rather quickly, the Devil may be awarded momentary blame, but it's almost as if nobody really, deep down, believes in the Devil. Even those who spend their lives worshiping the creator God mention the Light Bearer only in passing, usually as a tool to illustrate human failure. This viewpoint may possibly be a mistake."

Hiddleston: ~Two Weeks before Flyby

Mary Hiddleston felt incredibly stupid. That feeling was especially galling for someone who fancied herself as a person intelligent enough to earn a Ph.D. In a hard science, no less. She had felt that way for two days now, and she was getting annoyed with herself. This morning, Hiddleston had made the decision to accept her stupidity and get on with her life. With a few minor changes.

She had just finished typing an important message on her laptop. It wasn't just a message, really. It was a letter of resignation. Almost three months ago, she had gotten involved, intimately, and stupidly it turned out, with her boss. That was a bad decision. Then it got worse. Two days ago, she had discovered that she was not the only intimate involvement Director John House had been engaged in with a female employee. Humiliated, she had decided at once to cut all ties with House and his government research lab.

Until House, Hiddleston had not had much of a social life. She'd never married, nor even dated much. Now, at 38, she was wedded to her work. Not that she was that unattractive. Her light brown hair was cut short and permed, and she had a pleasant, friendly face. No, the problem rested with her social skills. Or, rather, the lack of them. Raised in a poor family, she had studied hard to earn a scholarship. When that happened, Mary threw herself into her university studies in a field that was dominated by men. Arrogant men at that. She'd had half-a-dozen rather fruitless dates while earning her doctorate. There was nothing of any significance after until House had convinced her to accompany him to a play three months earlier. That had started a relationship for which she was woefully unprepared. Her gullibility and naivete, along with her lack of experience, had turned around and bit her.

If nothing else came of the experience, she learned fast and was not about to make the same mistakes twice.

Upon arrival at her office, she had boxed up her personal effects before starting the message. Now all she had left to do was hit "send" and walk out the door. Yet her finger hesitated over the key, knowing that action would begin a new chapter in her life. She did not feel quite ready for that.

She was a scientist working for NASA in the main office in Washington, D.C. She spent much of her time searching newly discovered planets that seemed to be within the Goldilocks Zone of their respective star systems. Her goal was to search for indications of intelligent life on those far distant planets. She examined possible alien radio signals, the use of solar transuranics, evidence of a Dyson sphere, and such. So far it had been a mostly fruitless search. There was, of course, Przybylski's Star, HD101065, its blazing interior filled with transuranics which tend to not appear naturally, especially in the innards of a star. Then there was the famous Tabby's Star, KIC8462852, in which there was a slim possibility that its periodic dimming was caused by a Dyson sphere, or at least a modified sphere. She also studied FRBs, but fast radio bursts, although not well understood, appeared to be natural in origin.

Mary loved her job. There was always the possibility that the next star system she studied might nail down strong evidence of an intelligent civilization. But now, she could no longer stand to be in the same building with House. The thought of seeing him in the flesh, so to speak, made her almost physically ill. She was obligated to keep her mouth shut about the whole mess. House was also the President's science advisor, and Hiddleston didn't want to create waves that might end up hurting innocent parties.

She took a deep breath, pressed "send" and held back tears.

She took one last look around her office. She'd been there for seven years and would miss it. She'd miss working with some truly talented colleagues, many of whom had become close friends.

Mary had just reached the door and flipped off the lights when her office phone rang. She hesitated. She didn't have to answer it; Mary Hiddleston didn't work there anymore. Officially, however, her resignation hadn't yet been accepted. Reluctantly, she stepped back to her desk and picked up the phone.

"Hiddleston," she said softly.

"I'm not accepting it," John House said quietly.

"You don't have a choice," Mary said firmly.

"You can't leave right now. We need you."

"The feeling is not mutual. You and I certainly don't need to be talking right now. I'm hanging up."

"No, wait. One minute, please! This isn't about us, it's about your work."

"I can't work for you anymore, House. And you certainly know why." She moved the phone away from her ear.

"That's why I'm reassigning you to Chandara Bell over in radio-astronomy. Stay and you'll be working for her."

Hiddleston hesitated, then moved the phone closer. "Why the sudden need to keep me under your thumb at this particular moment. You really think something is going to change?"

"I told you this wasn't about us and I meant it. Look, I made a mistake, I admit it. More than one. I'm owning up to it. But this is not about us; that's all over and done with. Some of the people working for Chandara have picked up odd radio signals, and she wants you."

"What kind of radio signals? From where?"

"Where do you think? Out there..."

"FRBs?"

"No," he said loudly. Then, in a softer tone, "we're not sure what they are, but they're regular, they repeat, and they are complex. We've never received anything like them before."

"Another 'wow' signal?"

"That was a one-off," House said. "This one repeats. In fact, it's still repeating now."

"Why me? Why now? They've got a lot of good people working over there."

"They need your help. You've got expertise they don't have."

"Nonsense. There are others..."

"Not with your talent. All I'm asking is that you give it two weeks. You won't see me, you won't hear from me. If you still want to leave at the end of two weeks, I won't say a word."

Mary started to reply, but paused.

"Two weeks. Okay? We have a deal?" House pushed.

"You're a real piece of work, House, you know that?" Mary said bitterly. She dearly wanted to slam the phone down and walk out. It took an almost physical effort for that not to happen.

"As I said, it's not..."

"I know, it's not about you. About us." Another long pause, then a deep sigh. "Okay, I'll give it two weeks. If you call, or I see you, or someone even mentions your name, I'm gone. Got it?"

"Yes. I assume you have your personal stuff already packed up. Report to Bell. They have an office for you. And Mary...?"

"What?"

"Good luck."

Mary slammed the phone down and almost burst into tears. She picked up her belongings and exited the building. She was determined to never return.

Lang: ~Six Years to One Month before Flyby

The university auditorium was filled with relatives, friends, and spouses. This was an auspicious day, much different than an earlier day almost six years previous. That was when William Bonner had gotten the call. He would never forget that call, not ever. At the time, he was living with his teenaged son, Jarad. His ex, Marianne, had gotten custody of their daughter, Vickie, now a college student.

The families lived in separate states, two hundred miles apart. The parents swapped children once or twice a year for week-long visits, but otherwise, they lived separate lives. And that, too, would have ended soon. Both kids were growing up, looking forward to their own independent lives. Bonner thought about the unrealized opportunities caused by the split; the joys of family life that didn't happen, the events missed, or not shared. If wishes were dishes he could feed an army.

Bonner was a real estate broker. He specialized in exclusive residences and high-end commercial properties. He worked very hard and enjoyed the riches of his success. He did not begrudge the alimony and child support he paid to Marianne every month. The relationship with the remote half of his family was not overly intimate but cordial. His relationship with his son had often been somewhat less than cordial, but it was far from antagonistic or hateful. Jarad was headstrong and driven, but he respected his father. He had dreams of a sports scholarship and perhaps even a professional football career. Bonner urged more down-to-earth dreams, and the two argued about it from time-to-time. Jarad was, indeed, an excellent high school varsity running back. He was hoping for a football scholarship, and his chances had been good.

But that was then, before the phone call, before Bonner decided to kill another human, six years ago.

Today, William sat in the third row of a square of several hundred folding chairs among a crowd of excited, happy people. Up on the stage, young men and women, along with a few older candidates, passed in review and received the reward of their hard work; a Doctorate. The commencement would be followed, that evening, by a banquet and a hooding ceremony.

Bonner was looking back at 50, and his hair, it seemed, insisted on being a decade older. Well, he'd been through a lot, and the remaining strands of gray hair he thought of as a symbol of his survival. His skin was somewhat tan and already speckled with age spots. His middle sported the White man's paunch, but the gut was not the result of over eating or excess alcohol, but rather due to lack of adequate exercise.

His success derived from an uncommon persistence and attention to detail. He worked very hard to get his clients the best representation possible. Because of his reputation, he had many repeat clients. He drove a late-model Lexus with all the options, and lived in a nice, rather small, but not overly ostentatious home in a gated community near Logan Square. Bonner and Jarad had lived a comfortable life with no more than usual father-son disagreements. Until, of course, he had gotten that phone call six years ago. That's when it all changed.

Bonner shifted uncomfortably in the hard metal folding chair and waited until he heard the name, Ted Lang, announced. A young, tall, shaved-headed Black man strode across the stage, a determined yet somewhat sad look on his face. Bonner joined in the applause, but his was a subdued applause, almost as if he didn't know it was the right thing to do. But after he had gotten that phone call, he'd made a decision, and he was going to see it through. All the way. No half measures. The young man received his diploma and headed for the stairs. Bonner stood up.

Six years ago, he had vowed to send a message to that same young man. It took him a lot of time and money, and considerable effort, to set things up.

It all started with that phone call, six years ago. It was from a Chicago police detective, Tyce Davidson. It was about Bonner's son, Jarad. The boy had been found early that morning, shot to death, at the entrance to an alley in a rather seedy part of town. It happened at night, just before midnight. Jarad had been hanging out with friends and was probably on his way home. They found his car parked around the corner.

"How? How could this happen?" Bonner had asked the detective when he arrived to take a report. The officer helped William to a chair. He found himself confused and unsteady on his feet.

"It looks like he may have interrupted a drug deal going bad. From what we can determine, Jarad probably walked past the alley, saw or heard something, and turned to look. Bullet took him in the chest. We don't have the Coroner's report yet, but it looks like he died instantly."

Bonner gazed at the officer in disbelief, tears streaming down his face.

"Mr. Bonner, was your son involved in any kind of gang activity?"

Bonner shook his head. "He was just a regular high school student. Home almost every evening except when he hung out with friends. Never any trouble with any of them. Good boys."

"Did he use drugs?"

"Not to my knowledge. If he was addicted to anything, it was football and girls. I just don't understand. Why? Why him?"

"Wrong place, wrong time, I'm sorry to say. Just a freak accident. It happens that way sometimes."

Bonner wiped his eyes and leaned forward. "Yeah, I suppose it does, but...do you know who did it? Do you have a suspect?"

Davidson shook his head. "No leads right now. We have a bullet casing, but no prints on it. The lab is processing the slug as we speak. If we get a match, that might give us a lead, but..."

"I still can't believe he's gone. I don't know how I'm going to tell his mother, his sister." He held his head in his hands and sobbed. Davidson watched, emotionless.

At that moment, Bonner's shock and sadness were joined by growing anger. He made a commitment that day to find the guilty party, even if the police couldn't. And he'd make whoever did this pay. Oh, how he would make him pay!

He was aided in his quest by an astute and persistent attorney. Bonner had, several years earlier, taken out a $250,000 life insurance policy on his son. It had a double-indemnity clause for accidental death. While Jarad had been murdered, the attorney was able to convince a court that his presence at the scene was completely and totally random, a chance event. The murder was not planned, it was not an act of passion or anger, it probably wasn't even intentional. It was almost certain that Jarad and his killer did not know each other. Thus his death was deemed accidental.

Marianne got half the payment, and Bonner's $250,000 allowed him to curtail his real estate activities temporarily and devote most of his time to finding his son's killer. He cultivated a friendship with detective Davidson, which occasionally gave him access to what would otherwise be privileged information. He became a subtle fixture in the run-down neighborhood where the killing had taken place. He hired a couple of private detectives who weren't too keen on following established and recognized protocols. They were, however, very good and very discreet.

Despite six months of investigation, the police had turned up nothing. They hadn't even found the murder weapon.

"Where's the damn gun that killed my son, Tyce?"

Davidson shrugged. "You'd be surprised how often the weapon in a murder case disappears or is never found."

"I'm beyond being surprised. What I'd like to see is some action."

"You and me, both. I'd give a month's pay for one solid lead."

The detective's voice sounded disingenuous, but then again, Davidson was dealing with seventeen open murder cases.

Eventually, Jarad's murder was relegated to the warm-case file, still hope, but no suspects and no leads. Within the same six months, Bonner's PIs had supplied him with a name, and a face. A teenager named Ted Lang. Bonner began making plans. He had the kid followed, got as much information about Lang and his activities as money could buy.

Lang was a high school kid, a senior. He dealt drugs, but did not seem to be part of a street gang. He kept a low profile, and was evidently not selling to get rich, but generated only enough dollars to meet his immediate needs. He was pretty much a loner, did not have many close friends.

Once he had sufficient information, Bonner began trailing the kid himself. He spent two months watching and noting the places where Lang hung out, who he visited, where the boy lived. Lang was Black, of course. The neighborhood was predominately African-American and Hispanic, and most residents were poor. Murder was common. After two more weeks of shadowing the boy, he had a good idea of Lang's day-to-day routine. Bonner determined that it was time to deliver his message. He picked a time and a place, and made a few arrangements. He spent extra money for a used handgun that could not be traced to him. He bought a car from a gang-member-owned chop shop, with clean plates registered to a dead old lady. Bonner's name was in no way associated with either the vehicle or the weapon.

He knew this about Lang: His school grades were good, sometimes excellent. He continued to deal drugs, but sporadically. He sometimes carried a gun, most likely a replacement for the missing murder weapon. Police did not consider Lang a suspect in the murder of Jarad Bonner, and Bonner had not informed Davidson of what he had discovered. William had gathered all the information he needed without help from the police. Now it was time to deliver his message, and he was going to do it on his own terms.

One evening, early November on a Friday, he followed Lang to a coffee shop in a neighborhood a little better and a few blocks removed from the kid's own. It was cold out, and snow was predicted for the next week.

Bonner watched from his car as Lang entered the shop and stood for a while looking at the tables. He did not make a purchase, but eventually went to a table near the front window and sat down. The boy reached over and shook a cup left by the previous occupant. He took a drink and grimaced. Lang looked around, then took out his phone and began scrolling.

A few minutes later, William casually entered the shop and placed an order. When he got his cup, he quietly joined Lang, sitting down next to the boy. The kid looked up, a bit of surprise on his face. His eyebrows went up.

"You are Ted Lang." It was not a question.

"That so? You a cop?" The boy shifted a few inches away.

Bonner shook his head and with his hand under the table, pushed the barrel of his handgun into the kid's side. Lang stiffened and kept his hands on the table.

Very softly, Lang said, "You got the wrong guy, cop."

"I'm not a cop."

"Then what do you want? Who are you?"

"Listen carefully. You are going to be very quiet. We're going to talk. Actually, I'm going to talk. You're going to listen. Then we'll get up and leave. We'll get into my car and go someplace very dark and very, very private. Then we'll talk some more. Got it?"

Lang looked down at the gun, mostly hidden by Bonner's overcoat. He looked back up and nodded.

"What's this all about. Who are you?"

Bonner sighed. "You see, you got it backwards already. I talk, you listen. If you don't like it that way, I'll shoot you right now, five or six times. When the cops get here, you'll be dead. And it would take a very bad jury to convict me. I'm a well respected and relatively rich White man, and you're...well, I don't want to be racist, but you're making it hard. So let's start over."

"Okay, okay," Lang said slowly. "But can you put that gun away?"

"No. Now shut up and listen."

Lang spread the fingers of his left hand and nodded.

"My name is William Bonner," the other said quietly. "Means nothing to me."

"Until six months ago, I had a son named Jarad Bonner."

William stopped talking and looked at the young man, but saw no reaction. "He walked past an alley and saw something. He stopped to look. Someone in that alley aimed a gun at him and pulled the trigger. That someone was you."

As Bonner spoke, Lang's eyes got larger and larger. He opened his mouth to speak, but Bonner wagged a finger at him.

"Now that you know who I am and why I'm here, this is the part where we get up and walk to my car. We're going to go very slow and careful. Pocket your phone and stand up. Try anything, anything at all, and you'll have more holes in you than a golf course. Now up."

As he stood, Bonner hid the gun in his overcoat, but made sure Lang could see that it was still pointed at him.

Lang slipped the phone in his shirt pocket and slowly stood. He reached for his cup.

"Leave it," Bonner said, "and carry your coat on the side away from me."

Together, the two exited the coffee shop and walked across the street to Bonner's car.

"You carrying?" Bonner asked.

"Huh?"

"A gun. You got a gun on you?"

"No," Lang said. He started to elaborate but decided to say nothing more.

The doors unlocked at Bonner's approach. He followed the kid to the passenger's side. "Get in, put on the seat belt."

Lang got in and clicked the belt. Bonner closed the door then went around to the driver's side, eyes fixed on Lang. He entered the car with the gun in his right hand. He switched hands while securing his own seat belt, then started the car.

"You're going to keep both hands in your lap where I can see them. You make any sudden moves, and they will be your last. Understand?"

"Yes. But..."

"Questions later. I've got a message for you, but before I deliver it, you need to know everything, so there's no doubt. Now be quiet and stay very, very relaxed."

Lang shrugged. "You going to kill me?"

"Quiet."

Bonner drove away. He had already picked out a place nearby. There was an abandoned warehouse on a street of similar abandoned properties. This one was so dilapidated even the homeless avoided it. It had a locked chain-link fence around it. Or at least it did until Bonner had cut the gate lock earlier that afternoon.

When they arrived, Bonner inched his vehicle up to the fence. A gentle bump and the gate swung open. He didn't think anyone would notice until morning. By then...

The wooden warehouse doors had collapsed years ago. The interior of the building was a black cave filled with debris and fixtures that could not easily be removed. The roof was well perforated and close to collapse. He pulled the vehicle in, then turned left and edged the car far enough so that the vehicle lights would not be visible from the street. He turned off the engine.

Bonner took a deep breath, his eyes staring into the darkness. "Until six months ago, I had a son named Jarad. One evening, he was walking in your neighborhood and stopped when he saw something in an alley. His curiosity got him shot. Right in the chest. Dead before he hit the sidewalk. Does any of this mean anything to you?"

Lang turned stricken eyes to Bonner. "That...was your son?"

"Then you do remember the incident? That's good. Very good."

"Of course I do," Lang shouted. "It was an accident. I swear. I was selling this cat some meth, and he didn't like the terms. Things were getting tense, man, because I couldn't drop the price, and he don't want to pay what I needed. Then I saw a shadow out the corner of my eye. I turned and saw someone standing there, and I panicked. My finger jerked and the gun went off. The other guy, he vanished like smoke. I went up to...to your son." Lang's voice broke and he wiped tears away. "He was dead. Not even much blood. Then I panicked again. I threw the gun on the roof of the building and took off. It was all an accident, a horrible, terrible accident. I swear!"

"You were selling drugs, slime ball," Bonner growled.

Lang paused. "I'm sorry, man. I didn't want to kill him. I never wanted to kill anyone." He stopped talking and broke into uncontrolled sobs.

"But you did kill him. You murdered my son. You got to pay for that."

"You don't understand. Listen, man. Please, don't kill me! I only sell drugs to pay for my sister's meds. If I'm gone, she's got no one. Please, man. *Please!*"

Bonner was silent for a long minute. He thought about everything the kid had said.

"You're a drug dealer and a liar. That doesn't give you a free pass. And that sob story is as old as dirt. No. You got to pay." He raised the gun.

"Mister, I'll take you to her. I'll show you. You can see her. Please listen. My sister's got a condition. She's very sick. The meds are expensive. We got no insurance. We got nobody else. It's just the two of us. You kill me, she dies too. I'll take you to her. You can see for yourself. *Please!*"

Bonner was silent for a long time, processing Lang's flood of words. Finally, his gun wavered. "Okay, fine. We'll switch places, you drive. I'm keeping the gun in my hand. You try anything...you try to go anywhere except your apartment..."

"Okay, okay. I'll do whatever you want. Just don't use that gun."

"Stay where you are until I'm ready." Bonner got out and went around the back of the car. He opened the passenger door and waved the gun as Lang slowly moved over to the driver's seat. "Seat belt on. I don't want you jumping out." Bonner slid into the passenger's seat. Both men clicked their belts. Lang driving, they backed out of the abandoned warehouse.

Bonner kept a close watch on Lang as he drove back to the neighborhood near where the shooting had taken place. They stopped in front of a run-down apartment complex with eight sad-looking units.

"This where you live?" Bonner asked. He knew the answer, but wanted to see how the kid responded.

Lang simply nodded.

"If things are as bad as you say, how do you afford the rent? You make that much money from drugs?"

"I do some maintenance work for the manager, just enough to keep the code cops off his butt. Which isn't much of a problem, they hardly ever come around." Lang looked at the complex and smiled sadly. "Don't matter much, we're still two months behind in rent. Janetta hasn't been doing too well this month."

"Your sister?"

Lang nodded.

"Okay, let's get this over with. Hand me the car key. Stay in the seat until I get out. Don't undo your seat belt until I tap on the window. Got it?"

Lang nodded.

Bonner carefully exited the vehicle and hurried around to the driver's side. He kept the gun in his hand, and his hand along the side of his leg. He tapped on the window.

Lang opened the door and stepped out. "Apartment six," he said softly, "ground floor, on the left."

"Yeah, I know," Bonner said. Lang stopped and stared, but said nothing. Then he continued.

As they walked to the complex, Bonner noted it was in even worse shape than it had looked from the parking lot. Calling it a dump didn't come close. "So you go to school, take care of your sister, and do maintenance?"

Lang nodded. "I don't get a whole lot of sleep." He pulled a keyring out of his pocket and unlocked the door to number six. It was dark inside, and cold. "Over here," Lang said quietly. He led Bonner to a bedroom with a missing door. There was a peculiar smell emanating from the bedroom. It was not a pleasant odor.

"Janetta?" Lang whispered.

If the kid was going to pull a fast one, Bonner knew this was his last chance. He kept the gun ready. Then he heard a soft, feminine voice. "Teddy?"

"It's me, Baby. I'm going to turn on the light, okay." Lang's voice was soft and loving.

"Okay."

"I've got a visitor with me, so don't be scared."

"Who is it?"

"Uh, just a friend. He wants to meet you."

"How old is she?" William asked.

He heard Lang fumbling with a light switch. "She's ten, but she don't look that old."

Subdued light flooded the room. Bonner realized it was a low-watt bulb. Even so, Janetta squinted and complained.

He saw a thin, almost stick figure laying on the bed. Her eyes were large and moving, but the rest of her was so thin, Bonner couldn't see how she managed to still be alive.

"Who is he?"

"I told you. He's kind of a friend."

"He looks like a cop. And he's White."

"He's not a cop. Relax Jan, he won't hurt you."

Bonner slid the gun in his coat pocket. "I'm happy to meet

you, Janetta," he said softly. He kept his voice neutral. This was not going the way he'd planned.

The girl looked at Bonner. She didn't smile. He wasn't sure she was capable of it. He watched as Lang opened a bedside drawer and extracted a pill bottle. He poured some water and held the girl's head up so she could swallow the pill and the water. Lang silently showed Bonner the bottle. There were two pills left in it.

"Good girl," Lang said. He lowered her back to the pillow, then bent over and gently kissed her forehead. "Now you go back to sleep, okay."

"You won't leave?"

"Not for a while, Baby. I'll tell you if I got to go out, okay?"

"Okay. I'm a little bit hungry."

"I'll get you something in a few minutes. All right?"

"I'd like more soup. We got any crackers? Those... those little oyster crackers. I like those."

"I'll check, Jan. Maybe."

Lang led Bonner back to the living room, and they sat in well-worn overstuffed chairs.

"So..." Lang said, finally.

Bonner stared at the young man. Then he sighed. "You have placed me in an untenable situation. I think you know the reason I'm here is to blow your brains out. But of course, that is no longer possible. I could break your legs, but that would lead to consequences almost as bad as killing you. My goal is to make *you* pay, not your sister."

"I don't want you to kill me, Mr. Bonner. I would like to ask your forgiveness, but I know I don't deserve it. I did what I did and I can't change that." Lang sighed and looked bleak. "If you go into the kitchen, you won't find much food in there. The only way I can get food is to sell some dope or steal it, but if I do either of those and get caught, Janetta doesn't get her meds."

"How long have things been like this?"

Lang looked angry. He leaned forward, rested elbows on his knees, and held his head in his hands, staring at the ratty carpet. "How long? Since our mom died last year. We've just been getting by, and sometimes we ain't been getting by." He wiped an unwanted tear from his cheek and looked up at the older man. "Can you imagine, Mr. Bonner, how hard it is to get to sleep when all you've had to eat that day was breakfast. And a small one at that. And worse, all your sister can eat is soup, and there's only half a can left in the fridge. And I don't have to go look. There ain't no crackers."

"No, son, I can't imagine being that hungry. But I can imagine the pain. For months, I hurt from the loss of my son. I hurt bad, still do. And all I could imagine, the only thing that kept me going, was the pleasure of putting a bullet between your eyes. You deserve it, you know that, right?"

Lang nodded without hesitation.

Bonner pulled out the gun and looked at it. He sighed. "I came here to give you a message." He put the gun back in his pocket. "It's not going to be the message I had planned on." He stared at the young man until Lang became uncomfortable. Bonner leaned forward. "Okay, son, here's how it's going to go down. I'm going to give you a hundred thousand dollars, money from my son's life insurance. In exchange for that, you need to stop selling drugs. You need to graduate from high school, then I want to see you in college. Within six years, I want you to have earned a doctorate. In something. Doesn't matter what."

"I—I don't understand." Lang leaned back in the chair. He looked like he was about to collapse.

"I'm giving you money for school," Bonner said. He and Lang both stood. "You won't need to sell drugs anymore.

Whatever your sister needs, doctors, drugs, tests, get it for her. I'll pay for that, too. If the hundred thou isn't enough for you to earn a doctorate, I'll give you more. But you have to keep a squeaky-clean police record, and you got to earn that Ph.D. or else I find you and finish delivering the original message. Got it?"

"I still don't understand. You came here to kill me, now you're giving me money? What the..."

"I'm not giving you money, Lang, I'm buying my son's legacy through you."

"I—I can't...I don't understand."

"I don't, either. Not really. But this feels right. And I usually listen to my feelings."

"If what you're saying is real, how can I possibly thank you?"

"I don't want your thanks. I don't want your gratitude, ever. I only want your performance. And I want you to never, ever forget what you did to me by taking my son away. I want you to go to your grave remembering that, you understand?"

"Yes, Sir, I understand."

"Good. Now, call me tomorrow," he handed the kid his business card. "We'll get a bank account set up for you." He gave the kid all the cash in his wallet, a few twenties. "Go get some food, and some more pills. I'll be back tomorrow afternoon, after school gets out. Be here." Bonner turned and walked out the door.

Lang looked stunned, his hand out, still holding the cash. He kept opening his mouth, then closing it. Finally, he collapsed back into the chair, holding his head in his hands, his entire body shaking with sobs.

By late afternoon of the next day, he had a bank account. A hundred thousand dollars, just as Bonner said. And he'd made an appointment to see a specialist for Janetta. Bonner showed up the following day with keys to a basic late-model automobile. "Think about moving into a better apartment, with some damned heat in it. Go get yourself some new clothes," Bonner said, "and don't miss Janetta's appointment tomorrow."

"I won't," Lang said with a hesitant smile, which grew as he looked at the car keys in his hand. "No, Sir, I won't. And I'll get that Ph.D. Don't you worry about it." They walked to the door together.

Bonner turned and smiled. "Oh, I won't worry at all. I've still got my gun."

That was the last he heard from Lang for almost a month. He got weekly reports from the one detective still on retainer, and the kid seemed to be keeping up his end of the bargain. Before Bonner released the detective, he had him retrieve the gun Lang had tossed to the roof near where Jarad had been shot. Bonner made sure that piece of evidence would never be found.

Three weeks later, Bonner's phone rang at 2 a.m. He sat up in bed and looked for his phone, found it on the end table under the book he'd been reading. "Hello," he grunted.

Silence answered. Then, softly, "She's gone."

"Who is this? Ted? Is that you, Ted?"

"She was so small and innocent," Lang whispered, "Oh God, she won't know what to do. She barely had a chance to attend school. I can't remember the last time she got to play outside. She was the only thing in this world I had left." The voice broke into sobs. "Now I'm alone, man. Totally alone."

"No, you're not," Bonner said firmly. "I'll be over to see you in the morning. Now you try to get some sleep."

When he arrived the next morning, the little girl's room was empty. Lang said nothing, his grief-stricken face unable to maintain composure. Bonner put his arms around the teenager and held him for a long time, until the crying stopped. Then he sat the boy down and listened to him talk.

"My dad disappeared before I turned three," Lang said, staring at nothing. "When I was eight, Mama got pregnant again. She wouldn't tell me who the father was, got mad at me if I asked about it. I was in the waiting room when the baby was born. I got to pick her name, Janetta, after *Euphaedra Janetta*, an African butterfly. She was so beautiful. So small and so beautiful. We were poor, man, but we had a good life together. Mama worked two jobs. She didn't have no education, but she knew a lot. Then she got cancer, and Janetta got sick, too. Doctor once told me he thought it might be 'cause of the water in this hell hole part of town. Now they're both gone." He broke down again.

Bonner helped Lang make arrangements for a funeral, then, after considerable thought, moved the boy into his own home, into Jarad's room. Over time, as the months passed, they became almost father and son. At first, Lang was quiet and serious. He'd suffered too many shocks in his young life. He applied himself to his school studies. He graduated later that Spring with honors and a couple of scholarships. He attended a local college for two years where he tutored other students in advanced math and graduated at the top of his class. He then moved East where he'd been accepted by an Ivy League university. There he majored in astronomy and physics. His grade point average only once dropped below 4.0. Lang also insisted on working to help pay for his tuition, books, lab fees, and apartment. He shared the apartment with two other students. Bonner was amazed and pleased at how Lang stretched every dollar that touched his hand. The older man was prepared to pay all of Lang's education costs, but ended up spending very little.

Bonner watched his ersatz son grow from a quiet youngster to a confident young man. After a time, the kid began to laugh and even found the courage to pull a couple of innocent pranks on Bonner. The young man visited home during holidays and between semesters. While the older man would often chuckle, and his praise for the young man was frequent and sincere, they seldom laughed together. Despite everything they had gone through, there remained a gap between them. It did not unduly affect their relationship, but neither did it fade away over time.

Six years from the month Jarad had been killed, the commencement ceremony over, Bonner shook Lang's hand. "Congratulations, Doctor." His smile reflected both pride and joy.

Lang grinned. "I still can't believe it, Mr. Bonner. I've already lined up a job. In a few months, I'll be a Professor of Astrophysics." The grin faded. "I just wish my mom, and especially Janetta, could've been here to see this."

Bonner smiled. "You did them proud."

"How can I ever repay you?"

"You already have."

"When I get a job, I'll pay you back every dollar..."

"Don't. Pay it forward, instead. Find some other worthy person in trouble and help them. Do it in memory of Jarad."

"I will, Sir. I certainly will. Don't you worry, Mr. Bonner, I will honor your son in every way I can. I will never forget him, and I'll do everything I can to make sure the world doesn't forget him."

"Thank you, Doctor."

Smithson: ~Two Weeks before Flyby

Colonel Meyer spent a good five minutes hunched over his phone, intently talking with his associate, and ignoring General Smithson, his commanding officer.

Smithson managed to be patient, which was a struggle for him. By his way of thinking, the military was built on four foundations; discipline, training, culture, and protocol. Smithson saw them as four legs of a chair. Remove any one leg and the damn chair would tip over. Meyer, he determined, was missing a couple of those legs. How he'd ended up a colonel...

Smithson ran a hand over his short-cropped silver hair. His allocated time for nonsense was just about over. Meyer's phone conversation was low-pitched but sometimes heated. Finally he hung up. He stared at the phone for a moment, then sighed.

"Well," Meyer said finally, a statement, not a question.

"Colonel," Smithson said, "if you've got something more to tell me, please do so. I have another meeting in about five minutes."

"Harvey thinks he's found a message in that radio signal."

"He thinks?"

"Yes, Sir. It's a very simple message. Charted, it makes an extremely simple drawing, and displays some numbers."

"And you call that a message?"

"Well, yes, Sir. It's perfect for a first contact. It's simple and based on mathematics. We're hoping that whoever sent it will give us subsequent messages that contain more complex data."

"Don't you think it's a bit suspicious, Colonel, that this... mysterious...radio signal shows up at just about the same time that an asteroid is heading right for Earth?"

"What are you implying, General?"

Smithson smiled. "It could be that the asteroid is not an asteroid at all, but a giant alien spacecraft. What do you think about that?"

"Impossible, Sir. We have photos of that asteroid. They're not the best pictures, but it's definitely a rock, not a craft."

"Maybe it's a craft that's been designed to look like a rock. Have you considered that?"

Meyer looked skeptical. Then he changed the look to a thoughtful one so as not to unduly upset his commanding officer. "It's a possibility. We'll certainly look into it."

"Good. Now get out. I've got a meeting."

After Meyer left, Smithson poured himself a drink, the other half of his "meeting." That crap about alien craft disguised as an asteroid ought to keep the Commandant of Nonsense out of his hair for a day or two.

Now, he had to consider what action to take in the event the busybody scientists were wrong and that damned rock was headed for an impact with Earth. He didn't trust scientists. He didn't much like them, either. So he was going to consult with what he considered to be real scientists; Air Force fire control experts. They would tell him if it were possible to launch a nuclear-tipped rocket to intercept and destroy, or at least deflect, that stinking asteroid. It was his duty to advise the Joint Chiefs and the President, and he was, by damn, going to have answers before they started asking questions.

He picked up his old-fashioned land-line phone, which was totally secure, and called several experts. He set up meetings for the next day. Let the dreamers dream, he thought. His military scientists would give him a plan that worked. No aliens needed. After hanging up the phone, his unease turned to confidence. Asteroid? No problem.

Later that evening, Smithson headed home to his wife and teenage daughter, neither of whom were speaking to him at the moment, but for different reasons. He smiled grimly. Military discipline did not work as well at home as it did in his office. Both females knew they had to toe the line, but it sometimes took a while for them to realize it.

A military officer, even the one in charge of the whole base, was not entirely a free agent. He couldn't order civilian contractors to drop everything and come fix a leaky toilet. Nor could he interfere in a public school and somehow stop certain boys, and even some girls, from calling his daughter a few unflattering names.

The home on base was standard military housing. Anywhere else, its age, lack of repairs, and sporadic shoddy maintenance would label it sub-standard housing. On base, however, Smithson's home was quite a coup, despite its view of nothing more than a vermin-infested swamp in the back and an overgrown golf course in the front. It was reasonably clean and almost everything worked, although there was that leaky toilet upstairs and he suspected mold in one of the downstairs bathrooms. Nothing but the best for our nation's military.

His wife, Monica, was plain looking and a bit overweight. His daughter, Nora, was even fatter and uglier, and she knew it. Smithson smiled. He realized that many less-than-perfect looking people often made up for it by cultivating a winning personality. Others, including his wife and daughter, went the arrogant snot route. He suspected Nora had learned from her mother, although after 18 years of marriage, Monica had begun to trade in her own snot and arrogance for apathy.

Despite their lack of filial intimacy, she enjoyed being the wife of the base commander. The perks were adequate, and she had a knack for bossing around Air Force personnel. Thus, she was not well-liked, which caused her to be bored and lonely. And like everybody else in the family, she hated Louisiana. Monica was persistent in her nagging. Why couldn't her husband get a base a little further North, where the weather wouldn't be so hot and sweaty? And they probably shouldn't be living on base anyway, not with all those noisy jets flying around day and night.

Smithson had learned not to bring up the subject of bugs. Both the women in his home absolutely hated bugs, of which they had plenty both in number and variety. Monica would attack them with grim determination. Nora, on the other hand, ran screaming from anything larger than a flea, gums and butt cheeks flapping.

While Smithson and his spouse still slept in the same bed, he and Monica had not had intimate relations for a couple of years worth of months. Smithson had resorted to visiting hookers once or twice a month. He mildly wondered if any of them were Russian spies. He kind of hoped they might be. He smiled again. If any were spies, they certainly put out a lot of effort for no results. Smithson knew how to keep his mouth shut.

Kylie: ~Two Weeks before Flyby

After the bell, Kylie Janeway walked to the front of her Current Events class. Mr. Carter had told her to stay after. Kylie was 16 and bubbly-cute and quite full of herself. She was a sophomore at Lakeside High School in Redmond, Washington. Her grades were terrible not because she was stupid, but because she was a self-proclaimed "wild child" and didn't give a horse's ass about grades. She was often in trouble both at home and at school, sometimes for the same reasons.

"Thank you for staying, Kylie."

"Sure, Mr. Carter." She gave him her sexy kitten look, which he ignored.

He stared at her for a moment, then half-smiled. "I wanted to remind you that your report on the asteroid is due Monday."

"I'll remember."

Mr. Carter nodded. "Glad to hear it. If you do a good job, I can give you a passing grade for this semester. And it shouldn't be too difficult since your sister will be observing the flyby from the International Space Station. You have a unique opportunity, so don't blow it."

"Okay, Mr. Carter. I'll see you on Monday."

But she didn't see her teacher on Monday. She never saw him again.

Somehow, she ended up at a party. An older boy driving a red sports car saw her walking home and invited her to join him and some friends. She bounced on for several more steps, pretending to ignore him, but listening to his spiel. He was good-looking and had a nice, friendly smile. He had the hint of an accent, just enough to give him an exotic flair. He seemed to be college-age, which made him even more alluring.

He honked once, then looked at her expectedly. She stopped walking, put her index finger against pouting lips, and smiled.

He stopped the car. "Come on! You don't want to miss this. It will be fun."

"You really want me to come to your party?"

"Absolutely."

"Don't you want somebody older?"

"I want *you*, girl. Come on, get in."

"Where is this party?"

"At my fraternity house. It's not far from here."

Kylie thought for a moment longer. "So what's your name?"

"Chad. Chad Thomas." He crooked a finger at her and she walked over to the car window.

"It will be fun. You'll love it. Lots to eat, lots to drink, and some other stuff you might like." He winked.

What the hell. She ran around to the passenger side of the car and got in.

"Seat belt on," he said in a fatherly manner. She clicked the belt. Chad stomped the gas and squealed tires. Booming music erupted from the sound system. Kylie laughed and sat back. She dropped her shoes and put her feet on the dashboard, her dress sliding up and showing a lot of leg. Chad took several quick looks and licked his lips.

Kylie laughed again. It was the weekend. All she had waiting for her at home were yelling parents and a stupid report that would probably never get done. It was party time!

Despite her "wild child" persona, Kylie was still a virgin. She had gone down that road quite a ways several times with various boys, but had never "crossed the bridge," so to speak. Maybe Chad would be the one. She was in that frame of mind. She gazed at him while he drove, trying to make up her mind. He reached over and put a hand on her knee and she smiled back at him. Kylie was, if nothing else, confident that she could take care of herself.

They pulled up to a large, older, two-story house. A half-dozen cars were parked around the place. Chad eased up behind one of the cars and cut the engine. Kylie could hear music and laughter coming from the home. She could hardly wait to meet Chad's friends and get happy!

Chad unlocked the front door and held it for Kylie. "I'm back!" He shouted over the music, "and I found what I was looking for." He put an arm over Kylie's shoulder and led her into the living room.

Kylie was surprised to find all the other party-goers were male. She counted seven young men and no other women.

Someone turned down the music.

"Guys, this is Kylie. She's here to help us party!"

Kylie grabbed his arm. "How come there aren't any other girls here?"

"Oh, they'll be along shortly, don't you worry your little pug nose. We'll have some great fun while we're waiting." Kylie frowned. There was a strange vibe in the house.

Chad introduced his fellows. Someone handed her a glass filled with an amber liquid. "Drink up, Kitten," he said. Kylie took a drink while the boys watched, and got bubbles up her nose. She coughed and tried not to spray anybody, and was mostly successful. She took another drink and it went down better.

Several minutes later, she was relaxed and happy, sitting in a chair with Chad, cradled in his arm, listening to music and talk.

That was the last thing she remembered clearly.

The remainder of that night was a confusing sequence of visions. She was placed on a bed in one of the rooms, dimly lit. Each of the young men visited her that night, some of them more than once. She was only partially conscious and unable to protest or resist. When she seemed to be coming out of it, they gave her more amber liquid to drink. She cried. Sometimes she managed a scream, which got her slapped. But she was unable to rise from the bed or in any way attempt to escape the assaults. Sometimes she fell asleep but was awakened by pain or company.

She slowly regained consciousness the next morning to discover she was only partially dressed, laying in the yard outside. All the cars were gone. When Kylie got to her feet, she stumbled to the front door and pounded on it. There was no answer. She sat on the steps and cried.

Later, she decided to walk home. It was not easy because she didn't know exactly where she was, and she had no shoes. A few blocks away from the house, a police car pulled up next to her. The officer saw a disheveled teenager wearing nothing but a t-shirt, bloody underwear, and suffering from various bruises and cuts. He called for an ambulance and a backup.

Once in the police car, Kylie gave the officers directions and pointed out the house where the assault had taken place. It was empty. There was no sign it had ever been a fraternity house. Detectives were called in to search for clues. All the evidence, however, had been removed. In a dull, monotone voice, Kylie gave police descriptions of Chad and what she could remember of his friends.

At the hospital, Kylie was told that she had been drugged and then raped multiple times, and assaulted in other ways.

She was tested and probed, evidence was collected which would, hopefully, give police a DNA match. After an almost endless number of medical assaults on her dignity, she was told her parents were in the waiting room to take her home.

"I think you should spend one more night here in the hospital," her doctor advised. "But if you want to, I'll process your discharge and you can go home with your parents."

"Yes, please. I want to go home." Her voice was hoarse and her eyes still puffy from crying. She couldn't look at the doctor.

"Fine. I'll prescribe some pain medication. Keep yourself well hydrated. Use this cream," he handed her a tube, "on the abrasions and wounds. You're going to be pretty sore for a few days, but you don't seem to have suffered any permanent physical damage."

"Am...am I pregnant?"

The doctor shrugged. "Only time will tell. It doesn't look like any of the...subjects...was concerned with that aspect."

Kylie cried some more.

She dressed in clothes brought by her parents, then walked slowly to the waiting room. She really didn't want to deal with her mom and dad. She just wanted to climb into a hole and die.

Both Mom and Dad tried to hug her, but she pulled away. She did not want to be touched. Nor could she look them in the eyes. They said nothing of any substance, it was all just noise. She followed them out of the emergency room, head down. Once in the car, she lay down in the back seat and did nothing to stop the tears from flowing.

Ford: ~Two Weeks before Flyby

Ford opened the car door and Ana exploded in, squealing and hugging her mother. The driver got a car seat from the trunk and installed it next to Ford. Then it was on to the middle school for Cherise. Finally, the three of them were dropped at the condo where they had a two-bedroom unit on the seventh floor. On the drive home, Marsha had been fully briefed on the girls' day. They were so full of bubbling enthusiasm, it was like a shot of caffeine for Ford.

She couldn't keep a smile off her face as she ushered the girls through the doors of their building and into the elevator.

Ford unlocked the condo door and dropped her purse on a chair placed there for that very purpose. Shoes were next, followed by a deep sigh of relief. That carpet felt like a cloud.

"So, Ana Banana, what do you want for dinner?"

"I'm not a banana. And I want pizza." She plopped down in the living room, turned on the television, and went straight to the cartoon channel.

"We had pizza last night," Cherise said. "How about soup and salad, Mom?"

"I *hate* salad," Ana said indignantly.

"Girls!" Marsha said, loud enough to get their attention. "We're having soup and salad," she held up a finger before Ana could protest, "and leftover pizza. How's that?"

"I could do without the temptation, but okay," Cherise said with youthful dignity. She was a beauty, slender and athletic, sporting a one-tract mind and an artistic flair. Ana, on the other hand, was off in all directions at once, filled with energy and joy and a burning curiosity.

"Me too! Me too! Pizza and soup and salad, my favorites!" Ana said, jumping up from the floor and doing a dance.

Marsha laughed. "Okay. Cherise, homework. Ana Banana, turn that off and get your shower out of the way. When you're both done, dinner will be on the table."

"Okay, but I'm *not* a banana," the little girl giggled and ran off to the bathroom.

Ford grinned and watched as her kids happily went to work on their tasks. She couldn't describe how much she loved her kids. They were super. Happy, intelligent, and obediently disobedient.

Todd was their father, but Todd wasn't around much. He had a slight but consistent drinking problem, which had resulted in some tension. His real flaw, though, was an insatiable search for high adventure. Ford thought he might even have a subliminal death wish of some kind. He loved wing flying, once flew through the (to her) small opening at the mountain top of Heaven's Gate in China. He did bungee jumping off the tower in Macau. He'd hunted wild boar in Argentina with a bow and arrow. He visited primitive, and dangerous, tribes in the Amazon, and was a dirt-bike enthusiast who cheated death every time he rode. He'd broken several bones, and if they gave awards for concussions, Todd would have some major trophies.

In the early days, before the kids, when Marsha and Todd were together all the time, she got experience behind a camera by recording some of his daredevil stunts. She posted some of her work online, and it garnered her the attention she was looking for, and led, indirectly, to her current career. It got to the point, however, where she was no longer able to watch Todd narrowly cheat death over and over.

So Marsha and Todd decided early on that they would be on-and-off lovers. Her career aspirations and his love of adventure were too demanding and diverse, with not enough wiggle room to allow for an ongoing intimate relationship.

On one of his visits, she had gotten pregnant with Cherise. Seven years later, another visit gave them Ana. Now, he visited once or twice a year, stayed a few weeks, then was off scuba diving among sharks in Japan, or climbing a mountain nobody else had ever heard of. But he always remembered to send presents for birthdays and Christmas, sent money when he had extra. Otherwise, he did not involve his family in his relentless search for adventure.

Marsha expected that someday, she'd receive a phone call or an email message with news that the girls' father had killed himself in some totally off-the-wall method. Until then, she and the girls looked forward to his infrequent visits, and otherwise tried to get on with their lives without him. When she and Todd were alone, Marsha referred to him as the Black Indiana Knievel.

Ford popped five slices of pizza into the oven, and set a pot of tomato soup on the stove, both set to low. She made short work of three salads with her own home-made balsamic vinegar dressing that all three of them liked.

She then sat down and called a friend at a rival network. "Harry? This is Marsha Ford...yes, I'm fine. And you? That's great, good to hear it. Listen, I'm trying to find someone to talk to. Needs to be a scientist, maybe somebody who once worked on the SETI program. No...no, nothing specific. I just have some procedural questions that I need to get straight. What? Yes, of course. If something comes of it, I'll let you know. You got someone? Great! Can I get a name? Wait a minute. Let me write that down." She grabbed a pen and jotted for a few minutes. "Awesome, Harry. That's just what I needed. Thanks. I'll get back to you if I turn up anything. Okay. Take care. Bye."

Ford looked at the name on her pad. Mary Hiddleston wasn't someone she was familiar with. Harry told Ford she worked at NASA headquarters and searched for signs of intelligent life around other stars. Sounded like she might have just the information Ford needed.

She checked her food and kids, saw they were both still simmering. She checked the time, saw it was twenty before five, then called the number Harry had given her.

The phone rang three times. "Hello?"

"Is this Mary Hiddleston?"

"I'm sorry, Ms. Hiddleston is no longer at this office. Could someone else assist you?"

"This is Marsha Ford with WMSG News. Can you tell me how to get hold of Ms. Hiddleston?"

"I believe she was recently assigned to the Special Projects division at the Goddard Space Flight Center in Greenbelt. In one of the annexes, I think. Can I give you her new phone number?"

"Yes, please." She got the number and called. Since it was late afternoon, she expected to get only voice mail. She was surprised when the call was answered.

"Hiddleston. Can I help you?

"Hello. My name is Marsha Ford. I'm a reporter for..."

"I recognize your name," Hiddleston said. "What can I do for you?"

"I have some questions that you might be able to help me answer. Is there any chance we could get together for a quick interview?"

"Ms. Ford, I'm very busy, and I'm not interested in appearing on a news report. I'm sure you understand."

"I do understand, Ms. Hiddleston. At this stage, I'm only doing research. I can assure you that you won't be on camera, and your name won't be mentioned. I just need answers to some questions, and I need an expert to help me understand some concepts that are, quite frankly, beyond my ability to understand."

The other woman was silent for a time. "I guess that would be okay," she said, finally. "I don't see the harm in that. I have an hour available tomorrow at three in the afternoon. Does that suit you?"

"Perfectly," Ford said. "I'll see you then."

Dinner was awesome and fun. She laughed and relaxed, and wallowed in the warm loving presence and joy of her two awesomely beautiful children.

Dunbar: ~Two Weeks before Flyby

"Critics have said that if the Bible were the true Word of God, there should be science in it. Scientific principles, they say, don't change. I certainly agree. There should be scientific principles in the Bible if the God who created the universe is the same being who also inspired the Bible. Because that very God would certainly have also created those same scientific principles."

He pulled the line to wiggle the worm. He could see them thinking. Just a little wiggle, and he'd have a bite.

"But we've been told time and time again that no such science exists in the Good Book. Or have we been told wrong? Maybe we should take a closer look. The Bible tells us that our creator is a single being, God, expressed as a trinity; Father, Son, and Holy Spirit. This is religion (by-the-way, the word 'religion' itself means 'to join' or 'to bind'). Albert Einstein has taught us that our universe is made up of two things, expressed as four: Space-Time and Matter-Energy. This is science. In the first verse of the first chapter of the first book in the Bible, it is written *In the beginning*. There you go. That's time. *Then God created the heavens*. That's space. *And God said 'let there be light'* That's energy. Right after that, He began creating stars and planets. That's mass. So we find all of Einstein's four basic elements of existence are there in the very first words of the Bible."

That got a reaction.

He continued, "We've been told by scientists that approximately 13.8 billion years ago, our universe did not exist. There was a single object, we are told, a quantum singularity, existing within a void. We are told by some scientists that all the matter and energy that makes up our entire universe was contained in this singularity which, they hypothesize, was about the size of a tiny round BB. A highly compacted object, with everything compressed to the max. Density was infinite and the laws of physics were on vacation.

"Before time and space, before matter and energy, was the quantum singularity. So think about this: If density is infinite, and there is no space, does that mean time inside the singularity is irrelevant? If density is infinite, does space, time, matter, and energy merge into one? Is that not the exact definition of a singularity? So if our entire universe existed as a BB-sized singularity, wouldn't time, space, matter, and energy all be infinite? Just. Like. Heaven?

"Scientists tell us that at the end of infinity, this singularity became unstable and exploded, hence the Big Bang. However, in space there is no atmosphere to carry sound waves so *'let there light'* is a more scientifically accurate description."

He was losing some of his audience. Science and religion didn't mix well, and it's a stiff mixture to swallow. But this was stuff they needed to know for the rest of his hypothesis to work.

"Most of what makes up our universe consists of what scientists call *Dark Matter* and *Dark Energy*, which they hypothesize exists but have as yet found no reliable way to detect or measure. The stuff you can see and hold in your hands; stars, planets, galaxies, rocks, iPhones, etcetera, makes up only a tiny percentage of the total volume of the universe.

God, on the other hand, took somewhat less than 13.8 billion years to create the universe. He spoke it into existence, and it was. Here we have two separate and distinct creation events, one scientific and one religious.

"What if," he paused, "what if both creation events began with the same quantum singularity? One might assume that Heaven, the home of the creator God, existed before space, time, matter, and energy since these things were all created by God. And the Bible hints that God existed before the universe...or (scientifically speaking) before the singularity became unstable. What if this eternal quantum singularity and the eternal Heaven were one and the same? They both would have gone on forever had not something bad happened."

Whoa! That created a stir.

He continued, "What does the Bible say about Heaven? Some confuse descriptions of the New Jerusalem with the descriptions of Heaven. The New Jerusalem is described as a giant city which, it is said, will descend to the earth after Jesus comes again. The New Jerusalem is not Heaven, but it is from Heaven and therefore some of the descriptions may be useful to help us understand the characteristics of Heaven. Let's look at some of them. In Revelation 7:16-17: *They shall hunger no more, neither thirst any more; neither shall the sun light on them, nor any heat. For the Lamb which is in the midst of the throne shall feed them, and shall lead them unto living fountains of waters: and God shall wipe away all tears from their eyes.* In Revelation 21:4-6 continues this thought: *There shall be no more death, neither sorrow, nor crying, neither shall there be any more pain: for the former things are passed away. And he that sat upon the throne said, Behold, I make all things new...It is done. I am Alpha and Omega, the beginning and the end.'* In Revelation 22:5 there is this: *And there shall be no night there; and they need no candle, neither light of the sun; for the Lord God giveth them light: and they shall reign for ever and ever.*"

Dunbar stopped and gazed at this audience. There were no more murmurs of possible dissent. Everyone listened with their full attention.

"Are these verses a description of what it might be like inside a quantum singularity?

"Like that singularity, Heaven is eternal. Inhabitants will not be hungry or thirsty. There won't be death or pain. No need for a sun. Everything is being made new.

"Today there is debate among scientists as to whether our universe will continue to expand infinitely, or if it will contract back into the original singularity. Most believe the universe will continue to expand and radiate until it reaches a state of maximum entropy; a continuum with little or no mass-energy, no gravity, and probably no space-time. An endless, timeless, empty void if you will. A universe under control of a creator God, on the other hand, might reach a certain point in its expansion, then begin to contract to eventually reach its original singularity state. But, unlike Einstein's universe, God's universe was created for a purpose, that purpose being to purge itself of evil."

These were some heavy ideas for a simple church congregation. He paused again to let them assimilate the information.

"Now imagine, if it were possible, to be alive and conscious while inside a singularity the size of a BB, with infinite space-time and infinite mass-energy. Take it one step further and imagine that singularity under the control of a creator being. Imagine, if you can imagine it, a conscious quantum singularity."

He paused again. He saw people whispering to each other. He saw many heads shaking. They'd taken the bait, and he'd been toying with them on the line. Now it was time to reel them in.

"So how did our (godless) universe come into being? We are told that somehow, an infinite, everlasting, ultimately dense singularity became unstable, which resulted in a massive explosion. At the same instant relativity took over and mass-energy and space-time appeared. Most of this new universe consisted of dark matter and dark energy. In fact, the visible stuff we think of as mass and energy actually makes up only about one-half of one percent of the entire universe. We just can't see or detect the majority of the stuff in our universe, so we've designated it *dark energy* and *dark matter*. We are told that dark energy makes up about two-thirds of our universe and the remaining one-third consists of dark matter.

"Scientists tell us that the universe expanded, spherically, from the singularity, spewing out mass and energy, visible and invisible. Slowly, the universe as we know it began to form. Stars, planets, and galaxies started to self-create through the actions of energy, mass, and gravity.

"In the Bible, we are told that the creator God, in His Trinity, plus an unknown number of creations we call angels, resided in a perfect, infinite Heaven. Did the creator God exist before He created the universe? If so, did the Heaven in which He resided also exist before God created the universe? And if this Heaven existed before the creation of the universe, was it populated by both the creator God *and* the creations known as angels?"

He allowed the questions to hang. For a small moment, he stopped reeling in his audience. He gave them time to think about everything he'd said so far. He'd dropped a few bombs, but the real explosions were still to come.

Cranston: ~Two Weeks before Flyby

As David hoped, the clicks continued to repeat in the background. He looked at the line of dots and dashes in his notebook. They almost looked like a message of some kind. He realized that the number 55 could be factored into the prime numbers of 5 and 11. What if he put the numbers into a rectangular stack, five across and eleven down? As he plotted the data, he was astonished to see that the first five rows created a triangle pattern. Below that was a gap consisting of only dashes, empty space. The last three rows contained both dashes and dots. He thought about it for a long time, then it hit him. Dots and dashes, ones and zeros. It was binary! He was stunned to realize those last three rows, expressed as binary, were the base ten equivalents of 1,2,3,4,5.

By damn, it *was* a message of some kind. A very simple message, but multi-layered and complex nonetheless. But where in the world did it come from? He'd never heard of a cell phone receiving anything like that. He looked around the coffee shop. There were the usual half-dozen people engrossed in their laptops or cell phones, couples leaning close and quietly conversing, a couple of older people reading newspapers. No one else seemed to have a puzzled look on their face. No one had the shady, contemptuous look of an imagined hacker.

David turned his phone off, waited a minute or two, then turned it back on. Once the phone booted and reconnected, the clicks resumed. He turned off the wireless, and the clicks continued. That meant it was something on the cell phone radio frequency rather than data, which made it less likely, though not impossible, that he was dealing with some kind of hacker.

He called Dwight. "Dude, you got time before class to meet me here at the coffee shop?"

"Sure. What's up?"

"I need somebody to put my brain back inside my head. You're the only one I trust."

"Brains are my specialty. Be right there." Dwight drove an old pickup he called the "gumball machine" due to the fact that parts routinely fell off and the rust that remained was held together, as the boy put it, with various types and flavors of gum.

Ten minutes after he hung up, David heard the distinctive clatter of the other's truck. Dwight James met David in the coffee shop a few minutes later. James was tall, Black, and gay, and thus routinely faced a double-dose of discrimination. However, his winning smile and pleasant demeanor tended to deflect much of the animosity directed at his race and sexual orientation. It helped that he was an ardent student of the Krav Maga fighting style, and that he also played second base on the varsity baseball team.

James's life goal was in the field of medicine. As an adequate student, he would probably struggle with pre-med classes, but had no doubt he would eventually pass. When he omitted sports and applied himself, his grades improved significantly. He had the brains and temperament to become an excellent physician, he just needed the motivation. And, of course, money. James had a close relationship with an 18-year-old who had graduated the previous year and went on to college. They had plans to meet up next school year after James graduated, and room together at college. Assuming, of course, that James found a way to afford the tuition and all the other costs associated with a college education. So far, it wasn't looking good.

James and Cranston had been best friends since junior high school. Their relationship was close but platonic.

James looked under the table. "I don't see any brains lying around," he said, spinning the chair around to sit and lean up against the back. "Of course, you didn't have many of those things to begin with, so..."

"Can it. Check this out." He showed Dwight his chart.

"Interesting. But this little bitty thing made your brain explode?"

Cranston put his hands together, then separated them, fingers wiggling. "Boom," he said.

James laughed, but David remained serious.

Cranston was quiet for a long time, staring at the chart. "I think it's a radio signal, but I can't figure out why my phone is picking it up. It just doesn't look like something a hoaxer would bother with. It's too simple, and no way to cause trouble or steal money. I don't know why, exactly, but I'm beginning to think it came from somewhere besides Earth."

Dwight's eyes widened. "You tellin' me..." He used an index finger to point up.

"I can think of several other explanations, but that one," he glanced up, "seems to be the most logical."

"Nah, got to be another source. I ain't seen alien spaceships for at least a week. Dude, you gotta stop watching them old monster movies."

"I want you to listen to this," he held up his phone and turned up the volume. The dots and dashes continued, repeating every three minutes and eighteen seconds.

"You got that," Dwight pointed to the chart, "from *that?*"

"Dots and dashes and spaces in the first part, my friend. On and off, ones and zeroes for the second part. Binary code. Only, why is my phone picking it up?"

Dwight shrugged.

"How many languages you know," David asked.

"You mean if you count English?" Dwight answered, "Two. Couple more I can make out, but can't speak worth a..."

"This *is* language," David said firmly. "It's a message. They're trying to tell us something."

"Whoever *they* are." Dwight's eyes flicked toward the ceiling.

"Hey, you guys. Basketball season's over. Time to lighten up on the sports talk." The speaker was a thin, blonde beauty. Samantha Rivera was also a classmate at the high school. She and David were an on-again, off-again thing. Despite being strongly attracted to each other, they never allowed their relationship to fully blossom. Sam was headed to the West Coast for college, while Cranston had his eyes set on an East Coast school, which would separate them by an entire continent.

Other than an occasional date with David, Samantha was rather aloof. She lived with her mom, a stepdad, and his eight-year-old son. Her real dad had died five years ago in an auto accident, and her mom re-married two years later. While she got along with her stepdad just fine, they were not close, though she adored her step-brother. Samantha was a good, though not excellent student. She could have parlayed her looks and personality into extreme popularity, but instead, she maintained a low profile. She was a member of the Pep Squad, but not the leader. She had run for class treasurer, but lost. She participated in a few other extracurricular activities, but did not stand out. David often wondered about that, but didn't pursue the matter as he preferred her exactly the way she was.

Dwight looked up. "David's got a big headache. Brain exploded. I'm practicing some brain surgery. Tryin' to get that gray-matter back where it belongs."

Samantha laughed. She absconded with a chair from the next table and sat down. "You get it all back in there?"

Dwight shrugged. "No problem. Plenty of room."

Sam joined in the laughter. David ignored them.

"So, what's going on?" Samantha asked, taking a drink from David's coffee cup. She grimaced. "This stuff's cold."

"David's got a mystery," Dwight said.

Sam raised an eyebrow, so David explained the signals he was receiving and how using prime numbers he had extracted a coherent albeit mysterious message.

"And you think these signals are coming from somewhere other than Earth?"

"That's what I suspect," Cranston said. He reached for his coffee cup, remembered what Samantha had said about its contents, then put it back down.

"Can I listen?"

He handed his phone to the woman. "Hear the dots and dashes?"

"I hear 'em."

David laid out his chart so that she could follow along. She listened intently.

"How are you receiving this on your freaking phone?" She asked.

"I don't..."

Dwight snapped his fingers. "Didn't you download that SETI app a long time ago, before they shut it down?"

"Come to think of it..."

"Bet it's still running in the background."

"By damn," David said.

"You've had that phone since junior high," James said, "when you gonna get a new one?"

"Soon as I can afford it," Cranston said, "which will probably be never."

"You guys be quiet. I can't hear..."

David and Dwight leaned away from Sam and changed the subject.

"What's this about your Mom deep-sixing your college apps?" Dwight asked.

David shook his head. "I still can't believe it. The bitch grabbed all my applications before the mail was picked up, tore everything up, including the application fees. But I've made up my mind. No matter what, I'm going to some kind of school away from here and away from her. I don't know how I'm going to do it, I just can't stay here. I especially can't deal with that beer-bellied boyfriend of hers."

"I hear you, Dude."

Samantha began waving her hand urgently, interrupting the boys' soft conversation.

"What?" Dwight asked.

"Get over here! It changed. Listen."

David looked startled. "What changed?"

"The pattern. It's different now. Lots more dots and dashes."

David reached for his phone. "You're kidding."

He put the phone to his ear and sure enough, the pattern was different, and much longer. He listened intently for a moment, then flipped his notebook open and began feverishly marking down dots, dashes, and spaces. He did so for almost ten minutes, until he was sure the sequence had begun repeating. He'd filled two pages with the data. He listened to the pattern again, making sure he got everything right. His friends watched silently and did not interrupt.

He looked at the larger pattern, trying to make some sense of it. He tried the prime number trick again, but this sequence seemed too complex for that to work. There had to be another key, a logical but mathematical key. He knew it had to be included in the overall pattern. He noted a slight extra pause before the first dot. That was followed by a dash, another dash, a pause, two dashes, a pause, three dashes, another pause, five dashes, pause, eight dashes...then it hit him. "Holy Batman, Cow, this is the Fibonacci sequence," he said, a bit too loud for the coffee shop's subdued ambiance. He glanced around in embarrassment, but was too excited to really care.

"The Fibonacci sequence? What's that?" Samantha asked.

"Sounds like a disease," Dwight commented, "or a plate of fake spaghetti."

Samantha snorted a laugh. "Right. What the hell is fake spaghetti?"

James shrugged. "Faux noodles?"

"Same to you," Sam said. They both laughed.

"Okay, guys. Enough of that. This is important."

"So explain this fib a noxious sequence," James said.

David looked up, made sure only his friends were listening. "It's a mathematical sequence in which each number is the sum of the two previous numbers," he said softly. "It's a pattern that's found in nature, in music, just about everywhere. Get this, if you take the exact length of Earth's year, 365.242 days, and divide it by the Fibonacci ratio of 13/8 you get 224.7 days, which is exactly a year on Venus. The sequence is also called the Golden Ratio and a few other things."

"Now *I've* got a headache," Samantha said. "You walk around with *that* kind of stuff in your head?"

"Now I'm lookin' for *my* brain," Dwight added. "Sounds like magic."

"All of this data is another key, just like the first one," Cranston said. "The key tells us the next series is going to be larger, with more information. Once this ends, I'll bet we get a slew of dashes, dots, and pauses. They're getting ready to send something really complex."

"Who?" Samantha asked. "Who is going to send this?"

"He thinks they're aliens," Dwight said.

David looked up. "Right, it's aliens. I'm sure of it."

"You mean, like, little green men?"

"Well," David said, looking at his chart, "they probably won't all be, like, male types. And they probably won't be green."

Sam's look changed from wonder to concern. "If you're serious, and you're right, I'll need to talk to my Grandpa."

"He a scientist?" Dwight asked.

Samantha shook her head. "Not exactly. But if it's aliens, he'd know what to do."

David was still listening intently and writing.

"So, what now?" Dwight asked.

David thought for a moment. "Right now, the code is just repeating. Eventually, it will change again. When the next sequence comes in," he said slowly, "it's going to be orders of magnitude larger than the first one." He looked around the coffee shop. "This isn't the place to work on that. We're gonna need room. And paper. Lots of it."

"Can't you just input all that stuff into a computer?" Samantha said.

Cranston shook his head. "The data is going to come in as dashes, dots, and spaces. But what they're actually sending is going to be visual. We need to lay it out first, *then* input it into a PC."

"They got some of that kind of paper in the AP math lab at school," Dwight said. "Maybe we can get permission to use some of that." He glanced at his watch. "We're already late for English class."

"Brilliant, my friend." Cranston stood, "Let's go. When the second part of this message starts coming in, we need to be ready."

"I'm coming, too. This could be some serious..."

Ishmael: ~One Month before Flyby

Ishmael Hadad walked from the gym to English class. He was slender, with jet black hair that needed a trim. He was not tall and looked younger than his fourteen years. His eyes were black and his features Arabic, including what his father called the Middle-East Beak, a rather large, hooked nose they both shared. Ishmael had brilliant white teeth and a wide smile.

The middle-school was new to him, and he hoped he could make some new friends here. In reality, he belonged in high school, probably as a Junior. Despite his age, he was learning at a college level in many of his subjects. The family had recently arrived in the center of nowhere Texas from Saudi Arabia. And middle school was where the Office of Education had put him, based primarily on his age rather than his academic achievement.

While his grades were excellent, and he'd taken, and passed, numerous high school and college-level classes back home, he was stuck in middle school for the next two or three months. He wasn't sure he'd like it. These Texas kids had a tendency to look at him suspiciously.

Next year, his Dad had promised, he'd be taking upper-level high school and AP college classes. Ishmael's goal was to earn a Bachelor's degree before he turned sixteen. He couldn't do that in this school full of functionally illiterate cowboys.

"Hey! Mo-Ham-Head," someone called from outdoor tables near the cafeteria. This was followed by laughter. Ishmael looked and saw three male students, sitting on the table, feet on the bench. They watched him closely.

He put on a bright smile and walked over. "Call me Ishmael," he said.

The boys didn't react, obviously not getting the literary reference.

"You some kind of Moslem?" the one in the middle asked.

"I'm Muslim, yes."

"Well, Mo-Ham-Head, we don't know how you ended up here, but we don't like your kind. This here's an American school. We already got too many Blacks and Mexicans, and we certainly don't need no Moslems."

"I'm sorry you feel that way. I wish we could get along and be friends. But if not, I'll try to be quiet and invisible. You probably won't even notice I'm around. Okay?"

The one in the middle spit out a grass blade, aiming it in Ishmael's direction. "Not okay, Mo-Ham-Head."

"Why do you keep calling me that? My name's Ishmael, like in the book."

The kid on the left laughed. "This Arab thinks we read books, Chet. Catch a clue, Habib, unless you got a bomb on you somewheres, you ain't gonna have much fun in this school."

Ishmael opened his sweater. "See guys, no bomb, and just books in my backpack. So, you gonna tell me your names?"

"I'm Chet," the middle one said. "My dad's the Mayor of this crap town."

Chet pointed to the boy on his left. "That's Dod."

"My dad's the police chief," Dod said. "That means we get to do just about anything we want around here. Got it?"

"What about him?" Ishmael pointed to the one on the right.

Chet laughed. "That's Timmy. His dad's in prison." The two boys laughed and Timmy looked annoyed.

"Prison?" Ishmael said. "How come?"

"His Pop raped a Mexican girl."

"He did not!" Tommy replied hotly. "It was conceptial. I mean consexual, I mean consensual."

"She was fifteen, dumb ass," Dod said.

"She still wanted it," Timmy said.

"Yeah," Chet laughed, "right up until she started putting on weight, if you know what I mean."

"This is all very confusing, guys," Ishmael said, "I'd like to stay and talk, but I got a class. Nice to meet you."

"Dude thinks we met," Dod laughed.

Ishmael hurried off to his English class. He was truly confused. Much of the conversation didn't make sense to him. While he had an excellent command of English, the jargon and colloquiums were hard to decipher. Add in the central Texas drawl, and it was almost a foreign language.

English out of books was a lot easier to understand.

He had hoped this transition to a new home would be smoother than it was turning out. He was beginning to suspect his parents had made a terrible mistake.

Hiddleston: ~Two Weeks before Flyby

Mary Hiddleston didn't know very much about radio astronomy. Chandara Bell had welcomed her new employee in an offhanded manner, gotten Hiddleston settled into an office that made her old office look plush and new. Radio astronomy apparently did not warrant a large budget. Her new office was inside an older building near, but not within, the District. Here, she had no windows and she was going to miss her sink. No more making her own coffee. There was a small staff lounge one floor up. She had sampled the communal coffee there. It tasted like something out of an old septic tank.

No view, no sink, and she was appalled to find on her desk an antiquated Dell computer still running Windows 7. Previously, she'd done most of her work on a late model Apple iMac with dual 27-inch screens. Her 'new' PC had a single 19-inch monitor covered in dust and fingerprints and, she suspected, a plethora of ink marks. She hated people who used ink pens as pointers for their monitors.

Judging from the flatness of her office chair, and a lingering redolent odor reminiscent of a horse barn, Hiddleston surmised the previous occupant of the office had been a fat man with a methane problem. She sighed. While the smell could be tolerated, getting used to a single monitor was going to be torture.

Coincidentally, Bell was unhappy filling one of her coveted offices with someone who might not be an asset to her department. Hiddleston was there for one reason, and one reason only, and that reason had almost nothing to do with the long-term goals of radio astronomy.

To top it all off, the newcomer's salary came straight out of Bell's budget.

Chandara Bell was tall, stately, and middle-aged. She had been born and raised in Jamaica. She still spoke with a very slight Jamaican accent, but worked hard to suppress it. Her straightened black hair was streaked with gray and her eyes were dark blue. She had full lips and a bosom that drew stares. And she quite often resented those stares. It hadn't been an easy road for her, leaving family and friends in Jamaica for college in the U.S. She'd made the most of her opportunity, however. While she was still in high school, her father had sold his boat tour business, and then surprised his daughter by giving her most of the proceeds for her college expenses. That made Bell more determined than ever to make him proud of her. She excelled in college, and at graduate school, eventually earning a Doctorate and landing a coveted position with NASA. She'd started near the bottom and worked her way up. Two years ago, she'd been named Director of her division.

Her initial interview with Hiddleston was short and exhibited a wariness on both sides.

"I've read some of your papers," Bell told Hiddleston. "You're doing some interesting work, but I don't see..."

"Me either," Hiddleston replied. "I was told you were in need of my expertise regarding some radio signals you've received."

Bell smiled. "Not exactly. We didn't receive the signals.

That's not really our area of interest, either, but we've been asked to assist the military..."

"It's not really mine, as well. I know how to position and operate the TESS, but that's not really relevant to this situation."

Bell frowned. "I'm not familiar with that acronym."

"Oh. It's the Transiting Exoplanet Survey Satellite, a space telescope designed to look for exoplanets."

"Well, that kind of fits in with our mission. We're interested in radio emissions that come from much farther away than this particular signal."

"FRBs?" Hiddleston asked.

"Right. And other sources. That group of military types began receiving unknown radio signals a few days ago. The signals appear to be coming from space, but not too far away. The mean orbit of Mars would be the most distant origin based on the amplitude, orientation, and signal strength."

"So what are you telling me?" Hiddleston asked.

"Some of the soldiers think it's alien, and it's close to us. They really don't say as much in so many words, but that's the implication."

"And what do you think?"

"I think they've been drinking too much of their own kool-aid over at the Naval Observatory. But I can't dismiss it. If they're right..."

"I see. If they're right, we've got a major discovery on our hands."

"Other stations have picked up the signals, too. So it's not an issue with the receiving station. The signals are definitely real."

"And my job?"

Bell sighed. "I'm not quite sure how to define your role here. Quite frankly, I didn't request you. I took you on as a favor to a...friend, a favor that I'm beginning to suspect I'll end up regretting. No offense, but at the moment, you're a liability. Ideally, we need to confirm the signals, make sense of them, and then determine their origin. If we can frame those goals as questions, and answer them, then we get to the three hard questions. If aliens are originating the signals, who are they? Where do they come from? And what is their purpose for contacting us? That's six questions, total. How many of those do you think you can answer?"

Hiddleston hesitated. She was beginning to suspect that House had thrown her to the wolves. She decided to be straight with Bell. "I'm not sure that I can answer any of them definitively. With assumptions, maybe four out of six. They won't be answers, they'll be hypotheses."

Bell stood, gave her new employee a half-smile. "Good enough. Welcome aboard. I'll leave you alone so you can get to work."

Later that afternoon, Hiddleston received a phone call from a news reporter. Someone looking for background information. She'd had dealings with reporters before. What they said they wanted, and what they really wanted, were often two different things.

She tried to dismiss the woman, but found herself making an appointment for the following afternoon.

She was nervous about meeting with a reporter, especially since she had just moved her office and now worked for Bell, a woman she did not know well. This could easily blow up in her face.

The next day, Hiddleston started work by reading the non-classified reports from the military. They, of course, had redacted most of the details she needed. She placed a call to Colonel Roger Meyer at an Air Force Base somewhere in the alligator-infested swamps of Louisiana. She requested a meeting with him, in person if possible.

While she waited for Meyer to return her call, Hiddleston reviewed reports from others who claimed to have received the same radio signals. These reports were several days old, and while most of them suspected a message of some kind might be embedded in the signal, no one at the time had made any sense of the dots, dashes, and spaces contained therein. Was it a message? Or just random noise? And in the meantime, had anyone made progress?

Her phone rang. "Hiddleston."

"Hello. This is Colonel Roger Meyer, U.S. Air Force. I'm returning your phone call."

"Oh, yes, Colonel Meyer. Thank you for getting back to me. I'm with the NASA Radio-Astronomy office in D.C. I've read your report regarding the anomalous radio signals. I'd like to talk with you about it. Are you at liberty to provide additional details?"

"I'm not aware of any security classification pertaining to my report, although that may change at any time. Other departments may have slapped classifications on this data, but I, personally, am not aware of any. So go ahead and ask your questions. If I can answer them, I will."

Mary glanced at the redacted copy of Meyer's report and almost said something. Then she changed her mind.

"Any chance we might be able to meet in person?"

"I don't think that's a possibility. At this time, I'm stationed in Louisiana, Dr. Hiddleston, and I cannot possibly get away."

"I understand. Please call me Mary. In that case, what can you tell me about these radio signals you've been studying?"

Meyer was silent for several seconds. "First of all, we're convinced it's a real message. Yesterday morning, we found a coherent code in the signal."

"Interesting. Do you have any idea where this radio signal is coming from?"

Meyer hesitated again. "We're not sure. It could easily be some kind of a hoax, or some natural phenomena, although right now that's extremely unlikely. It could be some kind of bounced signal, but again we just don't know at this point."

"Could it be an LDE of a standard signal?"

"Not likely. It's repeated hundreds of times. And Long Delayed Echoes are just that, echoes. They don't typically repeat. In my mind, that points more toward a hoax than anything. Although we do not as yet have any strong evidence that it is a hoax."

"Have you considered the possibility that something has triggered a Bracewell probe?"

"We've thought about it, of course, but no one on our team has seriously proposed it."

"Does the message contain any kind of language?"

"You mean other than mathematics? No."

"And you've definitely confirmed that this signal is coming from somewhere off Earth?"

Dr...I mean Mary, the signal has been picked up by the ISS as well as ground-based radio telescopes. The Chinese have received it, the Russians and the Israelis as well. That's not an exhaustive list."

"Interesting. Anything else you can tell me?"

"Well..." Meyer hesitated again, this time for more than a couple of seconds. "I can tell you this. Recently, the radio signal has changed."

"Changed? How so?"

"The first message was brief and contained a reference to prime numbers as well as simple binary code. The new message is much longer and much more complex. My colleagues tell me this one is going to take some time to decipher, if, indeed there is anything *to* decipher. It could, after all, turn out to be just random noise."

"I see. Thank you, Colonel Meyer, your information has been extremely helpful. I'd like to ask if you'd be willing to send me the original message, and keep me informed of any additional progress your team makes."

"Subject to the whims of military protocol, I would be pleased to do that."

"Thank you, Sir. We'll talk soon, I'm sure. Goodbye for now." She disconnected the call and stared at her phone, thinking. Maybe this was more than just kool-aid after all.

Cranston: ~Two Weeks before Flyby

David and his two friends opened the door to the high school math lab. It was Tuesday, so no classes would be meeting in that particular classroom until 3 p.m. That gave them four hours, but Mr. Rayburn, the math teacher, wanted them out of the classroom no later than 2:30. That was a deadline the three were prepared to ignore, if necessary.

"Okay, guys, look for a big roll of graph paper," David said. "We want a really long sheet on this table."

While Cranston set up and booted his laptop, Dwight and Samantha searched for, and found, where the graph paper rolls were stored. James carried a roll over to one of the long, narrow lab tables and sent the end rolling all the way to the edge, where it rolled off and thumped to the floor.

"That should be enough to start with," he muttered to Sam.

"We got your paper ready," Samantha called to Cranston.

"Be right there," he said. His laptop had booted. He stood, pulled out his phone, and grabbed the notebook.

"Has the message changed yet?"

"Nope. Not yet." He listened intently for several minutes. Then Cranston suddenly sat up. "Okay, it stopped."

"And?"

"Hang on. Nothing yet...nope, nope...okay, okay, here it goes." He started writing in his notebook. He wrote for over an hour. Both Sam and Dwight took short breaks, but David remained hunched over his notebook, writing furiously. He suspected the data would repeat, but since he didn't know for sure, he made an effort to get it all down correctly during the first run.

"Okay," he said, taking a deep breath and dropping his pencil, "I think I got it all. We should listen one more time to check our work, but we'll run out of time. Let's start plotting this data." He moved over to the paper and attacked it with a freshly sharpened pencil.

Considering the amount of data David had recorded, if this *was* a message from aliens, they really had something to say this time.

Hiddleston and Ford: ~Two Weeks before Flyby

"Mary Hiddleston?" A slender African-American woman knocked softly on the door.

Hiddleston looked up from her computer screen. "Yes? Can I help you?"

"I believe we have an appointment. I'm Marsha Ford, WMSG Television News."

"Oh, right. Please, come on in. You'll have to excuse the office. I just moved in this week and things have been...hectic."

"No problem." Ford stepped in and sat in the only other chair, an antiquated metal folding chair with the words "St. Anthony's" stenciled on the back. The chair wobbled.

"I'd offer you coffee," Hiddleston said, "but what they make here I wouldn't give to a pack of rabid bats."

Ford laughed. "No problem. I don't drink much coffee anyway."

"What can I help you with, Ms. Ford?"

"I'm looking for background information on a couple of subjects." Ford smiled. "If I'm going to ask my interviewees the right questions, I need to know what I'm talking about, at least superficially."

Hiddleston smiled. "I understand."

Ford opened her notebook and looked at some handwritten notes. "Let me ask you this, first. You've heard about the asteroid headed our way?"

"Of course," Hiddleston said with a slight nod. "Who hasn't?"

Ford leaned forward. "You think it's going to hit us?"

Hiddleston shook her head. "From everything I've seen and read, it's going to be a near miss. But that's really not my area of expertise, so my personal opinion certainly isn't definitive."

"Of course," Ford said, "but it's a question I'm asking everybody these days."

"I understand. Anything else?" A bit of impatience had entered her voice.

Ford was slow to ask the second question. "I have heard rumors that various stations are picking up odd radio signals. From space."

Hiddleston sat back in her chair. "I've heard rumors like that as well," she said slowly. She leaned forward and, as carefully and as unobtrusively as possible, closed the file folder that was open on her desk.

"You think there's anything to it?"

"Earth is bombarded with radio signals from space all the time. Neutron stars, pulsars, quasars, even entire galaxies emit radio signals."

"We're not talking about those kinds of radio signals," Ford smiled, but it was not a friendly smile. "We're talking about a specific sequence of signals from within our own solar system. I've heard hints that experts think there might be a message hidden in the signals. Can you tell me anything about that?"

Hiddleston sighed. She stared at Ford for a moment, then reached over and reopened the file folder. "You are not to use my name. Is that understood? And I want you to know that I really don't like doing this. This has got trouble written all over it."

"No name. Agreed. I've got other sources who will talk on the record, but I need to know what questions to ask them. And, Mary, it's important that you know I protect my sources. Vigorously."

"Okay. Good enough. This is second-hand information you understand. I spoke with a member of the U.S. Air Force and he confirmed that the signals have been received and that they had, indeed, found a message."

"Alien?"

Hiddleston shrugged. "I don't think anybody knows the answer to that at the moment. It's certainly a possibility, but there are several other possibilities that are much more likely."

"So the message isn't a clear 'take me to your leader' type?"

Hiddleston laughed. "Hardly. It's mathematical in nature, which is logical since math is a universal language that could be understood by any advanced civilization. Or, in some cases, even a primitive one like ours."

Ford chuckled. "I see. But you don't know what the message was, exactly?"

"Not a clue. I haven't seen the original data."

Ford paused and looked uncomfortable. "Mary, let me be frank with you. I need a name, a contact who is familiar with the radio signals and who can answer the questions that you can't, and for the record."

"I'm sorry. I can't do that. I could end up in some very hot water. Or worse."

Ford leaned forward. "I hear where you're coming from. But I have a job to do as well. I just need a name. No one will ever know who gave me that name, no matter what. I'd go to jail before I revealed any of my sources."

"I'd rather not," Hiddleston said, frowning, "you don't know the trouble that could cause."

"I understand. But if this turns out to be a legitimate alien signal, the consequences could be, well, unimaginable. I think people have a right to know. They have a right to be part of this discovery whether it leads to aliens or some teenager in his parents' basement." She paused again. "All I need is a name. Just a name. Please."

Hiddleston sighed. She leaned forward in her chair. "I'll give you four words, nothing more, and you did *not* hear it from me. That's all I'm going to say. So don't bother asking."

Ford smiled. "That's all I need."

"Colonel Roger Meyer, Louisiana." Hiddleston stood, followed by Ford.

"That's fine. That's perfect. Anything else you can share with me?"

Hiddleston shrugged. "No. I'd say there is a possibility that some additional data may be received in subsequent messages."

"Mary, you almost make it sound like this has already happened." Ford hadn't asked a question. She left the statement open.

Hiddleston didn't bite. "I don't have any confirmation of that." She nodded toward Ford's notepad. "He would know. Ask him."

Ford nodded. "Fair enough. Well, it's been a pleasure talking with you. Perhaps we can speak again, soon. You've been extremely helpful."

"I don't think that's going to happen. I've told you all I can." Hiddleston shook the other woman's hand. She was happy the meeting had finished. She didn't think she'd shared enough information so that someone could point fingers at her.

As Ford exited the office, she was trembling with excitement. Hiddleston had shared much more information than she expected. All she had to do now was find that Colonel Meyer and see if he could be talked into doing an interview on the record. That was extremely unlikely, but it didn't hurt to ask. And Ford was prepared to be extremely persistent.

Back at home, she spent some time with her kids, watched part of a movie with them, then fired up her computer. She searched for Colonel Roger Meyer and found him listed as a research scientist at Barksdale Air Force Base in Louisiana. She found him listed in the base directory, but with only a general department phone number. She'd have to wait until morning to call him.

Marsha stifled her excitement, forcing herself to spend some quality time with her girls. They played Yahtzee for a while, then watched the rest of the movie, with promises they'd watch the sequel the next evening.

She was up early the following morning, ate breakfast with her kids, and packed lunches for both of them. She rode the Uber with them to school and daycare, then back home. She killed an hour doing various random searches. Late that morning, she called for Colonel Meyer. Knowing his name got her transferred to his office. Once there, however, a receptionist became reluctant to put her call through.

"I just need to ask him one question," she said.

"I'm sorry, Miss, Dr. Meyer is very busy right now," the receptionist said speaking in a heavy Louisiana accent. "He specifically told me he's not taking phone calls or reading emails today, at all."

"I'm sorry to hear that. I have some new information about strange radio signals. I thought he might be interested in talking to me." It wasn't a lie, exactly, just a matter of perception.

"I see. Okay, please hold. I'll check with him."

After a few moments, a man picked up the phone. "This is Colonel Meyer. To whom am I speaking?"

"Colonel, my name is Marsha Ford. I understand you've received a strange radio signal, perhaps more than one, possibly from space, and that there might be cryptic messages embedded in those signals."

"Ms. Ford, with whom are you affiliated."

Ford sighed. That question had come just a little too soon. Time to lay it on the line. "Colonel, I'm a reporter for a television news station in Maryland. I really need to talk to you, or someone in your office, on the record, about these radio signals. I need someone I can interview for a news report I'm doing."

Meyer was silent for a time. Then he surprised her. "That's a bit unusual, but I see no harm in it, Ms. Ford. We would need to do it remotely as I am unable to leave for obvious reasons, and I doubt you would want to travel all the way to Louisiana."

"That would be fine, Colonel. Can I call you right back using my computer VOIP? This will allow me to record our conversation for later broadcast."

Meyer agreed and gave Ford his personal cell phone number. "I have a meeting in an hour, and we've been very busy, so our time is limited. I hope that's okay."

"That's fine, Colonel. We should be done in plenty of time. I'm hanging up now, and I'll call you right back."

She ended the call and set up her PC to record the phone

call. She fitted a headset over her ears and tested the microphone. Meyer answered the call almost immediately.

"This is Marsha Ford with WMSG News. I'm speaking this morning with Colonel Roger Meyer, U.S. Air Force. Colonel Meyer is a research scientist stationed at Barksdale Air Force Base in Louisiana. Good morning, Colonel."

"Same to you, Marsha. How can I help you?"

"I've heard several unconfirmed rumors that diverse locations, including the International Space Station, have reported the receipt of some unexplained and strange radio signals that appear to be coming from space. Can you confirm that?"

"Yes. Such signals have been received."

Ford pumped a fist into the air.

"Some people are convinced that the signal source is alien in nature."

Meyer chuckled. "That's certainly a possibility, but not very likely. The signals are probably reflected signals sent from somewhere on Earth itself."

"Have you deciphered the signals? Is there a message?"

"Well, Marsha, our researchers have, indeed, found a mathematical message, for lack of a better word, embedded in the data. We're studying that message as we speak."

"Do you think there's a possibility additional signals might be forthcoming?"

"Uh," Meyer hesitated, "that's certainly a possibility. We are monitoring the same frequency around the clock."

"But you're certain no additional signals have been received?"

Again the hesitation. Ford's intuition was ringing a bell. She'd deliberately used the plural at the beginning of the call, and Meyer hadn't corrected her.

"I don't have any information about that at the moment. If

such a signal is received, we will certainly assess it for any additional messages."

"Don't you find it a little odd, Colonel, that these signals are received only a few weeks before Earth is expecting a very close encounter with a giant asteroid?"

Meyer chuckled. "It's a bit unusual but certainly not exceptional. Coincidences are more common than most people realize."

"So you don't see a connection?"

"Not at this time, no."

"What do you think the impact might be if these radio signals really do turn out to be from aliens?"

"That's a hard question to answer, Marsha. If the source is proven conclusively, it could change our entire perspective of the universe. Such a confirmation would have profound repercussions here on Earth as well. Just knowing there is intelligent life elsewhere in the universe would impact all of our various societies and religions."

"Thank you, Colonel Meyer. I've been speaking with Colonel Roger Meyer of the U.S. Air Force." After a moment of dead space, "thank you, Colonel. I appreciate your time and information."

"You're certainly welcome."

After a few more pleasantries, Ford ended the call.

She couldn't stop smiling. That was a short but very productive interview. She forwarded the recording to her work e-mail. After a quick lunch, she called an Uber and headed for the studio. After this interview, she'd have to clear some space on her bookshelf for some major awards.

Later that evening, she watched as her pre-recorded interview with Colonel Meyer aired. The repercussions were almost immediate. Suddenly, news of the asteroid flyby took a back seat to news of possible alien communication.

Tito told her later that the station received calls from every major network, and a whole bunch of minor ones. Ford's interview had gone viral on social media. She thought about her bookshelf, and decided she'd put the Pulitzer right there in the middle.

Dunbar: ~Two Weeks before Flyby

"The Bible tells us that there was a 'war' in Heaven. Lucifer and one-third of the angels rebelled against God, were defeated, and were cast down to the Earth. That's Earth, as in our planet right here." Dunbar stomped his foot.

"The traditional timeline goes something like this: God creates the heavens and the Earth, then plants and animals are created on Earth, then He eventually gets around to creating humans in His image. Sometime later, at a time that's not clearly defined, there's this war in Heaven, and Lucifer and his angels are cast down to an already created Earth. We are told that one-third of these invisible angels were cast out of Heaven. Logically, then, that leaves two-thirds of these beings still in Heaven or, perhaps, elsewhere in the Universe. Interesting that the approximate ratio of dark energy and dark matter roughly equates to the ratio of 'good' angels versus 'bad' angels.

"We are told in Rev. 12:4 *And his tail drew the third part of the stars of heaven and did cast them to the earth.* In verse 7 '*there was a war in heaven; Michael and his angels fought against the dragon; and the dragon fought with his angels. And prevailed not; neither was their place found any more in heaven...And* verse 9: *he was cast out into the earth, and his angels were cast out with him.*"

Dunbar cupped his chin in thought. He waved a hand at the congregation. "Maybe this timeline is all wrong. And there are some other problems as well. The first thing God does after the Big Bang is to fashion the Earth. Wait a minute! Shouldn't that make Earth the center of the universe? That can't be true, can it? Well, if you search deep enough into the science behind the beginning of the universe, you will eventually find an admitted confirmation that no matter which direction you look from Earth, the universe seems to be expanding away from us exactly as if our planet were, indeed, Ground Zero for the Big Bang. In fact, scientists have had to create a convoluted series of mathematical equations to explain this anomaly—why it appears as if we are the center of the universe, but of course, scientifically, that couldn't be the case. In science, there is nothing special about the Earth. However, if we look at it from God's point of view, no convoluted math was ever needed. Earth *is* and always has been the center of the universe."

Another stir rippled through the audience. Danny held his breath for a soft moment. The fish was out of the water. Now it was time to get it in the net.

"Ignoring that traditional timeline, we find that the Bible tells us Lucifer is already on Earth very shortly after its creation. We know this because he shows up in the form of a serpent in the Garden of Eden to tempt the newly-created Eve. So traditionally we assume God creates the heavens and the earth, and sometime thereafter there's a war in Heaven. But what if we've got it backwards?

"Let's assume for a moment that the Heaven we're talking about was the eternal home of God that existed before creation of the universe. Let's further speculate that the quantum singularity from science and the Heaven where God resided are one and the same. If so, we have science and religion meeting once again. In the eternal pre-universe singularity something became unbalanced and the whole thing blew up, and we ended up with an evolving universe. In the eternal pre-universe Heaven, something became unbalanced and there was a war in this Heaven which led directly to...creation of the Universe. The term Lucifer means 'light bearer' or 'light bringer.'

"Think about that for a minute. What are the first four words God utters in the Bible?"

He paused, looked expectantly at his audience. Then someone said, "Let there be light."

He pointed to the speaker. "Exactly! What if the war in Heaven took place before creation of the universe, before there was light? Before space-time and matter-energy existed? Back when there was only a BB-sized quantum singularity? *That's* where and when the war took place!

"When God says *Let there be light*, to whom was He speaking? What if He was speaking to the *Light Bearer*, Lucifer? What if the only way to expunge Lucifer and his evil angels from Heaven was to explode Heaven? Create light, powered by physical reactions rather than the spirit of God? What if, think about this now...what if the entire universe was created by God so that He had a place to cast out Lucifer and his rebellious angels? Evil, contained to this place which we call Earth, where that evil was isolated and could eventually be defeated and eliminated. Whereupon the universe, Heaven, would could again be made new, i.e. a new singularity.

"And, finally, what if Earth was primarily created not for us, humanity, but to contain Lucifer and his evil onto one tiny speck of this new universe that is otherwise filled with billions of planets and life forms that have never known evil?

Dunbar went on quickly, while his audience still reeled from what he'd just said.

"So who was Lucifer? In Ezekiel 28:15: *Thou wast perfect in thy ways from the day that thou wast created, till iniquity was found in thee*. So Lucifer was created perfect, but iniquity–or sin–or an imbalance, was found in him and he was cast down to Earth with one-third of heaven's angels."

Murmurs were going around the congregation. He didn't want to lose them.

"Somewhere along the line, *we* are created in the image of God. There are several interesting aspects about the Biblical creation of humans. First of all, there are two creation stories. The first begins in Genesis 1:26 *Let us make mankind in our image, after our likeness...* The second happens in Genesis 2:7 *And the Lord God formed man of the dust of the ground, and breathed into his nostrils the breath of life; and man became a living soul.* Many Biblical critics look at these two versions and assert they are two separate and unrelated creation stories, written by two different people (or groups of people) at two different times. Another way to look at it is that the first human creation verses were an overview, and in Genesis 2:7, the Bible goes into detail. In this second detailed version, God creates man, then immediately places him in a protected garden. And from there God says, in verse 9 *And out of the ground made the Lord God to grow every tree that is pleasant to the sight* and in verse 19, *And out of the ground the Lord God formed every beast of the field, and every fowl of the air...*"

Danny held back the most critical facts, for a moment. "Before we go any further, let's skip ahead to chapter 3 verse 1: *Now the serpent was more subtil than any beast of the field which the Lord God had made. And he said unto the woman, Yea, hath God said, Ye shall not eat of every tree of the garden?*" By this time Lucifer and his evil angels had already been cast down to Earth, sometime during, or before, the seven days of creation. There is no way to nail it down any finer, so our speculation that Earth was created to contain evil Lucifer and his rebellious angels, must float, or sink, on a rather circumstantial boat.

"So the Garden was under God's control, but the serpent was crafty enough to infiltrate it. Lucifer is often portrayed as either a snake, serpent or a dragon. Look at how often the serpent/dragon motif is used throughout ancient history when referring to either evil or a god-like being. Virtually every ancient civilization refers to dragons in their mythology. In South and Central America, we have the gods *Kukulkan* and *Quetzalcoatl*, feathered serpents who bring–guess what?– knowledge and learning to their subjects. Interesting that our scientists now tell us that many dinosaurs were, themselves, feathered. Depending on the location, dragons in legends are often portrayed as evil fire-breathing, or protectors of riches and bearers of wisdom and power. Bearers, if you will, of the knowledge of good and evil."

Oh yeah, that caused a stir! No time to let down now.

Smithson: ~Two Weeks before Flyby

"Hope" Smithson watched an online replay of Marsha Ford's interview with Colonel Meyer. He had a hard time not flinging his laptop across the room. He called his receptionist. "Hannah, I need to speak with Colonel Meyer right away. Get him for me, now please."

"At once, General."

Five minutes passed before his intercom beeped. "General, Colonel Meyer isn't available at the moment. He went to the medical clinic for his biannual Covid-19 shot. He should be back within an hour."

"That's fine. Please make sure that he gets my message immediately upon his return. I want to see him soonest, got that? Oh, and please make the same clinic appointment for me and put it on my calendar, will you? Sometime early next week."

"Yes, sir. Will do."

Smithson watched the news report again and shook his head in misery. His officer in charge of nonsense just became his officer in charge of butt pains. He desperately wanted a drink, but he resisted. He needed a clear head for the upcoming confrontation.

An hour passed before his receptionist buzzed and told him that Colonel Meyer had returned and was ready to meet.

"Please send him in," Smithson said. "And Hannah, hold all my calls unless it's someone, you know, like the President or Admiral Ardmore. Thanks."

He watched silently as the Colonel entered, a tentative smile on his face. Meyer saluted, which Smithson ignored. "General, I heard you wanted to see me?"

"Sit down, Colonel. I'm pleased to see you remembered your service cap this time."

"I try to learn from my mistakes, Sir. Sometimes it's not easy."

"Indeed," General Smithson said with an icy emphasis. Meyer sat stiffly, sensing tension in his superior officer's polite demeanor.

"May I ask what this is about?"

Smithson sighed and glanced at his computer screen. "I was watching your, uh, interview, on this morning's news. It seems to have created quite a stir. All the network news stations have picked it up, and it has blown up all over social media. You must enjoy being a celebrity of sorts."

"I wouldn't know, Sir, I haven't had a chance to see it myself."

"Perhaps you were busy checking your emails?"

"I haven't had a chance to check my emails for the past couple of days. We've been quite busy."

"I understand. Perhaps, then, you've also been too busy to check your daily briefings?"

"Well, I've glanced at them, of course. But..."

"Then perhaps you are not aware that your work on the radio signals was designated Top Secret two days ago? Did you happen to miss that section of your briefing? It was on the first page, at the very top, in bold print. The one with the red border? And, I suppose, I wasted my time sending you an email inviting your attention to the briefing."

"Well, I, uh..." Meyer stopped when he realized the significance of what the General had just said. "I'm sorry, General."

"Do you understand the position you have put me in? Not twenty-four hours after I designate something Top Secret, I'm stunned to see that same classified information revealed to the public at large in a news interview. In a totally unauthorized interview, I might add." His voice became louder as he spoke.

"General, I..."

"I've had a call from the Chairman of the Joint Chiefs already this morning. I'm expecting a call from the President at any time, for the love of Pete. And there are probably others who want their turn to rake my butt over some burning coals."

"I'm very sorry, General. If there's anything I can do..."

"There is. I want a full written report on everything that led up to that interview, and your part in it. If my butt's going to have burning blisters on it, yours is, too. I want that written report on my desk within five hours. Printed, not e-mailed."

"But General, my work..."

"Don't worry about your work, Colonel. You're going to be very busy. All calls about your interview will be directed to you. And you are to stonewall, understand? It was all a big mistake, and you repeated information that turned out to be erroneous. Got it?"

"Sir? You want me to lie?"

"Yes, Colonel. I want you to lie. That's an order, and I expect it to be carried out."

"But...but General, I have important work to do. The second message..."

Smithson held up a finger. "Forget the second message. For the moment, telling lies is your work. And get that report to me. It will be used with other relevant facts to determine if you will be charged with treason, or not."

"Treason? Sir, are you serious? A guilty verdict could mean..."

"Execution? That's correct, Colonel. However, I trust we can sidestep that unpleasant conclusion. But, Colonel Meyer this is a very serious matter. Your irresponsible disregard of military protocol might have earned you life in prison. If you're lucky."

"General, I don't understand. Life in prison?"

"It's a distinct possibility. There will be a court-marshal and you will be assigned legal representation. Your guilt or innocence, and possible punishment, will be up to the court. Now get out. You have four hours and fifty minutes to get that report to me. And, Colonel, you are restricted to this base. You are as of this moment, relieved of any other duties other than what I've just assigned to you. And you will not speak to anyone about this, other than as I have directed you. Do you understand me?"

"But...yes, Sir." Meyer stood, saluted, and walked out.

Ishmael: ~Two Weeks before Flyby

Ishmael waited nervously until his father arrived home from the chemical lab.

"Dad, can I talk to you for a minute?"

His father sighed. "Okay, son. Give me some time to get washed up. Then we can talk." He smiled, but it was a tired smile. Almost as if he knew what was bothering his son.

A few minutes later, they met in Ishmael's room. They sat on the bed next to each other.

"Okay, Son, what do you need?"

"Dad...? I'm sorry, I hate to bother you. But..."

"Out with it, child! It's almost time for dinner."

"I don't think I'm going to like this school."

"How so?"

"Some of the kids aren't very friendly. And a few of them act like they don't want me anywhere around."

Dad sighed. "I understand, Son. It's never easy moving from one place to another, especially from one country to another, one culture to another. It hasn't been easy for me, either. Your mother and sister are making adjustments as well, although they don't have as much contact with the people here as you and I do."

Ishmael looked uncomfortable. "How do I do this, Dad? How do I make friends when people won't even talk to me?"

Dad roughed his son's hair. "You just have to be patient. I know that's not the answer you wanted to hear. But sometimes you just have to tough it out, deal with it, endure it. Eventually, some of the kids at that school will accept you when you become a natural, normal part of their day. Then, slowly, you'll begin to make friends."

"And if you're wrong?"

Dad sighed again. "Look, Ish, you're only there two-and-a-half months more, then it's summer vacation, and you probably won't even see those kids. When you go back to school in the fall, you'll be in a more mature environment. I've already made arrangements."

"But that still doesn't give me any friends now, Dad. I had so many friends at school back home. Why can't...?"

Dad's voice became harder and impatient. "We're not back home anymore, Ishmael. We're here now. This is our home. We have to make the best of it. It's not easy for any of us. We're not only strangers here, but also different. We look different, we act different, and our accent is different. This is a place where people don't trust different. But it will all work out eventually. You'll see. Just be patient."

Ishmael sighed. He understood his Father. He agreed with him. But he still wanted things to be more like home. "I'll try, Dad."

"Good. Let's go eat. I'm starving."

Cranston: ~Two Weeks before Flyby

It took longer than the three students expected to plot the latest radio signal data, there was so much of it. Then David made himself take the time to check his work. It took an hour-and-a-half for all the dots, dashes, and spaces to cycle through once again. David was nervous because they were running out of time.

Just before their 3 pm deadline, with an impatient math teacher standing over them, tapping his foot, the three had finished marking up half a roll of graph paper. They stood looking down at all the plot points.

"I don't get it," Dwight said, rubbing his chin.

"Look here, it's the same thing, over and over again," Samantha commented, moving down the table.

They had about thirty graphs of essentially the same thing. Yet each "page" was preceded by a series of dots, one for the first page, two for the second, three for the third, and so on until the last page had 30 dots on it. Each of these dot sequences was followed by a long sequence of other dots, dashes, and spaces, but each set was oddly similar. David was familiar with redundancy, but this didn't seem right.

"Okay, you three. Out," Mr. Rayburn said, clapping his hands. "I've got a class and students will be arriving in two or three minutes."

"Okay, it's time for us to go," David said. "Let's grab all these sheets and we'll head for the study lab. It's usually empty this time of day. We can work there." Obviously, the three were cutting regular classes that day. All three of them considered the sacrifice a worthy one. And considerably more exciting.

Once in the study lab, they used the old rusty paper cutter to separate the pages and put them in order. As with the first communication, this series resulted in crude images. At the top left, a small circle. To the right were two triangles that overlapped slightly, almost like a company logo. At the bottom right, a large curved line. The three stood looking at the sheets, trying to make sense of them.

"So what have we got here?" David asked. "The same picture 30 times."

"I don't know, but it's got to mean something, Dude."

"Each image has to be different, somehow," Sam said, "the dots at the top tell us that."

While they stared at the sheets of paper, Samantha plugged in an earbud and brought up a news website on her phone. David glanced over, then chuckled.

"What?"

"You're going to watch the President speak? That old geezer..."

"Hey," Samantha said. "I like listening to President Dickson's press conferences, okay? He reminds me of my grandfather."

"Hope grandpa is smarter than that pathetic duck," Dwight said.

"Be nice," Samantha whispered, then turned away from the two boys.

While they spoke, David picked up sheet number one and sheet number thirty and set them next to each other. "Look," he said softly. Samantha glanced at the sheets, then once again turned away to concentrate on her phone.

"What am I looking at?" Dwight asked, bringing up one sheet, then another.

"There's a difference. Look at the triangles. They're in different positions, but just barely."

"You're right. As the numbers get larger, the lower one is more separated from the upper one. And look at the little round circle. It moved a tiny little bit, too."

David looked up at his friend. "So there are differences. Why? What does it mean?"

"You got me by the..."

"Guys, quiet! The President is talking about the radio signals."

"Holy guacamole, what's he saying?" Dwight asked.

Samantha waved a hand for quiet. "There was some kind of news report, but he's trying to downplay it. He says the military doesn't think it's from aliens. Mostly just a lot of reassurance."

Dwight shook his head. "Man, this is all too much for me. I'm goin' home and play me some video games."

Cranston slapped his friend on the shoulder. "That's it, Mr. James! You're a genius!" he shouted. "These sheets," he pointed to the table, "are the frames in a very short video." He laughed as he began gathering up the papers. "It's a freaking *movie!* They sent us a movie. Dude! Tell me they're not aliens!"

Smithson: ~12 Days before Flyby

"Hope" Smithson followed the Chair of the Joint Chiefs into the White House. He didn't really want to be there. These meetings hardly ever ended in his favor. The two were escorted into the Oval Office. President Dickson rose from his desk and walked over to meet the two military officers. "Sophie, Hope, glad you could make it."

"Mr. President."

"Sir."

"Please, sit." Dickson waved them to one of the facing sofas, and he took the other. On the narrow table between them, ensconced under a glass case, was an ornate light blue vase. The President noticed Smithson admiring it.

"Like it? That's my Ming vase, gifted to me by President Qishan during our summit last month. Beautiful thing, isn't it?"

"Stunning," Smithson said. He had little appreciation for art, but Chinese vases were an exception. Some of them transcended even art, and he considered them to be ceramic poetry. He shifted his eyes away from the vase and back to the President.

"So, what have you got for me, guys?"

Admiral Ardmore leaned forward. "General Smithson tells me his people are convinced the radio signals constitute a message from aliens."

"Interesting. And what is *your* opinion, General?" The President asked.

"Sir, I'm committed to keeping an open mind. But I have to listen to the, uh, experts on my staff. This latest message almost rules out a hoax or something natural."

The President looked at the military advisors with a penetrating stare. "What does it all mean?"

Ardmore looked at Smithson, who shrugged. "We're still working on the message itself. We're not quite sure how to interpret the data, but we're working 'round the clock. We have to consider every possibility. We need to keep in mind, Mr. President, that this is all happening at virtually the same time a large asteroid is about to make a very close approach to this planet."

"You think the two are somehow connected?"

Smithson sighed. "I sincerely hope not. But we have to consider it. What if the aliens maneuvered the rock into a position where it actually impacts the Earth? They could take out virtually our entire planet with one blow."

"You really think that's what's happening?"

"Again, Mr. President, none of us has an answer to that. But if it's true..."

"Yes? Then what?"

This time it was Admiral Ardmore's turn to shrug. "The only thing we can do. We nuke the asteroid if we can. We actually have some simulations based on that very scenario, but they have a tendency to end badly."

"Seriously?"

Smithson leaned forward. "There's another possibility, Sir. If five or six nations all launch nuclear-tipped missiles at that thing we could do...something."

"You don't sound convinced."

"Mr. President, it's one damn big rock. And it's moving really fast. We'd need to launch, like, within the next week or ten days to do any good."

"Can we do that?"

Ardmore said "No" and Smithson said "Maybe."

"I don't like the sound of that," Dickson said softly.

"Yeah, well, we don't, either."

"And why would the aliens send us a message, essentially warning us of their impending attack?"

"Arrogance," Smithson said. He looked at Ardmore, then back to the President. "Perhaps." He always wanted to have answers for his superiors, but this time his responses didn't sound like answers.

"Or it could be an attempt to see how well we can protect our planet. It would certainly give them a good assessment of our capabilities," Ardmore added.

"I'd like to think that someday we might have a slightly better handle on those capabilities," Dickson said.

Ardmore spread her fingers. "There are a number of variables to consider, Mr. President. As a planet, we're not very well prepared for this kind of situation. It shouldn't be that way, but it is."

"Well, how do we rectify that?"

"Time and money, Mr. President. That's always the answer. And it's always the two things we don't have enough of."

Dickson shook his head. "Much as I hate to admit it, Admiral, I'm afraid you're right. Anything else you want to add?"

"Not at this time, Mr. President."

The President nodded and stood. "Thank you, gentle, uh, persons. I expect you to keep looking for a solution. This includes attempts to communicate with those aliens if, indeed, they exist. We'll need the best scientific minds we can find on this. So let's get this information de-classified and out into our academic and scientific communities as soon as possible."

Admiral Ardmore started to say something.

The President held up a hand. "I know. You'd prefer to keep the information privileged, but in this case, I'm overruling you. We need answers and we need them fast."

"As you wish, Mr. President."

"One last thing. And I'm talking to both of you, now. I expect to be kept in the loop. I don't want to get any more of my briefings from the nightly news. Understand me?"

Smithson and Ardmore saluted their Commander-in-Chief and exited the office.

"Damn," the President said softly, taking his seat at the desk. "Aliens and asteroids and no easy solutions. Damn."

President Dickson rotated in his chair and gazed out the window of the Oval Office at a brilliant blue sky. He was a tall man, thin, Lincolnesque in stature. He even had a neatly-trimmed beard. He was in his mid-60s and in the first year of his first term as President. He had an ambitious agenda. The last thing he wanted to deal with was asteroids and aliens.

He swung the chair back to his desk and opened the upper right-hand drawer. He pulled out a Bible, thick with use and time. He held it in his hand for a moment, feeling the power of the words without having to look at them. Dickson was a deeply religious man, but he consciously tried to avoid injecting his faith into his decision-making processes. Sometimes it was hard, like now. He studied the two words on the cover for a long moment, then placed the book back in its resting place. He should have felt comfort, but this time it didn't seem to work.

It was time for his next meeting.

Rylee: ~One Week before Flyby

Rylee Janeway rested her helmet against the headrest. In 30 seconds the Virgin-X Heavy Lift Vehicle would fling itself away from the Earth into low orbit. Four hours later, it would dock with the International Space Station.

Rylee was ten years older than her sibling, Kylie. Why her parents waited ten years before burdening the family with another child was beyond Rylee's comprehension. She also couldn't stand the fact that they had rhyming names. They weren't twins, after all. And, while Rylee was not plain-looking by any means, her little sister turned out to be a ravishing beauty with almost everybody remarking on the fact. Despite this, Rylee held an affection for her little sister. At least she did until recently, when the teenager had turned into a real whirling son of a horse's butt.

Because she always enjoyed school, Rylee breezed through high school, then surprised everyone by seeking an appointment to, and being accepted at, the U.S. Naval Academy in Annapolis. While Kylie was wowing everyone with her looks and annoying them with her lack of discipline, Rylee graduated tenth in her class and was commissioned an officer in the U.S. Navy.

Rylee became a fighter pilot, although she did not see combat action. She served one tour on the U.S.S. Nimitz before transferring to the Johnson Space Center in Houston, Texas, for astronaut training. Unfortunately she did not qualify for the astronaut program, failing two of the more rigorous physical tests. She had resigned herself to a career that would get her no closer to space than the maximum altitude of a fighter jet. It was a bitter disappointment, and she had almost resigned from the Navy.

Now...she was on her way to the International Space Station to observe and attempt to photograph the approaching asteroid as it passed through Earth's upper atmosphere. She had been selected from a group of ten Navy pilot volunteers who'd also had at least some previous astronaut training. Her college experience with high-end digital cameras and video editing software gave Rylee a slight edge, and she was selected. The fact that she was five feet eight inches tall and weighed less than 120 pounds might have had something to do with it as well. Weight was always a prime consideration with rockets, and tall people were not well-suited for the International Space Station's rather cramped quarters.

She'd wrangled a front-row seat to the most amazing celestial phenomenon in recent history.

"Let's just hope that thing doesn't hit the space station," her father, Roger, had said.

"Dad," Rylee laughed, "it's not even going to be close. We're only two-hundred or so miles up and we'll be well behind the asteroid's passing."

"Well, anyway, you need to be careful."

"Don't worry, Dad. I'm just a passenger in the rocket, and I'm on the ISS for one purpose only. After it's all over, I'll be coming home after the next docking in five or six weeks."

That was then, when her selection hadn't seemed quite real. This was now...

The countdown had reached the last 10 seconds. Nine, eight, seven...

The blast pressed her down as the four cryogenic liquid methane and liquid oxygen powered engines ignited, generating three Gs as it began pushing itself away from Earth. As it expended fuel and became lighter, the rocket increased its speed until it reached an escape velocity of 11.19 km/s. The main launch vehicle separated with a jolt, and the docking module's engines took over with a one-minute burn to place the craft into the proper orbit. The main stage would land near where it had launched in Florida, to be used again a few months down the road. Freefall allowed Rylee to turn her head slightly to look out the viewport. She watched as the sky became dark blue, then purple, then black. The stars came out.

The Virgin-X HLV carried a maximum of two pilots and three passengers. This launch was fully manned. In addition to Rylee, a Russian Cosmonaut named Leonid and a Brit biological scientist named Carrie endured the launch on each side of her. For the pilots, this was a routine flight. For the passengers, it was the trip of a lifetime.

Dunbar: ~Two Weeks before Flyby

Dunbar continued: "God creates the earth, then He creates a garden on this new earth—the earth itself is not the garden. Why? Because Lucifer was already on earth, Earth was created to confine Satan. So who's in control of Earth? Who was in control of it from the very beginning? You got it: The Devil himself. You want to know where Hell is? Take a look out these windows.

"Doubts? Take a look at these verses: In 1 Peter 5:8: *Be sober, be vigilant; because your adversary the devil, as a roaring lion, walketh about, seeking whom he may devour.* In Job: 1:7, '*And the Lord said unto Satan, Whence comest thou? Then Satan answered the Lord, and said, From going to and fro in the earth, and from walking up and down in it.*' In Matthew 4: 8-9 Lucifer claims the Earth is his to give away: *Again, the devil taketh (Jesus) up into an exceeding high mountain, and sheweth him all the kingdoms of the world, and the glory of them; And saith unto him, All these things will I give thee, if thou wilt fall down and worship me.*'

"How could Satan offer to give all the kingdoms of Earth to Jesus if it wasn't his to give? I think we often fall into the trap of looking at Satan as a boogie man or another word for a bad hair day. But if God is real, if Jesus is real, then Satan is as real as that person sitting right next to you. Turn and take a look at your neighbor. Then imagine it."

The speaker paused again. Many of these concepts were brand new to Christians. He had to give them time to digest them.

"Why would God make man in his own image? Once again, perspective changes things. What if Satan and evil were here first, before humans were created? Here, on a planet surrounded by and infested with evil, might it be that God needed some force to monitor and counteract that evil? Perhaps God created humans to be that force. The only way He could ensure the survival of such a creation was to place them in a protected environment, and make them in His own image so that there could be a connection between humans and God. This allowed God to later send us His Son in *our* image.

"Makes you wonder if the whole concept of sexual reproduction was built into life on earth for a single purpose; to allow the Son of God to be born, to secretly infiltrate a planet in the grip of ultimate evil.

"So here we have evil in charge of the earth, and a creation in the image of the Creator in a semi-protected garden with plants and animals as the Creator wanted them to be. What was the rest of the world like? With the majority of the earth under the control of Satan and his forces? Think about that for a moment.

"If God really needed to infiltrate the evil world outside the garden, He would need to embed his humans into that outside world, somehow. Get them out of the garden and into the real world. How best to do that? The Bible tells us how it happened.

"First, let me ask you a question: What fatal character flaw caused Lucifer to rebel against God? Do you think maybe it's a giant ego? He not only believed he could take the place of God, but he thought he could do a better job. And he convinced a third of the angels in Heaven that he was, indeed, better than God. Yeah, pretty big ego.

"'Whatever you can do, God, I can do better.'

"So Lucifer has Earth. God has a garden, an outpost on Earth, *and* the rest of the Universe. But I think God also had a plan. I think He created humans in His image, in His likeness, but not quite. He also, purposely, left the back door to the garden unlocked, so to speak, knowing who would slither in.

"Could God have done this on purpose? Watched as Lucifer sneaked in? Smiled as Lucifer deceived Eve into eating the Forbidden fruit? Because it was all according to the plan? He had made man in His image, in His likeness, almost, but not quite. There was one more step in the process. This required deceiving the great deceiver to make it work."

Dunbar took a deep breath. Everything he'd said up to this point was preparation for his next point. Brains were going to explode.

"And then there's that damned apple, the forbidden fruit; the whole reason Lucifer left the realms of evil he ruled over, and infiltrated the stronghold of his greatest enemy. It was all because of that apple. Lucifer, egotist, was looking to sabotage God's creations and at the same time cultivate allies for his own cause. So at the very beginning of human existence, we were involved, unwillingly, in a universal war between good and evil. Between, let's face it, warring gods.

"Look at it from a scientific, evolutionary perspective.

"Evolutionists will tell you that the first species of human predecessor evolved in Africa and spread throughout the world from there. Evolutionists tell us that homo sapiens sapiens, that is, us, dropped in about 40,000 years ago, having evolved from these primitive hominids. What they don't like to tell you is that cro-magnon man, again, us, and our cousins, Neanderthal and one or two others, really don't fit the evolutionary pattern. Why? Because the development of the human brain grew larger and more complex than any other species, and at a much faster rate than evolution is supposed to work. Homo sapiens sapiens basically means the wise man who knows he is wise. Yet why are we here and Neanderthal isn't? Is it because we ate of the tree of the knowledge of good and evil, and the Neanderthal didn't?

"Dr. Isaac Asimov once wrote *The human brain is the most complex bit of organized matter we know of anywhere in the universe.*

"So what is the price we paid for this highly evolved and complex brain? Dr. Carl Sagan tells us, *So far as I know, childbirth is generally painful in only one of the millions of species on earth: human beings...Childbirth is painful because the evolution of the human skull has been spectacularly fast and recent.*

"Because of the size of our brains, human babies are born in an embryonic state, unlike just about every other living thing on Earth. Even so, childbirth is almost unbearably painful for the mother. A chimpanzee is born, causing discomfort for the mother, but not a lot of pain. The baby chimp is born with fur, able to move about, find and eat food, grasp and hang on to its mother. A human baby, on the other hand, is pretty much a waste of space, a useless blob until he or she is about three or four years old. That's because our heads are too big, we have to be born before we're ready, before our arms and legs are developed enough to support us. Moms, can you imagine giving birth to a four-year-old? That's the way it should happen. But we don't fit the evolutionary pattern. There's something different about human beings. And it even gets stranger.

"Before the first few books of the Bible were written down, experts tell us, they had first been passed from generation to generation orally. So we don't really know how old these stories are. This small group of nomads, with their unique singular God, so different from all the other gods extant at the time, finally developed a written language and wrote down their holy books. We are told that these people were so primitive that they didn't really know where babies came from, had not made the connection between sex and pregnancy.

"Hold onto your hats, now. In Genesis 3:16, God tells Eve her punishment for eating of the tree of the knowledge of good and evil: *I will make your pains in childbearing very severe; with painful labor, you will give birth to children* (NIV). So it seems that these primitive nomads who had never heard of evolution somehow knew all about evolution. Because they realized that the sudden increase in human intelligence, and the size of the human newborn's cranium, would result in painful childbirth. In other words, evolution science and the first book of the Bible match perfectly. And somebody, way back in the mists of time, knew about this.

"Anyone who has trouble believing in God has to explain this to me: Humans quickly evolve self-awareness with an unprecedented increase in the size of his brain, which, in turn, results in painful childbirth. In the first book of the Bible, written by ignorant nomads, it says that by eating from the tree of the knowledge of good and evil, humans became as gods (increased intelligence, self-awareness), and were thus cursed by, you got it, painful childbirth."

He paused again, looking over his audience. He saw open mouths, heads shaking, people engaged in whispered conversations. But they couldn't deny what he'd said. They couldn't argue against it. Science fact and religion matched exactly. And that religion came from so far back in time, there was no reliable way to date it.

"I'm not done yet. We've still got a ways to go. Keep your hands on those hats. Let's stay in Genesis chapter 3 for a minute, and see if we can figure out God's plan regarding His newly-created humans.

"You remember what happened. God told Adam and Eve they could eat anything they wanted in the garden, except from the tree of the knowledge of good and evil.

"What if God actually wanted Adam and Eve to eat from that tree. Because Adam and Eve were homo sapiens, wise man. But they didn't yet know they were wise. Look at it logically. If we were made in the image and likeness of God, wouldn't we know the difference between good and evil? I think so. And I think that was God's intention. But He stopped short because Earth was (and still is) the domain of the Devil, and the Devil needed to think he had pulled one over on God. And God—well, God also had something up His sleeve.

"When told they couldn't eat the fruit of that particular tree, what do you think they dwelled on? How do you get a teenager to do something? Every parent knows the answer to that question: Tell them not to. Did telling Adam and Eve not to eat from a particular tree only serve to focus their attention on that very tree? Did God leave the back door of the garden open knowing that Satan would sneak in and tempt Eve? Because when Adam and Eve ate from the tree of the knowledge of good and evil, they were finally complete, homo sapiens sapiens. The wise man who knows he is wise. The wise one who suffers painful childbirth. We humans were at that moment fully in the image of God. This gave God the excuse He needed to kick Adam and Eve out of the garden and into the evil world, taking with them that unique connection to their Creator. And once outside the garden, these wise humans would be a connection to God in a place where He was not welcome."

Someone in the back of the sanctuary got up and walked out. A few others moved restlessly. Dunbar knew he was treading on thin ice. Too many new concepts, some of them very close to offending his listeners. But they hadn't heard anything, yet.

Lang: ~Ten Days before Flyby

Two weeks after his elevation to Doctor of Philosophy, Ted Lang moved out of his apartment into a small rental home in Maryland, within a few miles of the National Observatory in D.C. He had secured a position at a nearby university in the Department of Astrophysics, specializing in research on the nature of red dwarf stars. He had a light teaching load, mostly supervising TAs and a cadre of visiting professors. He only taught one class a week and substituted where needed a couple of times a month.

During this first three months, Dr. Lang wrote and submitted for publication several peer-reviewed research papers, including his Doctorate thesis. His department head put him on the fast track for tenure, a challenge that appealed to Lang. He looked forward to a long and productive career as a Professor, something he could only have dreamed of before... well, before Bonner.

One morning his phone rang.

"Hello?"

"Are you Ted Lang?"

"Speaking."

"Hello, Dr. Lang. My name is Mary Hiddleston. I've read your thesis, and I was impressed. I think you're doing some really good work. I believe we should talk, and I'd like to ask you to pay a visit to my office in D.C. at the NASA radio-astronomy annex offices."

"That's interesting. May I ask what this is about?"

"I'd prefer to not discuss it over the phone, but it's important that we speak. Can you be here at 3:30 this afternoon? I understand you're fairly close by."

"Today? Well, I don't..."

"I'll have a car sent over to pick you up. Trust me, it's very important." The phone line went dead.

Lang stared at his phone screen, then stuck it back in his pocket. Then he pulled it out again. He needed to cancel a couple of other appointments.

Then he sat down at his computer and did a search for Mary Hiddleston. As he scanned the entries, his eyebrows became elevated. "Fascinating," he murmured. He spent the rest of the morning grading papers. After lunch, he briefly worked on a research paper, but his mind kept returning to Hiddleston's strange phone call. So he gave up and played computer solitaire for an hour.

There was a knock at his door at exactly 3:00 p.m. When Lang opened it, two tall middle-aged White men greeted him with no-nonsense expressions. They wore identical black suits, and various bulges behind their coats suggested to Lang that they were both armed. He recognized the "cop look" from his youth.

"You are Ted Lang." It was not a question.

"Doctor Ted Lang, yes."

"Sir, may we see some identification?"

Lang showed the two his driver's license and his university ID. After a close examination, they seemed satisfied that he was the genuine article.

One of the men returned Lang's ID cards. "Sir, will you please come with us."

Lang returned to his desk and grabbed his coat and a laptop. "Can you guys tell me what this is all about?"

One "cop" shook his head. The other said, "We're not at liberty to discuss anything. Please come with us."

Lang stepped between the two and out the door. He turned to close his door, but one of the "cops" had already taken care of it. They escorted him to a black SUV illegally parked directly in front of the building. Lang took the passenger's seat and one of the "cops" sat behind him. The other one drove as if he owned the road. Neither spoke.

After about 20 minutes of either ignoring or fighting traffic, they pulled up to a rather dilapidated building with a faded NASA insignia on the front of it. The three men exited the vehicle.

"Your phone," one of the men said, holding out a hand.

"Really?"

"And we have to ask you to leave your computer in the vehicle," the other added.

"You're kidding. Where am I supposed to write my notes?"

"You won't be taking any," the first man said. The second took Lang's phone and laptop and placed them in the black SUV. He then took up a guard position near the main door. The second man opened the door. "Please come with me, Dr.

Lang." Lang noticed a very slight emphasis on the word Doctor. He wondered if the two men were a tad racist, or if they were just accustomed to dealing with people at a much higher level, and found his junior status a bit arrogant. He decided, for the moment, to assume the latter.

Lang followed the "cop" into the building. While the facility was an annex office for NASA's radio telescope operations, it had obviously seen better days. It needed painting and better lighting. They descended a flight of stairs and down a dark hallway. The place smelled musty.

"In here," the man-in-black said, holding a door open. As Lang entered, the man took up a sentry pose outside the door, visually examining the room before he swung the door closed. This was going to be one of the strangest meetings Lang had ever participated in, he felt sure.

"Doctor Lang," a woman's voice said, brightly, "please come in. Take a seat. The furniture in this dump isn't much. I'm afraid that chair wobbles, but it's all I've got."

Lang smiled and sat in the metal folding chair. "Not a problem. My butt has seen worse," he said. He pointed to the closed door, "what's with the secret service escort?"

Hiddleston laughed. "They take security very seriously around here. For the moment, they're protecting people, us, rather than information."

"Why do we need protection?"

"Maybe preventing panic is a better description. There's a lot of misinformation out there, and there are some who tend to act on what they think they know."

"I see," Lang said. "At least I think I see."

"By-the-way, I'm Mary Hiddleston. I'm sure you've seen the news reports and the press conferences that have taken place today?"

"I'm sorry? I haven't seen a news report all day, my schedule is...or was...pretty full. Has something happened?"

Hiddleston laughed. "You might say that. Turns out that Top Secret military information was leaked to a television news reporter yesterday, and it has absolutely blown up. Then about an hour ago, Air Force General somebody-or-other, announced the top-secret designation was being removed. He said the information was now available to researchers the world over."

"What kind of information are you referring to?"

"Mostly about radio signals from space. Signals with a message. Just about everyone thinks the signals are from aliens."

Lang stared at the woman for a moment, his mouth open. "You're kidding, right? You're not joking?"

Hiddleston shook her head. "I wish. And it's happening at about the same time that a giant asteroid is headed right for us."

"I *have* heard about that," Lang said. "But unless I'm mistaken, it's supposed to miss us."

"That's what they say. But some people, in very high places I might add, are just a little nervous that these aliens, if that's what they are, show up at the same time as the asteroid."

Lang shook his head in disbelief. "I find that all very fascinating, but what's that got to do with me? Why am I here, Ms. Hiddleston? Excuse me, Dr. Hiddleston."

"Please, just call me Mary. You're here because the U.S. Air Force, and myself, need help making sense of a second message that has been received within the past week. We think you might be able to lend your expertise and help us figure out what we're looking at."

"More radio signals from space?"

"Exactly."

"You really think this stuff could be from aliens?"

"I'm trying to keep an open mind, and I hope you can too..."

"I'll do my best. What's in that message?"

"That's the problem. We're not sure. It's similar to the first one in a fashion, but contains much more data. Here, take a listen." Hiddleston turned up the volume on her speakers and activated an mp3 file sent to her by one of the Air Force researchers.

"This first part is the header. I'm sure you'll recognize it."

Lang listened for a moment, then began nodding. "It's the Fibonacci sequence. Part of it, at least. It gets so far then begins to repeat."

"Right." Hiddleston stopped the playback. "But that's just the header, something to get our attention. Now listen to this one."

The second sound file was much longer. Lang listened intently, at least in the beginning. The dits and dots and spaces were almost hypnotic after a while.

"This is much more complex," Lang said. "Have you tried graphing it?"

"I think some of the Air Force geeks are working on it. The President just gave a press conference on this very subject, so I suspect there are a lot of high-level mathematicians and scientists working on this now from all over the planet. It would be beneficial if someone from this country cracked the message, if you get my drift."

"From what I can make out of the sounds, it's fairly complex, and other than a sequentially increasing page header, it seems to repeat every so often, but with very slight differences."

"Differences?"

"Yes." He pointed to the computer. "Listen to the first set, then the last. The alterations are very minor, but definitely there."

"You think those minor differences are significant?"

Lang cupped his chin in thought. "There are numerous sets of almost identical data. You can tell because of the increasing tag. Interesting that each set is almost identical to the ones on each side. Consequently, I believe that even small differences have to be important. Or else why make them?"

"That's interesting. I don't know if anyone else has caught that. I had a feeling about you..."

"Can I get a copy of this file? One that I can take back to my office?"

Hiddleston turned to her computer. "Tell me your e-mail address and I can send it to you right now." Lang told her his address. "There, as of now you have your own copy. Both messages."

"Thank you, uh...Mary. When I get back, I'll graph out the data and let you know if I come up with anything interesting."

The two stood and Lang got ready to leave. Before he turned, Hiddleston put a hand on his arm. "The military is thinking of trying to nuke the asteroid."

"That's absurd. They think they can actually do that?"

"Obviously they do. Part of our job is to make sure they understand the consequences."

"Yeah. If they succeed in breaking that rock into pieces, some of the chunks will almost certainly be flung into Earth's gravity field. Instead of one great big impact, we could have a bunch of medium and small impacts. 'Small' being a relative term." He shook his head.

"Dr. Lang, I hope you work fast. We're running out of time."

"From asteroids to aliens. Amazing," Lang shook his head.

"From the frying pan into the fire," Hiddleston said softly. "We'll talk soon. It's been nice meeting you, Dr. Lang."

"Call me Ted," he said. "I'm just barely a doctor." He left the building in a daze and was escorted back to his office by the Men in Black. This time, he was happy to have them along.

Had he driven himself, he would have been too distracted for his own good. He almost left his laptop in the SUV.

Ishmael: ~Ten Days before Flyby

His doubt that his father had made the right decision, moving to a small town in a place not known for its tolerance, continued to grow. He suspected the three boys were toying with him about their lack of reading. Ishmael assumed that everybody read books. He couldn't imagine falling asleep at night without first reading something.

Ishmael's dad worked in the fertilizer business. He was a chemical engineer, and a good one. His services came high, but his employers got what they paid for. Currently, he worked for an agricultural research lab in charge of testing new fertilizers for use in the parched Texas midlands. It was a one-year assignment and should be sufficient to tide the family over until their permanent resident status had been confirmed.

Besides himself and his parents, Ishmael had a younger sister, Jala. She was seven and incredibly beautiful. She definitely did *not* have a Middle-East Beak. Ishmael suspected she was smarter than he. She was already reading some of the college textbooks he'd finished.

After a week at school, he still had not made any real friends. Some students would nod and say "hello," but he barely knew anyone's name. He felt lonely and isolated except when he was with his family. Back home in Saudi Arabia, he'd had many friends and school was a happy, joyful experience. Everybody knew everybody else. Of course there, the students were all boys; girls had their own schools.

Ishmael found it odd, but oddly thrilling to attend school with girls, bare headed, and many of them very assertive. He found it difficult to look at the girls, and was too shy to speak to one. Still, he managed "hello" and "how are you?" in the rare opportunities where he felt it was appropriate. He also noted that in this American school, there were no classes in religion, unlike the schools back home.

He still had trouble understanding the Texas drawl and much of the local slang. But he learned quickly, and began to pick up, and use, some of the local argot.

He occasionally saw the three boys he'd met on his first day, although they all but ignored Ishmael. Sometimes they'd loudly shout "Here comes Mo-Ham-Head," and then laugh.

Ishmael confessed to his dad that the term seemed derogatory and it made him uneasy.

"They're probably just making fun of our religion out of ignorance. When you have a chance, talk to them. Ask them about their religion."

"I don't know if that would be such a good idea, Dad, but I'll think about it."

The family was Islamic, but not devoutly so. They observed Ramadan and did not eat pork, but they did not typically attend services at a Mosque. The nearest Mosque here was over fifty miles North in Lubbock. Occasionally the family found Dad kneeling on his sajjâda, facing Ka'aba and praying. However, both parents were relatively progressive and embraced diversity.

In fact, it was a Jewish executive at NASA, Gerald Spitzer, who was responsible for the family's move from Saudi Arabia to nowhere Texas. Many years earlier, Hadad and Spitzer had met at a university in, of all places, Thailand, and had become good friends. Spitzer was the family's immigration sponsor in the U.S.

Ishmael was too small and too studious to play sports. He even avoided the haphazard play during recess and lunch periods. Instead, he liked to spend time in the school library, reading. Since the school's offerings were rather sparse and tended to be outdated, he typically read from his tablet.

One night, Father took Ishmael and Jala exploring in his battered work pickup. They went out into the country beyond the lights of the small town. When it was very dark, he parked in a field next to an old empty farmhouse and barn. As with so many others in the area, this property had been abandoned many years ago. If his work panned out, they could put some of these old farms back into production.

The old truck had a worn mattress in the back. Ishmael and Jala spread a clean sheet over the mattress and lie down to look up at the stars. Their father walked over to the house to explore. He wouldn't be able to see much with the tiny flashlight he held, but still, it was an adventure.

Jala was delighted to see so many stars.

"Look!" Ishmael said, pointing, "a shooting star." The small meteor flashed across the sky and disappeared.

"What's a shooting star?"

"It is a small rock from space," Ishmael said. "It burned up when it fell into Earth's atmosphere. It's called a meteor."

"Well...maybe it wasn't a meteor."

"Oh?"

"Maybe it was an angel."

"I didn't see any wings on it."

"Maybe it was an angel without wings."

"And what would you do, little one, if that angel landed right next to us?"

Jala giggled. "I'd ask it where its wings were, and how it could fly without them."

"Look, there's another one," Ishmael said.

"The sky is full of angels," Jala exclaimed softly. "Look at them. So many of them are just watching us. Waiting."

"Waiting for what?"

He felt his sister shrug. "Maybe they're waiting to see if we know how to be good."

"Could be. I think you've already convinced them."

Jala turned toward her brother. Ishmael could see her eyes shining, two dark pools with their own stars twinkling inside.

Silently, the two gazed back at the heavens. They saw more shooting stars. Here, in the dark, away from the bright lights, the sky was alive with tiny burning meteors, and looking back at the two children, an unimaginable number of twinkling stars.

Sometime later, they heard their father's shoes crunching dirt and gravel, walking back to the truck. "How are you two doing?"

"It's wonderful, Father. How can the night be dark when there are so many stars watching us?"

Father laughed softly. "That's a good question, Jala. It's getting cold. Let's go home and think about it."

That was the last night of happiness for Ishmael. Later in the week, he decided to make a suicide bomb.

Ford and Smithson: ~Ten Days before Flyby

"This is Marsha Ford reporting live from Barksdale Air Force Base in Louisiana. I'm speaking with General Harris Smithson, leader of the research team investigating the strange radio signals from space. The General is also representing the United States in a global effort to deflect the approaching asteroid using nuclear weapons. General Smithson, do you really believe that nuking the asteroid can work?"

Smithson smiled. "Our confidence is high that we can deflect the asteroid, if we can hit the damn thing. Five nations have committed to joining us..."

"Can you tell our viewers which nations?"

Smithson paused. "China, Russia, Great Britain, Israel, and France."

"General, it's my understanding that the asteroid will approach Earth at tens of thousands of miles per hour. How can you expect to reliably hit something going that fast?"

"It won't be easy, trust me," the General chuckled. "We, in the U.S. at least, will be using a relatively new Artificial Intelligence computer guidance system to plot and launch our asset. We are very confident that we can hit the asteroid exactly where we want to hit it."

"And what will be the results of that nuclear explosion? Or explosions. Do you want to break up the asteroid, or deflect it in some manner?"

"That's a very good question, Ms. Ford. What we'd really like to do is both. If we can bust the asteroid into several pieces, they are less likely to be pulled into Earth's gravity field. If we can deflect the entire asteroid away from us that would solve the entire problem."

"And what if, General, some of those pieces do end up impacting the Earth?"

Smithson waved a hand, "Of course that could potentially cause destruction should one or more of these chunks hit near an inhabited area. But remember, most of the pieces will burn up in Earth's atmosphere. For rocks that might reach the surface, well, two-thirds of our planet's surface is water. The likelihood is that any pieces pulled in would burn up or impact water."

"Tsunamis?"

"Possible, but unlikely. And remember, this scenario is only if the rocket from the United States is less than successful. There will be five other attempts by the associated nations. When all of this is over, that asteroid will be little more than rubble. We think we can do this. We're confident of success.

And if we get the rubble we expect, we'll have the best global fireworks show in recorded history."

"Thank you, General. Now about those radio signals?"

Smithson chuckled again. "We believe the radio signals originated on Earth, were directed at and have been bouncing off the surface of the moon."

"So you don't believe they're alien?"

"Anything's possible, but in this case, very unlikely. We will, of course, continue to study the data, and we'll be on the lookout for the source. It could turn out to be alien, but I'm not optimistic."

"We've been speaking to Air Force General Harris Smithson. Thank you, General. This is Marsha Ford reporting. Back to you, Terri."

Smithson: ~Nine Days before Flyby

Colonel Meyer stepped into the room. "General? You asked for me, Sir?"

"Ah, yes. Come in Colonel. Have a seat."

Meyer sat stiffly on the edge of his chair, waiting for the pronouncement of his trial.

"Relax, Colonel. I'm restoring you to duty, no restrictions. All charges against you have been dropped."

"Dropped, Sir?"

"Yes. In reality, no charges were ever filed as I had not yet finished my investigation. So your service record remains clean. I'm sure that will meet with your approval."

"Of course, Sir. I'm just a little confused as to why."

"No mystery, Meyer. The President has ordered all information regarding the asteroid and the radio signals to be declassified immediately. So there are no longer grounds for prosecuting you."

"Oh." Meyer sat silently for a while. "I believe that was a prudent move, Sir."

Smithson grimaced. "I don't think so. You used poor judgement, Colonel, and that needed to be addressed. But I'm certainly not going to oppose my Commander-in-Chief, and I'm of the opinion that you have learned your lesson. So you're off the hook, Colonel. You may resume your normal duties immediately. You may also take a couple of days of leave, if you wish."

"Thank you, Sir. I think I'd rather get back to work, if you approve."

"Your choice, Colonel. Dismissed."

Meyer stood and saluted, then got out quickly. Once outside the door, he heaved a sigh of relief. Now he could devote his worry to the radio signals. And, of course, the asteroid.

"Davis," Smithson said into the intercom. "I want Major O'Brien over here immediately. Get him for me, will you?"

"Right, General."

Fifteen minutes later, Major Kurt O'Brien knocked and entered. He stood at rigid attention and saluted. His uniform was clean and pressed. He held his service cap tightly at his side. Smithson returned the salute. "At ease, Major. Have a seat."

"Sir! Yes sir!"

Smithson smiled. Now *here* was an officer. O'Brien knew how to comport himself and show respect to a superior officer. O'Brien ought to be a Colonel, Smithson thought, and that half-witted Meyer busted all the way back to First Lieutenant. This was, of course, not an action he could justify so he just had to live with it. At least for the time being.

O'Brien was a nuclear weapons fire control specialist on loan from USNORTHCOM at Peterson Air Force Base in

Colorado Springs. It was O'Brien and his team that would actually launch the nuke.

"You got my memo, Major?"

"Yes, Sir. You wanted my department to finalize our calculations."

"And have you done so?"

"General, we can, with high confidence, launch an Earth-based modified Atlas 5 in a trajectory intersecting the target asteroid. Our chances of actually impacting the asteroid are somewhat less, and range at about 55 to 60% probability of success, Sir."

Smithson's eyes widened. "Have you factored in the use of our artificial intelligence system?"

"Yes, sir. In fact, the percentages I just quoted you were determined by the A.I. itself."

Smithson tried not to show his surprise. "Did it explain why the percentages were so low, Major?"

"Sir, that is our job. I will endeavor to explain."

"Enlighten me, Major."

"Well, Sir, as you are aware, the asteroid is headed toward us at a very high velocity. While our target is a very large asteroid in relation to most other asteroids that pass near us, it is in respect to the size of the Earth itself, quite small. A fast-moving, relatively small target presents a range of problems, and a high number of potentially negative results. All factors considered, that is the best scenario we could expect. In actual practice, our chances may be somewhat less than prediction."

"I see," Smithson said.

"We could improve our chances," O'Brien said, "if we were able to launch the Atlas from a point above Earth's atmosphere. But, of course, that is beyond our current capabilities."

"So there is no certainty that you could hit that damned rock."

"I'm afraid not, Sir. And we wouldn't actually want to hit it anyway."

"Say again?"

"Our hope is that the asteroid is a bunch of smaller rocks traveling in concert. If we detonate our explosive about, say, 20 meters above the surface we could try to deflect the pieces without blowing it apart. If, on the other hand, the object is a solid chunk of rock, iron, nickel, or other dense materials...well, that's another story entirely."

"How so?"

"Imagine launching a standard grenade from a helicopter at a fully-loaded out-of-control 18-wheeler. Even if you can hit it, regardless of its velocity, you won't have much of an effect. Throw several grenades, it still won't stop the truck's trajectory. Standard grenades simply aren't powerful enough."

"You're not giving me much confidence here, O'Brien. You're saying that the efforts of six nations would have little or no effect on this asteroid. Is that what you're saying?"

"Once again, it depends on the asteroid's composition. But essentially, Sir, you are correct for a worst-case scenario. We will be launching our missiles from the surface of the Earth. Our dense atmosphere causes aiming problems. Even minor deviations in launch control will increase exponentially with distance, and once our assets are in space and on their way to the asteroid, control signal lag increases as the missiles fly further from Earth. If we plan to hit that thing out beyond the orbit of the Moon, signal delay can reach two or three seconds. Double that for feedback confirmation. So we have opted, instead, to attempt our impact after the asteroid has traveled well within the orbit of the Moon. That scenario, of course, gives us much less time to correct errors or react to new information. Sir."

Smithson sighed and threw his hands in the air. "So what the hell am I suppose to tell the President?"

"All you can tell him, Sir, is that we will do the best we can. We think we can hit it, but..." O'Brien spread his hands and looked worried.

Dunbar: ~Two Weeks before Flyby

"God needed to send his creations out into the rest of the world, that which was ruled over by Satan and his fallen angels. It was the only way to infiltrate the enemy's territory. Using this plan, God revealed to the rest of the universe that Satan was truly evil, a liar, and a deceiver. And it was Satan's fault that these new creations, these humans, who were now God's chosen people, were let loose into the world.

"Let's go back a little to Genesis 1:11 and 12: *And God said, Let the earth bring forth grass, the herb yielding seed, and the fruit tree yielding fruit after his kind, whose seed is in itself, upon the earth: and it was so.*

"Sounds a little like DNA, doesn't it? When human beings get together and make a baby, it doesn't come out a hippo. When we plant an apple seed we expect to get an apple tree, not a grapevine. That's genetics, more science. Why would God put genetics into the Bible? Could it be that someone, outside the garden, was messing around with genetics?

"God was the creator of the universe, and the being who was in charge of Earth wanted to take God's place. The one in charge of Earth had an ego the size of the Pacific Ocean."

A short pause. Then, "Let me ask you this question. God created the universe, He created humans. But can Lucifer, Satan, the Serpent, create stuff, too?"

He heard a chorus of "no"s from the audience. They were all certain they knew the answer to *this* question. Unfortunately, they were wrong. He was treading on very thin ice now. He smiled.

"*Of course he can!* In fact, you and I can create stuff. Give an artist a blank canvas and she will create a stunning scene. Give a carpenter a bunch of wood, and he'll make you a wonderful cabinet. Give a farmer seeds, and he'll create a thousand acres of corn. We can *all* create stuff. What we can't to, and what Satan can't do, either, is create stuff out of nothing. Only God can do that. But the Devil *can* create stuff out of something. And if God was concerned with genetics maybe it's because Satan, himself, was an accomplished genetic engineer.

"What if, outside the Garden of Eden, Satan was showing off his ego? Changing things, making them bigger, more evil, more spectacular? God created alligators and ostriches. Could Lucifer have taken God's creations and genetically engineered the age of dinosaurs? Taking the animals God created from nothing and turning them into monsters? Why does every ancient civilization on earth have legends of dragons and giant beasts? Lucifer saying to the universe, 'Look what I did! Look at the choppers on that thing!'

"Maybe dinosaurs were here on Earth because the Great Evolutionist made them.

"And when he saw that God had made man in His likeness and Image, Lucifer was determined to make his own intelligent bipedal humanoids. And maybe these are what our evolution scientists are digging up; Satan's failed attempts to make a human. And Lucifer was persistent. He got close with the Neanderthals and the Denisovans and probably others we haven't found yet. It is known that Homo Sapiens Sapiens interbred with these other human types. Some of us carry portions of their DNA within us. Some of us, perhaps importantly, don't.

"Dinosaurs, strange and awful plants, giant insects, humans that weren't. Is this the world into which Adam and Eve found themselves after being expelled from the garden? And we ended up with layers and layers of Satan's failed experiments, drowned and buried during the Great Flood. Today we dig up their fossils and are amazed at the seeming age of the earth! And in other cases, we pump out their remains in the form of oil.

"Through Adam and Eve, and their descendants, God's presence influenced the world that was the headquarters of evil.

"It also kind of explains why the Bible was concerned with humans not 'lying with beasts' if some of those 'beasts' had almost the exact shape and form of humans. Gives a whole new meaning to the phrase 'chosen people.'"

Two more members of his audience got up and left. Dunbar heard the soft buzzing of quiet conversations. It was time to hit them with the mind-blower.

"Beginning in Genesis chapter 5, we have the 'begats' ending in Noah. The 'begats' also sound suspiciously like a genetic breeding program. Here's another question. Do you think Lucifer would try to sabotage God's humans with a little human genetic engineering here and there? Not making his own humans as he had done before, mind you, but wrecking the ones God had made? Making them, perhaps, evil and nasty and violent? Perhaps the purpose of this part of the Bible was to record the generations of those who weren't re-engineered by Satan, those who remained as the Creator God had made them.

"In Genesis 6:2 we learn *that the sons of God saw the daughters of men that they were fair; and they took them wives of all which they chose.*

"When it says 'sons of God' in Genesis 6 could it mean more results of Lucifer's engineering? Go to verse 4: *There were giants in the earth in those days; and also after that, when the sons of God came in unto the daughters of men, and they bare children to them, the same became mighty men which were of old, men of renown.* 'Sons of God' could also mean 'creations of God,' which includes Lucifer, the evil angels, and even the genetically modified primitive hominids that were the results of Lucifer's experiments. We know, today, that Homo sapiens sapiens interbred with Homo sapiens neanderthalensis, and some of us are descendants of that mixing. Another match between science and the Bible?

"Throws out an entirely new visual when we mix in the mother of all mad scientists.

"In Genesis 6 verse 7: *And the LORD said, I will destroy man whom I have created from the face of the earth; both man, and beast, and the creeping thing, and the fowls of the air; for it repenteth me that I have made them.*'

Dunbar stopped again. "You know where we're headed with this, right? In verse 9, we find that Noah, at the end of the 'begats,' was a 'righteous man' and in the King James version, it says *Noah was a just man and perfect in his generations...* Which, if we turn it around, means all the other 'begats' other than Noah's line were somehow imperfect. All the animals and birds out in the world that God had created were, somehow, now imperfect, and He regretted what had happened.

"Here we have the end result of a genetic experiment, a method to keep God's chosen people, along with the plants and animals He had originally created 'perfect'.

"In verse 11: *The earth also was corrupt before God, and the earth was filled with violence.* And whose fault would that be? So God had Noah build his ark and sent to him the animals that were as He had created them, perhaps leading them directly from the Garden itself to the ark. No dinosaurs. No giant insects. No strange plants. No semi-human creatures.

"Take a look at Genesis 9:4, *God demands an accounting from each animal and each human being* (NIV). Really? An accounting? Why? Because, if you keep reading *...for in the* *image of God has God made mankind.* And God goes on to establish His covenant with Noah and his descendants, *and every living thing that came out of the ark with you...* This 'accounting' might just be a test of genetic purity.

"After the flood, the dinosaurs were gone. The strange plants, insects, and humanoids created by Satan were gone, wiped from the face of the earth. Imagine all those plants and insects buried by the Flood, turning into what we find today of their remnants as oil. Which is another strange thing. Today when animals die, they decompose because of the actions of certain insects, and bacteria. There isn't much left over to make oil. We'll get back to this later, but what if back before the Flood, there weren't these insects and bacteria that feed off dead flesh, and when animals died, they didn't decompose as they do today, but instead were eventually buried and compressed into oil? No proof, just a thought.

"The literal story of Noah and the Ark indicates that earth's total population after the Flood was eight. But could they have been eight families or eight genetic lines, rather than eight individual people?

"Some anthropologists tell us that human DNA does not have the diversity of a large and growing population dating from the time of Cro-Magnon's first appearance. They speculate that sometime during the early history of humans on earth, some event or series of events (speculated as, perhaps, the eruption of a super-volcano) seriously reduced the total number of humans from, perhaps, several million, to a population of a thousand or even less. Today, we are all descended from this small population of survivors.

"Once again, in the Bible, we have a small population of humans surviving a cataclysmic event, and in science, we have a small population of humans surviving an equally cataclysmic but unknown event. I don't know why, but it seems that Science and the Bible keep bumping into each other."

Kylie: ~Nine Days before Flyby

The day after Kylie's return home, a pair of police detectives visited the Janeway family, seeking any additional information that might lead them to the seven men involved in the girl's assault. Kylie sat in the overstuffed chair by herself, staring at the floor. Her parents took the love seat and the officers sat on the sofa.

"From what we've learned so far," Detective Emily Carlson said, "there appears to be two other instances similar to yours, Kylie. One took place a week ago in Bellevue and the other one a month ago in Tacoma. The victim in Tacoma was severely beaten and is still in the hospital in a coma."

Detective Mark Wheeler added, "It seems they break into an abandoned home, make it look like a fraternity house of some kind, then lure an unsuspecting young lady to a 'party.' And you know what happens after that."

Carlson gave her partner a dirty look, then softened as she looked back at Kylie. "We haven't been able to get a DNA or blood-type match. Is there anything you can remember, Kylie, that might help us find them?"

Kylie shook her head, still focused on the carpet. "I–I don't remember much. I wish I could help. They gave me something, I wasn't really conscious." She glanced up at the cops, then looked away.

"We think they gave you gamma-hydroxybutyric acid," Wheeler said. "It's a common date-rape drug known by a bunch of unflattering names. We'll know more once we get access to your lab results."

"Try to remember, Kylie. Anything at all," Emily said, "no matter how insignificant it might seem to you could be the one little piece that breaks this case open."

Kylie looked at the female detective. "Well," she said slowly, "I did notice Chad seemed to have a little bit of an accent. The others might have, too, but they didn't speak much."

Wheeler wrote in his notebook. "Would you say it might be more of a French accent, or maybe German?"

Kylie shrugged. "It sounded almost...Russian, maybe."

"That's good. That will help. Anything else?"

Kylie shook her head, then gazed back down at the carpet, hugging herself and rocking.

Kylie's dad stood up. "These other victims. Did either of them provide you with any useful information?"

Emily shook her head. "The first one has still not regained consciousness. The other one, about the same as we got from your daughter. It's hard to get accurate information from people who have suffered such a traumatic event. We think they might be immigrants from somewhere in Eastern Europe, early twenties, and morally deviant. Unfortunately, they keep moving around. We're not quite fast enough to catch up with them."

"When you do catch them," Roger Janeway said, looming over the two detectives, "I'd like you to do me a favor."

"Yes, sir?"

"Shoot every damn last one of them," he said forcefully. "Shoot 'em. Shoot 'em again and again. Don't stop until you run out of stinking bullets," he finished with a shout.

Kylie's mom stood and held onto her husband. Kylie watched her father with wide eyes. She had never seen him that angry before. His passion did something to her, deep inside. She started crying again.

Cranston: ~Nine Days before Flyby

Four days after receiving the second message, David and his friends had made little progress in deciphering the data.

David had been gone two of those days attending a math competition at Rockhurst University in Kansas City. He had been so distracted by the message that he placed only third.

Upon returning home, David, Samantha, and Dwight had met at study hall to catch up and continue discussing the pages David had plotted. It made no more sense to them now that it had earlier. They broke for lunch, then returned to their project. David spent much of that afternoon searching the Internet for others who might have made some progress. If anyone had, they were not posting it online.

That evening, after David got home, he parked his car in front of the house and walked quietly up to the porch. He wanted to avoid confronting his mom, and he especially didn't want to run into Biff-the-Belly. All he wanted was a quick dinner, then to his room where he could resume studying the alien message in peace.

He unlocked the door and entered quietly. The house was silent, then he heard a muffled giggle from upstairs, and a deeper mumbled voice. Curious, he eased himself up the stairs and stood just outside their bedroom door. He heard a third, strange, voice, and deduced it emanated from their computer, probably a YouTube video.

"See that?" He heard Biff say, "Bill-what's-his-name, you know the billionaire computer guy? He's giving a secret talk to the CIA about vaccines with microchips he wants to have embedded in us. He's evil."

"Why microchips," Janet said with a slight giggle.

"So they can control us. They can use them chips to tell us where to go and what to do."

"Why?"

"Control, Babe. They want your freedoms."

"Okay." She didn't sound convinced.

"Here, watch this one. This one's about chemtrails."

"Chem whats?"

"You know, that white stuff that comes out of the back of jets. This here guy's an expert and he says them chemtrails before now were just practice runs. In a few days, they'll be criss-crossing the entire Earth with them."

"And why would they do that?"

Biff laughed. "They're gonna use them to slow down that asteroid. They want it to hit the Earth."

"Who's 'they'?"

"You know, Babe, rich people. The Illuminati, people with all the secret knowledge. They got everything set up underground. When that thing hits, it will destroy all of civilization, then they'll come out and take over. We'll all be slaves."

"Sounds like he's got it all figured out. But..."

"What?"

"If the asteroid hits, won't we all be dead? We can't be slaves if we're all dead."

"Just watch the freaking video, okay? It's all in there. Not everybody is gonna die."

"I hope we survive, Biff. What if he's wrong?"

"No way, Babe, that guy knows what he's talking about. Right now FEMA is setting up concentration camps where they will house the survivors who aren't rich."

"And that's where Bill-what's-his-name is gonna inject us with nanobots?"

"You got it, Babe. Everybody needs to listen to this guy. Our country needs to wake up and smell the outhouse."

"Well, you certainly smell like an outhouse, Biff. Get your butt out of this bed and go take a shower. Sheesh."

David shook his head in disgust. Only an idiot would believe everything they saw on YouTube. Of course, he already knew Biff-Bubble-Butt was a major league idiot. Still shaking his head, he sneaked back down the stairs.

In the kitchen, he put a pot of water on to boil, grabbed a package of ramen noodles, a boiled egg from the fridge, and a stalk of green onion. He chopped the onion into small slices, peeled the egg, and tossed most of the yolk into the trash. The rest of the egg he broke into pieces. When the water boiled, he dumped everything into the pot, along with the seasoning pack, and waited for his dinner to heat to a boil.

"Well, if it isn't the lost boy," his mom said from behind him. "I thought I heard someone fumbling around in the kitchen."

David tensed, but didn't turn around.

"Look at me when I'm talking to you! And where the hell have you been all day?"

He turned around and saw his mom and Biff standing in the doorway.

"School, Mom. It's a school day, remember?"

"Don't lie to me, you pathetic weasel. I called the school and they told me you didn't show up for any of your classes, just like last week. What's gotten into you, Boy?"

"You called the school? Why?"

His mom laughed. "Hard as it is for you to believe, Sugar, I'm still responsible for you."

"Yeah, that's a laugh. You haven't been responsible for anything since Dad died."

Biff stepped forward. "You don't talk to your mother like that. Now answer her question."

"I *was* in school. I'm working on a special project, so I didn't attend classes today."

Mom looked up at the ceiling. "What a liar."

"I'm not lying. I was in the study hall. You can ask Samantha or Dwight. They were with me the whole time. They'll tell you."

"So you want me to ask two other worthless students to back up your worthless lie? Not gonna happen, pal."

"I'm not..."

"Shut up. You're grounded for two weeks. You go to school and nowhere else. Now get to your room. I don't want to see you until you leave for school in the morning. And you miss any more classes, you'll be grounded for a month."

David laughed humorlessly. "Why do you all of a sudden care if I go to school or not?"

His mom smiled. "I get home school money for you, baby chick, and after school care. Each month. Can't have you missing school, or they might take notice and stop the flow of free money."

"How can you do that? I'm almost eighteen."

"Biff, here," she patted his shoulder, "he told me how to do that. Biff knows a lot of stuff, and you should appreciate him more."

"Mom, I don't need daycare. I'm not a child."

"The government don't need to know that, Sonny," Biff said. "They think you're a little tyke."

"You two are a real piece of work, Mom. You guys make a sewer look like a mountain spring..."

"That's enough!" Biff shouted, stepping forward. "Any more of your mouth and I'm going to slap you into next week."

David laughed. "Your arms aren't long enough to reach past that belly, Burrito Butt."

Biff growled and lunged for David. Janet stepped in front of the older man. She turned her head and shouted, "Go to your room, David."

"I haven't had my dinner yet, Mother dear."

"You don't get dinner," Biff snapped.

"Relax, Dear. Don't spoil everything," Janet whispered into Biff's ear, but still loud enough for David to hear. "Remember, once we get rid of him, we can apply to be foster parents. We'll get paid to have little kids do all the work around here. We'll live like kings."

"Yeah. Well, when does he get tossed out on his ear?"

"Soon, Dear. Soon."

"Not soon enough for me," Biff growled.

David laughed. "Not a chance, Bernard. Remember, you and Mom burned all my college apps. I'll be living here until I retire from burger flipping." He grasped the handle of the pot. "Now you two lovebirds go vegetate in the living room and watch some brainless reality show on TV while I eat my dinner. Or, I can throw this pot of boiling water in your faces and send you both to the emergency room. Your choice."

Silence held sway for a long moment. "Come along, Janet. We'll let him eat, then I'll kill him in his sleep. I will. I'd love it." They turned and left the kitchen, whispering and giggling.

David sat at the table and tried to relax while his noodles soaked in the hot water.

God! He hated living here.

He managed to slurp down most of his food, but the noodles had turned to mush. After dinner, he went to his room. It was located off the kitchen and down a flight of rather steep stairs in the partially-finished basement. He had a private bedroom, even his own bathroom, and his Mom never went down there. He didn't think Biff-Blubber-Butt would even fit down the narrow steps.

As David descended the stairs, he took a deep breath and smiled. He was happy to have this own small refuge where he could relax. He didn't know if he could have tolerated sleeping on the same level as those two.

David pulled out the graph papers that he and his friends had worked on earlier. He was convinced it was a thirty-frame video. The difference between frame one and frame thirty was small, and any movement would be minor. Yet he knew it must hold answers. It *was* a message, he was sure of that.

The asteroid was due to pass Earth in just over a week. He

realized if there was any connection, it needed to be found very soon, or it would be too late.

He assembled the sheets and riffled through them. There was movement, but the paper was too imprecise to study minutely. Earlier at school, David had scanned each sheet into his PC, saving them as jpg files.

Now, he imported them into his video editing program, giving each frame a fifth-of-a-second span. The entire video would last about five or six seconds.

He saved the project, rendered it into an MP4 file, then took a deep breath, and clicked on "Play."

What he saw still mystified him. The two triangles in the upper left moved slightly, and the small circle moved a tiny bit to keep pace. The large crescent in the lower right did not move at all. How could this be a message?

He slowed the playback and watched it again. This time he noticed that the two triangles did not fully keep pace with each other. They moved in tandem, but at the end, separated a tiny bit in the process. The second triangle moved ever so slightly away and down toward the right.

That had to be the clue he sought. It had to be, there was virtually no other movement in the video. Now he only needed to find out what the two triangles represented.

Ishmael: ~Nine Days before Flyby

The week began with the same barely veiled hostility from Chet, Dod, and Timmy. Every time they saw him, they called out "Hey, Mo-Ham-Head" despite his attempts to convince them that it was offensive to him.

"We follow the Prophet Muhammad. The way you pronounce it is offensive. What if I made fun of your Jesus."

"We'd pound you into the ground, Mo-Ham-Head," Chet said.

Some of the other kids were starting to pick up the epithet.

After school, the three boys sought out Ishmael. "Hey, Ham-Head," Chet called.

"You talking to me? What do you want now?"

"Come with us. We want to show you something," Dod called.

"I can't go with you. I'm on my way home." Ishmael joined the three boys. "What is it? What do you want to show me?"

"Come on. It's a little walk out of town. Won't take long at all. And don't be afraid. We're not gonna do something, like, bad, or somethin'" They almost seemed to be friendly, so Ishmael decided to go with them. The four walked South, along the main road out of town, then took a side road that hadn't been maintained.

"So what do you want to be when you finish school?" Timmy asked.

Ishmael smiled. "Either an engineer or a physicist."

"Sounds hard. No wonder you read so much."

"How about you?"

Timmy looked up. "I think I'll join the Navy."

Dod laughed. "You can't even swim, dimwit. You need to swim to join the Navy."

"Okay, then I'll join the Air Force. I don't have to flap my arms and fly, do I?"

"In your case, it would probably help."

Chet laughed and kicked a rock.

Out of town, they came to a run-down abandoned shack with several large trees. Out back were the remnants of a barn that had collapsed years ago.

They stopped halfway between the two buildings.

"We dug this hole last year, take a look," Chet said. The hole was about four feet in diameter. Ishmael couldn't see how deep it was, maybe two or three feet. The hole was lined with a section of corrugated steel that had seen better days.

"What is this?" Ishmael asked.

"It's our personal, private zoo," Chet said. "Go ahead, look inside."

As Ishmael leaned over, something moved in the deep shadow. He heard a peculiar buzzing sound.

"Know what that is?" Chet said softly next to Ishmael's ear.

The Arab boy shook his head.

"It's a rattlesnake," Dod said. "We caught him two weeks ago. We keep it in here, bring it water and mice or rats every week or so."

"I've heard of rattlesnakes. Aren't they..."

"Yeah," Chet said, "they're poisonous. Bite you, kill you dead."

"This is, like, our third one," Dod said. "After a while, they die in there, then we have to go find another one. Plenty of 'em around here."

Timmy laughed. "Once old lady Simmons yelled at us for messing up her garden. So we took her dog, tied a rope around it, and tossed it in this here snake pit."

"After it was dead," Chet said softly, chewing on a length of straw, "we pulled it out and dumped it in her garden."

"How could you do such a horrible thing?" Ishmael said, stepping back from the pit and gazing at the smiling boys.

"The old lady forgot her place. We had to teach her. Most people around here know their place. We even got some Black families living in town, we can't call 'em what they really are or we'd get in trouble. But they know their place. If they forget, we teach 'em."

"How do you get away with that kind of activity?"

"Ha!" Dod laughed. "You forgot who our dads are."

"So why are you telling me all this?" Ishmael asked. "And why'd you show me that horrible snake?" He backed away from the pit a few steps.

"You see, Mo-Ham-Head..."

"Don't call me that!"

"There you go, that's your problem, see. You keep forgetting your place. You don't listen so good." Chet stepped toward Ishmael, "Like I said, we don't want your kind here. We told you that, and you ain't been listening," He gave Ishmael a soft shove, sending the boy back toward the road a few steps. "Now it's time to listen. You and your family don't pack up and get out of town, we just might have to toss you in that pit."

"But my dad's job is here. We can't move. I can't make my parents move."

Dod clucked. "That's too bad. The other day, we saw your little sister with your mom downtown."

"Maybe we should teach you a lesson," Chet said, spitting the straw into the pit. "We toss your sister in that pit, why then you'd be happy to move, or you'd be next. Ya think?"

Ishmael was too shocked to respond.

"Maybe you better go home and have that talk with your dad," Timmy said softly. "We ain't gonna give you much longer to get the hell out of town."

Dod gave Ishmael another little shove. "Y'all heard what he said, right?"

Ishmael glared at the three Texans. "Oh, yes. I heard. I will go home and I will speak to my father." He started walking back toward town, then he turned back. "You three will pay for this. I swear you will pay. You threatened my sister? That was a mistake." He turned and walked away, ignoring their laughter and jeers.

When Ishmael got home, he didn't speak to his father. This was his problem, and he'd solve it. And he knew just how he would go about it. Out in the garage, left there by the previous owner, was an old, worn-out fishing vest with lots of little pockets on the front for various lures and bait.

The next day at school, he grabbed a block of clay from the art class. Students were allowed to take blocks of clay home when working on school projects. Ishmael used the clay to fashion several round narrow pieces of clay that fit the vest's pockets and protruded an inch or so above each pocket.

Next, he got some colored wire his dad kept in the bottom of a toolbox. He cut the wire to size, then poked various strands into the clay. Then Ishmael got the cigarette lighter button from their car, which nobody used. He attached the colored wires to the lighter. If one did not look too closely, the vest, clay, wires, and button resembled a suicide bomber vest filled with plastic explosive.

Before going to bed that night, Ishmael checked some information on his computer. He searched specific times for different locations, adjusted for various time zones, based on estimates from scientists. He was in luck. The timing would be just about right.

He hid the jacket in his room. A few days later, Ishmael took the vest with him to school. He kept it in his locker until school was out, then he went into the boy's bathroom and put it on under his long Winter coat. It was a little warm for the coat, but he didn't think it would cause undue attention. It was almost time to send those three boys a message they would never forget.

Lang: ~Eight Days before Flyby

Ted Lang listened to the files Mary Hiddleston had sent him the previous afternoon. The main one was a very long file and made no sense. He went back to the original radio message and listened to it again. Then he reviewed the Fibonacci signal. After listening to the third file again, he began making notes and plotting the data.

After several hours of intense work, he had a series of thirty plots of just about the same thing. There were minor differences, but the images didn't really make much sense. A circle, two triangles, and a large crescent.

If he believed all the hype, Lang had to consider that this information came from aliens, hard as that was to accept. Looked at in that light, he began to wonder what relevance, if any, the signals had to do with the incoming asteroid. He looked at his work again, and his eyes widened as a possible relation occurred to him.

His phone rang. "Hello?"

"Hiddleston here. Dr. Lang, have you had a chance to review the radio signals?"

"Yes, I have."

"Anything?"

"Possibly. After studying the messages, I think I've identified two of the elements. I believe the large crescent at the bottom right represents the Earth."

Hiddleston didn't answer.

"I also think that the small upper left circle might be a representation of an alien spacecraft."

"Interesting," Hiddleston said. "That was something I hadn't considered. What about the two triangles?"

"I don't have a clear picture," Lang said. "Perhaps the two triangles designate something about the alien ship, or perhaps the location of their home planet. Something like that. But I don't understand why there are two of them."

"Hmm. Well, that's more than my people have come up with. Our military colleagues are busy trying to decide if they can nuke the asteroid, so they haven't had a lot of time to think about aliens."

"They believe they can hit that thing and do something?"

"Evidently."

"You agree with their assessment?"

"I'm a little concerned the military has made up their minds that the asteroid is going to hit Earth and that a nice, big, fat explosion will save us all. Every astronomer I've consulted still maintains it will be a near miss. I'm hoping the military doesn't know something we don't."

Lang chuckled. "That would be embarrassing."

"We've got eight days before we all know. Thanks for the information. I'll pass it along to our colleagues."

"If I come up with anything else," Lang said, "I'll get it to you soonest."

"Great. Wouldn't it be amazing if that circle really did represent an alien spaceship?"

"Amazing, yes," Lang said, "but I'd really like to know why they're here and why they keep sending us mysterious data. There's a message in there. I'm just not quite seeing it all."

"Give it some time," Hiddleston replied. "Everything will become clear. Bye for now."

Smithson ~Eight Days before Flyby

"Mr. President, based on information from my team of experts, I'm not convinced that a preemptive nuclear strike on the asteroid is warranted or even possible." The President didn't respond at once. Smithson looked at his phone to see if he was still connected.

"General, are you telling me that we can't hit that asteroid and deflect it away from the Earth."

"I wouldn't exactly put it in those words, Mr. President. All our observations to date are still telling us the rock will miss

Earth. I'm concerned that attempts to deflect it, may in fact push the asteroid closer to Earth, making impact more likely."

"So doing something might make things worse than doing nothing? That what you're saying?"

"Essentially, Mr. President."

"You are aware, are you not, that Admiral Ardmore is urging us to proceed with the launch. She is of the opinion that the alien radio signals are warning us of an impact..."

"Sir," Smithson interrupted, "even if she's right, we only have a 50 to 60 percent chance of successfully hitting our target."

"But there's a chance, General."

Smithson sighed. He hated working with politicians. They had to consider so many more things than just military strategy. Dickson and Ardmore were, essentially, nothing more than politicians. Their aim was to make the best possible political decisions, while his was to make the best military decision. If he were to fail, the politicians would blame him. If he were to succeed, the politicians would take credit.

He had considered all the data and percentages, and decided he wanted to let this damned asteroid pass by without interference.

"General, I will certainly express your opinion when I meet with the leaders of the other five nations. Once we've looked at all the facts, we will make our final decision. That's all for now. Thank you, General." The phone line went dead.

Smithson sighed. He thought he knew what the final decision would be, and he didn't like it. He didn't like it at all.

He keyed his intercom. "Daniel, I want to see Colonel Meyer and Major O'Brien in my office."

"Right away, Sir."

Twenty minutes later, the two officers were seated in Smithson's office, looking uncomfortable.

"Both of you, independently, have convinced me that our chances of hitting that asteroid are insufficient to warrant a launch. The President and the Chair of the Joint Chiefs are equally convinced that multiple launches from six nations is the proper and prudent course of action. Somehow, they have become convinced that this rock is going to impact Earth. I don't believe that is the case, gentlemen. I need something from each of you, some kind of evidence that I can take to Admiral Ardmore that will convince her to join me in lobbying the President to call off the launch. We have five days before launch countdown begins."

O'Brien and Meyer looked at each other. O'Brien spread the fingers of his hands.

"What evidence are you looking for, General?" Meyer said, leaning forward.

Smithson barked a laugh. "Any evidence that will work, Colonel. And I need it quickly, if you don't mind."

Meyer saluted and left. O'Brien hung around. Clearly, something was on his mind.

"Yes, Major?"

"Sir. Permission to speak freely, Sir?"

"Of course, Major. What's on your mind."

"It's my considered opinion, Sir, that we should go ahead with the launch. I believe the radio signals are, in fact, from aliens and that they constitute a warning. The only warning that makes sense is that the asteroid is going to hit us, despite all of our calculations indicating the opposite."

"Hmm. While I don't necessarily agree with you, Major, you make a good case. We will proceed with our launch preparations. We'll hold off making a final decision until just before the final countdown. Does that suit you, Mister?"

O'Brien smiled. "Yes Sir! I don't think you'll be sorry, Sir."

"That's to be seen. Now get to work. Dismissed."

O'Brien saluted stiffly and marched out of the office.

Cranston ~Seven Days before Flyby

The next day, David met with Samantha and Dwight in the study hall during lunchtime. "Last night I made a video of the images," Cranston said quietly, looking around to make sure no one else was listening. "I want both of you to look at it and let me know what you think."

"Sure, Dude. I can be a film critic."

"Let's see it, David."

First, he showed them the video at normal speed, which lasted about a second. Then he slowed it down.

"That was fast, even in the slow mode," Samantha said.

"Blink and you miss it. No academy award for you, Bub," Dwight said.

"Barely anything moves except the two triangles," Samantha observed. "That must make them important."

"There's only four elements. It *can't* be that hard," Cranston said in frustration.

"Okay, okay," Dwight said, shaking a finger at the screen. "This is from aliens, right? And them puppies are somewhere out in space, right?"

"Yeah. What are you getting at?"

Dwight looked at the other two. "That big crescent at the bottom. Guys, that's got to be the Earth."

"And the small circle?" Cranston asked.

Dwight shrugged. "No clue."

"But I think Dwight's right," Sam said. "The crescent represents Earth."

"How about the two triangles?" David asked. "That's got me stumped."

Samantha smiled. "So what's that thing up in the sky, heading right for us?"

The two boys looked at each other, then at the girl. "The asteroid."

"So you're saying the triangles represent..."

"The asteroid!" Sam whispered intently.

Dwight stared at the screen again. "Then why are there two of them?"

Rylee ~Seven Days before Flyby

Once the module had successfully docked with the ISS, the passengers moved into the so-called "reception" area where they were assisted by other crew members in removing their spacesuits. The suits would be stored until needed for the return trip.

Rylee was happy to get the thing off so she could scratch. Her stomach was busy protesting the free-fall environment, and she was sufficiently nauseous that she swallowed a pill. The poor Brit was not handling it well. She was dropsick and kept retching. The Russian, Leonid, looked on, unaffected, with superior disdain for the weak Western women. He'd been to the station twice before, so he was an old hand. The newcomers were then given a tour by the current station commander, Navy Captain Niles Knoblock.

Presently, Rylee's symptoms subsided and she found herself tired and excited at the same time. The three were led further into the space station and were given a chance to gaze out a window at the Earth. It was the most beautiful sight Rylee had ever seen. They watched, mesmerized as Africa slowly passed before them, replaced by Arabia, India, and the Near East.

Later they were assigned sleeping quarters. Rylee knew the facilities for sleeping were restrictive, but she had a difficult time imagining how she was going to slide into a sleeping bag in an area about the size of a refrigerator. The typically larger men did it every "night" so she knew it could be done. The bag had bungee cords to keep the sleeper from floating around. She felt it would be like sleeping in a coffin, but found that microgravity helped make a tiny space feel a bit larger. And sleeping in a no-weight environment was like lying on a feather bed without the feathers.

The bathroom was another affront to her sensibilities, but Rylee was pleased to find the bathroom itself was of a reasonable size. The whole elimination thing was based on the concept of a vacuum cleaner. Pee was recycled and used again, yuck. And no showers! Just a bag of warm, soapy water and a towel.

The habitable area of the space station was barely that of a standard-size American home. She wondered if she'd be able to stand the cramped place for the next five to six weeks. Space was infinite, but the invaders were confined to a tiny rat maze with no cheese.

Lang ~Six Days before Flyby

Ted Lang watched as the thirty frames played on his computer screen in slow motion. He'd watched it a hundred times, over and over. He'd already decided that the large crescent represented the Earth. But what about the little circle? It could possibly represent the Moon, but it seemed much smaller than it should be in relation to the large crescent in the lower right.

He hadn't yet really thought about the two triangles. He'd leave them for later.

He tried listing the facts and assumptions. The radio signals contained definite messages. They were probably from space. There was a strong possibility that the signals were alien in origin. He had to consider the possibility that there could be a connection between the aliens and the asteroid that would burn its way through Earth's skies in just a few days.

So where were these aliens? So far nobody'd nailed down the exact point of origin of the radio signals. It almost seemed they were not in a static location, but moving. What else was moving? Well, the asteroid, of course.

A circle, two overlapped triangles, a large crescent. These elements contained a message. Lang was sure of it.

What if the triangles somehow represented the asteroid? If the aliens were warning Earth about the giant rock, perhaps they were...

Lang slapped his forehead. *Of course*!

He immediately called Mary Hiddleston. She answered on the second ring. "Ted. You got something."

"Possibly, Mary. I think the crescent represents earth."

"Yeah, that was our assumption as well."

"I further believe the two triangles somehow portray the asteroid."

"Interesting possibility. Anything else?"

"I think the little circle near them represents the alien spaceship. I think maybe it's pacing the asteroid."

Silence followed that revelation.

"Mary? You still there?"

"We need to get our best telescopes searching the area of the asteroid. We need to look around, see if we can find that globe. Your alien spaceship, see if it's really there. By damn, Ted, I think you might be right! I think that little circle could very well be the source of our radio signals. It's a damned spaceship. An alien space ship. Holy crap!"

"Glad I could help," Lang said with a laugh.

"It's aliens," Hiddleston said. "They're really there. I almost can't believe it."

"I know it's hard," Lang said, "but we need to confirm it before we run in circles and celebrate."

"Right. I need to make some calls. Now we only need to figure out one more thing."

"That is?"

"The triangles representing the asteroid. Why are there two of them?"

"Hmm," Lang said. "Good question."

Cranston ~Four Days before Flyby

David kept looking at his video, slowing it down and speeding it up, his friends resting on his shoulder. Earth, a space ship, and an asteroid.

"Why two triangles?" Dwight asked for the tenth time.

"I wish I knew," David replied.

They watched the video again. And again.

"Two triangles," David whispered, then shook his head.

"One plus one is two," Samantha said softly.

David stopped the video. He looked at the girl, and his eyes widened. "Holy puppy poop, Cat Woman, that's it! That's the whole reason for the radio signals. That's why the aliens are here. That's what the warning is all about!"

"You lost me, Dude! A warning about what?" Dwight asked.

"Look. We know the asteroid is going to miss us, right?"

"That's what the experts say," Sam replied.

"What if..." He took a deep breath, "what if there are two asteroids, one right behind the other. The second one wouldn't show up on our sensors because they're too close together and going too fast, and the one in front is headed almost right at us, hiding the one behind it!"

"But all those science types should have seen it," Dwight said. "They got, like telescopes and radar and tricorders and, you know...other stuff."

"Yeah," David said. "But they wouldn't see the second asteroid because they're not looking for it. If they did see it, they'd assume it was all part of the same asteroid. They'd never expect two of them."

"Okay...so what now? What's the real purpose of the message?"

"Did you notice in the video how the second triangle begins to move slightly away from the other, down toward the crescent that represents Earth?"

Nobody answered. He showed them the video again.

"Two asteroids. One misses us, the other one..."

"Hits us, dead on," Dwight finished.

"How could that happen? They're both close together. If one misses us, the other one should also," Sam said.

"I don't know how, but when they get closer to Earth's gravity field, one of them gets pulled in. At least that's what the aliens are trying to tell us. They should know, they're right next to those rocks. Maybe the second one has more mass."

"So the message really is a warning," Sam said softly.

"Now that we know the whole message, what do we do? Dudes, we're running out of time!"

"We need to tell someone, someone in authority." David looked around for his phone, found it behind his laptop. "How do we call NASA?"

"If we call, we'll just get a receptionist who will laugh and hang up on us," Dwight said. "We're just high school kids."

"Maybe somebody else has figured out the message," Sam said hopefully.

"We can't rely on that. We need to talk to someone." He did a search for NASA phone numbers. "Hey! Look! NASA's got a Planetary Defense Coordination Office. And here's the number."

David called the number. As they feared a receptionist answered. "Hello. My name is David Cranston. I have some vital information about the asteroid that's headed our way. I need to speak to someone in charge."

"You and about a thousand other crackpots. I'm sorry, Director Spitzer is unavailable. I can take your number and he may call you back sometime next week."

"But that's going to be too late. He needs to know about this now!"

"I'm sorry, there's nothing I can do."

"Is there anyone else there I can talk to? Any other departments? This is critically important. I'm not a crackpot and I'm not joking."

"Okay, your name's David. Who are you with?"

"With? Uh, no one. I'm a high school student." The line went dead.

"Crap, she hung up on me." David looked at his friends with a wild look in his eyes.

"We need to call, like, a university or something."

"We're running out of time. I think the missile launches are scheduled to begin in just a couple of days!"

The three students sat for a long moment, looking at each other.

Samantha sighed and pulled her phone out of her purse. "Damn," she muttered, "I hate you guys, I really hate you. Okay," she sighed, "let me make a call. I know someone. He'll listen to me."

"But can he do anything to help us?" David asked.

Samantha tapped her screen. "He should," she said dryly as she held the phone up to her ear, "he's the President of the United States."

Smithson ~Four Days before Flyby

Major O'Brien called his fire control experts together. "Ladies and gentlemen, we now have fire control authorization, we are go to launch. And I have some important news. President Dickson just announced an unprecedented agreement with Great Britain, France, Israel, Russia, and, just now, China. They have all placed their own fire control authority for the designated missile launches with us. I don't know how the President managed to negotiate such an agreement, but he did. He convinced England, France, and Israel that our A.I. fire control system was better than the one in China. Whatever magic Dickson worked, we got Russia next, then China joined."

He smiled and continued. "I guess one coordinated effort is better than several independent launches. We will fire our own missile first, then China's, followed by the ones in Russia and Israel, and lastly Great Britain and France, as the Earth rotates each missile launch site into optimum position."

His men and women applauded and shouted. When they quieted, O'Brien said, "It is our proud duty to save the world. We have already received fire control data from the other nations. Your next duty is to enter that data, run it in, and check for accuracy. Once that's confirmed, we integrate the results into our A.I. system. We will be making dry runs until fifteen hours before the first launch. Once we've integrated all the data, you will be granted a four-hour break. Twenty-one hours from now, we will begin to launch our missiles. If we succeed, we will be the heroes. If we fail, five other nations will blame us for that failure. So let's not consider failure. Okay, let's get to work."

Kylie ~Four Days before Flyby

"Baby, can I come in?"

"I can't talk about this right now, Dad. Please. I just want to be alone."

"I understand. But please let me come in. You don't have to talk. I just want to tell you some things that I think you need to hear."

"But Dad, I...oh, go ahead. Come on in. Tell me I'm a miserable brat and I deserved what I got. You see, I already know what you're going to say. I've said it to myself a thousand times." She started crying again.

"Are you finished?"

She nodded and wiped her eyes with her fists. If her father needed to yell at her, now was as good a time as any. She couldn't feel any lower no matter what he said. Might as well get it over with.

Roger entered his daughter's room and sat on the edge of the bed. He didn't look at her.

"I've been doing a lot of thinking lately," he said softly.

Kylie remained silent. She stared at the ceiling.

She glanced at her father. "You going to kick me out, Dad? I...I understand if you do."

"No. No, Honey, never." He sighed deeply and tried to smile. "I'm going to try something new. I'm going to try loving you unconditionally." He looked at his daughter and Kylie was surprised to see tears in his eyes. "Your Mom and I, especially me, we've been unfair to you, all your life I think."

"What do you mean, Daddy?"

"Your sister, Rylee, she was a great student in school. She was smart, fun to be around. For the first ten years, she was an only child, the ideal child. We couldn't have asked for better behavior. Then you came along. You were so beautiful." He looked down at his daughter. "You still are. But I think we expected you to be another Rylee, another perfect child. But you aren't Rylee."

"I'm sorry, Dad. I can't be what I'm not." She looked away.

"You nailed it, Baby Girl. You're not Riley. Your mother and I wanted you to measure up to your sister, but that's impossible. You're reasonably close to your sister, but I think you rebelled against her by rebelling against us. You needed to do that, I see that now. You're not interested in science or the other things she's interested in. But you have your own interests, your own talents, your own value. All three of us living in this house need to realize that. You're never going to be a straight-A student like Rylee. And we should never have expected you to be."

"So what am I? Just a dummy with a pretty face?"

Her father smiled. "I used to think that, I'm sorry to say. No, Honey, you're so far from being a dummy that it makes me cry just to think about it."

"What am I good for, Dad? My grades are lousy, I hate school."

"I don't think you do. I think what you hate is trying to follow in Rylee's footsteps in school."

"I..."

"Look at your room," Dad swept his hand. "Your walls are filled with the most awesome artwork I've ever seen. When they called to tell us you were in the hospital, I came in here, hoping to see you lying on your bed, texting your friends. You weren't here, of course. So I looked at your work. I stared at it for the longest time. You know what I found?"

Kylie shook her head.

"I found love. I saw it in every work on your wall, and I'd missed it, never saw it. You've got such an amazing talent. I never really looked at it before, and I don't think you ever did, either, because it wasn't something that Rylee would do."

"But Rylee..."

"Rylee couldn't draw flies in an outhouse," Roger said.

Kylie couldn't help a small giggle.

"You're both so different. When it comes to this sort of thing, when it comes to dealing with people, just making friends, you've got it all over Rylee. Believe me, Baby Girl. And we almost lost you before we'd ever found you. It took *that* to wake me up, and I'm so sorry you had to go through sixteen years of my failure to see you as you."

"Oh, Daddy..."

"I love you, Baby. And from now on, I'm going to love you no matter what you do. I'm going to love you for who you are, not what I think you should be. I don't deserve it, I know. I've been bad for so long that I don't know if you can ever forgive me. But I'd like another chance. Will you give me that? Will you let me love you as my beautiful, wonderful daughter, Kylie?"

"Oh, Daddy, yes, of course I will. There's nothing to forgive. I've been a real butt these last few years. I can do better..."

"No!" her Dad said sharply, his hands on her shoulders, staring into her blue eyes. "No, Honey. Just be you. That's all I'm asking. Besides, you're already the best, so how can you do better?"

Without another word, the two hugged. They hugged for a long, long time. Neither said a word. The weight of years lifted from them both, and they just held on to each other.

Dunbar ~Two Weeks before Flyby

He could tell his listeners didn't like the assertion that the Devil was in charge of the Earth. It just didn't fit in with their Biblical teachings. But there it was...

"Despite the cleansing of the Great Flood, who was still in charge of the Earth? Naturally, the ownership of Earth had not changed.

"The Fallen One simply and predictably started his work over. In Genesis 11:3-4: *And they said one to another, Go to, let us make brick, and burn them throughly. And they had brick for stone, and slime had they for morter. And they said, Go to, let us build us a city and a tower, whose top may reach unto heaven; and let us make us a name, lest we be scattered abroad upon the face of the whole earth.'*

"Gee, I wonder who was in charge of *that* project? Someone wanting to make a name for himself? Someone who thought he was just as good as God, and maybe was searching for a way to get back into heaven? Was it Satan that got humans to build such a tower?

"After Satan's attempts to take God's living things and make them giant-sized, and failing, after the Flood, he decided to go in the opposite direction. Viruses, bacteria, and diseases can destroy all the creations of God, including humans, faster and better than predatory animals. We see these microscopic forms as part of the natural and normal processes of life. When animals (and humans as well) die they decompose. Maybe, just maybe, that was new, a post Flood attempt by Satan to attack God's creations. Coincidentally, perhaps the unclean warnings and hygiene rules of Leviticus and elsewhere in the Old Testament are there for a good reason. Suddenly, there were unclean things on the Earth, some of which could not be seen by the naked eye, but could kill just as quickly as the bite from a T-Rex. As such, humans would have no experience dealing with viruses and bacteria because they didn't exist before the Flood, so God had to provide some hard and fast rules to protect His people. There is no scientific evidence for this, but it makes a lot of sense.

"Part of Lucifer's plan had always been to subvert God's creations, first through Adam and Eve, then Cain and Abel. Later on, after the Flood, the attempts, overt and covert, began in earnest.

"With some exceptions, the remainder of the Old Testament is a recounting of God's chosen people. In the time when Moses leads his people out of Egypt, God provided direct but covert intervention in myriad ways, including a burning bush, pillar of fire, and cloud of smoke, on Mt. Sinai and thereby via the Ten Commandments, providing food and water as the Israelites wandered 40 years in the desert, keeping them separate and isolated, genetically pure, from the non-Chosen people.

"The Ark of the Covenant, one of the most mysterious, mystical, and possibly mythical artifacts ever created was built on direct orders from God.

"During this time, it became clear that Lucifer would not give up, sowing the seeds of dissent, doubt, and rebellion among a people who were, daily, witness to miracles and the presence of God. They escaped Egypt by the parting of a sea, were provided with food and water, and still they complained.

"The Chronicles of these people are related in much of the Old Testament, though God later operated less directly and more through prophets.

"Much is made by critics of the Bible regarding God's cruelty, often wiping out the enemies of His people, including women and children. In a world controlled by pure evil, God's unusual focus on protecting the purity of His chosen people becomes a little more understandable. God created humans in His own image, cultivated a pure strain in a most inhospitable environment, and in a massive flood tried to eliminate the rest. Later on, God used similar methods on a smaller scale, to protect and mold a few people that He had created and needed to keep pure, for the singular purpose of planting the sword of Good into the heart of evil.

"A specified homeland, altars, temples, the sanctuary, the Ark of the Covenant, these were all used to focus God's followers on their mission. Now there was no Garden of Eden as a refuge. It had been replaced by the Ark of the Covenant. Inside it were the tablets containing the Ten Commandments, God's law, and key of His character.

"God's chosen people were not only chosen but cultivated, trained, prepared. They certainly weren't devoid of the influences of evil, they certainly were not immune to failure.

"I once read a book by a Biblical scholar (who was, himself, an Atheist) complaining that Jesus, the Son of God, had promised his Disciples that the Kingdom of God would manifest itself within their lifetimes. And, in this author's eyes, the Kingdom of God didn't appear, so Jesus could not have been the Son of God."

Dunbar stopped for a moment and shook his head. "When I read that passage, it struck me as odd that this Biblical scholar, for all his learning, missed the entire manifestation of the Kingdom of God. What am I talking about? Christianity as a religion did not exist during the time of Christ. The movement began to grow some time after his crucifixion and resurrection. During this time, the gospels that make up the New Testament were, if not written down, at least passed along orally.

"The New Testament, and the religion it inspired, *is* the Kingdom of God that our Biblical scholar searched for and couldn't find. The religion became the largest, most powerful, most far-reaching movement in the history of our planet. Not a perfect kingdom, to be sure, because of who was still in charge of Earth. Even so, at the beginning of this movement, Jesus declared that by following Him, adhering to His teachings, everyone who believed could receive the mantle of 'Chosen.' It was no longer a genetic inheritance, but a spiritual one.

"Once again, Satan's emphasis shifted. This time, his goal was to infiltrate Christ's church and bend it to his will.

"We think of Devil worshipers as people who choose to worship evil, doing evil deeds and calling up demons to wreak havoc. While there are misguided people who purport to be such followers of Satan, they are few in number and shunned by almost everyone.

"Satan doesn't work like that. He is in charge of the Earth after all. His ego is too large. There is a reason he is called the great deceiver and it's not because of some dim practitioners worshiping goats. No, Satan created his own Christian religion, teaching the gospel, helping people, holding services, attracting millions of followers. This church teaches the words of Jesus, but then subtly (and sometimes not so subtly) alters them, weakening the connection between humans and God. Satan's church focuses on tradition and ceremony, appearance, and pontificating rather than the humble worship of the Savior, who saw Himself as nothing more than a lamb.

"The Earth is the battleground between good and evil. Even Jesus had to sneak in via the back door, so to speak. And there were immediate attempts to kill Him.

"Once again, Satan's plans were used by God to take the next step, to open up the ranks of His chosen people and offer the opportunity to everyone who accepts Jesus, including you and me."

It was time to wind this down. Dunbar took a deep breath.

"So when people despair of the evil in the world today, and ask 'why doesn't God do something? Why does God allow these things to happen? Where is God when children are tortured and killed?' You now have the answer. God isn't in charge of this world, Lucifer is. The rest of the Universe? That's God's domain. Earth is where He has imprisoned evil. Humans are here to keep Satan occupied so that in the end, the New Jerusalem will arrive on Earth and allow those humans who follow Jesus to escape. This giant city will keep everyone safe until God disposes of evil, and then in the final act, God will re-create the quantum singularity. The entire universe will shrink down to the size of a BB. Space and time, matter and energy will cease, once again, to exist. And Heaven will be eternal.

"Now, having said all that, let me leave you with a final message. We pretty thoroughly investigated the ruler of this world. But what about the character of He who rules the remainder of the universe? In 1 John 4:8, we find an answer: *He that loveth not knoweth not God; for God is love.* And if God is love, all the other creatures in the entire universe, except Earth, can also be similarly defined...as love.

"Thank you, ladies and gentlemen. I will be in the lobby to answer any questions. There, you can also purchase my books or get information about my online presence. Peace be unto you."

There was a polite round of applause. But it didn't last long. Some of the people were too lost in thought, others were busy looking for their brains.

Ford ~Four Days before Flyby

"This is Marsha Ford with an update on the asteroid situation. The United States military has announced plans to launch a coordinated missile attack against the giant rock. Fire control experts using the latest Artificial Intelligence computer program will begin their launch procedure within forty-eight hours, the countdown will begin at that time, with the actual launch of the first missiles in approximately 60-hours from now. We've just received word that the other nations planning similar launches have given fire-control authority to the United States. In an unprecedented action, even Russia and China have turned over their launch control to the U.S. Air Force. The missiles of each nation will be launched as the Earth rotates that portion of its face to the asteroid. The U.S. will launch first, followed by China, then Russia and Israel, and finally Great Britain and France. The hope is that the coordinated effort will result in the giant asteroid being blown into pieces, or at the very least deflected away from Earth. These actions are being taken even though experts have stated and continue to assure us that the asteroid is not, repeat not, on a collision course with Earth. General Harris Smithson has stated that the launch is merely a precaution. The General declined to add any new relevant facts regarding the strange radio signals that have been received by numerous stations in the past few days. Some think the signals are alien in origin and may contain a warning to mankind. Others still maintain the signals are fake. WMSG News will have live updates as they become available."

Cranston ~Four Days before Flyby

Samantha's voice had suddenly become small and high pitched. "Hi, Grandpa...it's me, Samantha." She listened for a moment. "I know. And I wouldn't have called you if it wasn't important. Yes. Yes. I know. But I have a friend, he's a math guru. He...well, he thinks the asteroid is really two asteroids, flying close together. One of them will miss, but he thinks the other is going to hit the Earth. No. No, Grandpa, he's as sane as you are. He thinks the two triangles in the latest alien message represent the two asteroids. One will pass us, but the other will drop into our gravity field and hit."

There was a long pause while Samantha listened. "Yes, Grandpa. I understand what you're saying, but we think the experts are wrong. That little circle in the last radio message? My friend, David, thinks that represents the alien space ship. No, he's very nice. He's a responsible young man. We've dated a few times, but...no Grandpa. We're just good friends. At least right now. What? Well...okay."

Samantha held the phone out to David. "He wants to talk to you."

Cranston's eyes grew wide. "The President wants... to...talk...to... *me?*"

"Yes. And hurry. He's very busy."

David took the phone and gingerly placed it to his ear. "Mr. President? Yes, this is David Cranston." His voice squeaked for the first time in five years. He cleared his throat. "Yes, Sir. Yes. Math is kind of a hobby for me. Yes, Sir, the three of us deciphered the last message, and we realized it was a short one-second video. Yes...no, I think it's real. It has to be. Yes, Sir, two asteroids. The video shows the one in back moving slightly away and down. What? You want us to do what? All three of us? Well, I'm sure we can. In three hours? Yes, Sir. We will be ready. Okay. Thank you, Mr. President." He handed the phone back to Samantha. "He wants to talk to you again." When Sam took the phone, David stared at his hand in disbelief.

Sam took the phone and continued speaking with her grandfather.

Dwight was wide-eyed and trying hard to keep silent. He was not very successful. They moved away from Sam. "Are you serious? You were just talking to the freaking *President?*"

David shook his head. "Yep. And he wants us in Washington, D.C. He's sending a special plane for us. We need to be ready in three hours."

"Are you serious? Did I wake up in the Twilight Zone or something?"

They heard Samantha saying goodbye, and she pocketed her phone.

"How in the holy name of Ned are you the President's granddaughter?" David asked.

"You don't even have the same last name," Dwight accused.

"Guys, hold it down." She looked around. Luckily, the study hall was empty, except for the teacher at the front, busy on her own phone. "Nobody was ever supposed to know. And I'm counting on you two to keep this a secret. Anybody else finds out, I'm in deep horse pucky. I'm using Rivera, my stepdad's name. Otherwise, I would have been placed in a private school and have secret service goons following me everywhere."

"I can't believe it," Dwight said, "you actually know the President. Totally rad. If it was me, I would have soaked that for all it was worth."

Samantha shook her head. "Not me," she said forcefully. "I just wanted to have a normal high school experience. If nobody knew, I could ditch the guards. I could be myself and have friends and participate in school activities. And it worked. I was so careful to stay under the radar. Until you, Mr. Cranston, forced me to break my cover. I don't know whether to thank you or slap you silly."

"You're welcome to do both. But can you wait until all this is over? We need to go home and pack, then get to the airport."

"No, David, someone is on the way to meet us here and take us home. Then they will bring us back here so a helicopter can take us to the airport. There will be a jet waiting to fly us to D.C. We meet with the President in four or five hours from now."

The three fairly ran to the front of the school. The principal popped out of his office as they ran by. "Hey, you three, hold up. School's not out yet. You're not allowed to leave the campus!" They slowed, but kept going toward the door, opened it, and stepped outside.

"Wait up, guys. I'm not going to tell you again..." His voice trailed off as three black SUVs drove up, screeched to a halt, and the back doors popped open. Men, almost identical, each dressed in black, sunglasses, and no-nonsense expressions got out and stood beside the door of each vehicle. The three students ran across the lawn, split up, one to each SUV. Each one slid into the back seats of their respective vehicle, which then drove off. Just before they turned the corner, David took one last glance at Principal Evans and saw mostly open mouth. The three vehicles split up, headed for three different homes.

The black SUV containing David pulled up in front of his home. "You've got ten minutes to pack, son, so get a move on," the man in the back seat told him.

"Right."

David ran to the house then down to his bedroom. He heard his mother calling to him, but he ignored her. He pulled his worn carry-on bag from the closet and threw in enough clothes for the next few days. He stopped and thought for a moment, then added his good pants, a dress shirt, his one somewhat formal jacket, and his good pair of shoes.

"David!" His mom called from the stairs, "What the hell are you doing home from school? You are in so much trouble, you little jerk, I'm tempted to let Biff have at you."

David ran up the stairs. "No time, Mom. I'll be gone for a few days."

"Gone? Where? Hey, get back here!"

David ignored her. When he reached the front door, he opened it and started out. A large, beefy hand reached out and pulled him back into the living room. "Your mom's talking to you, Dickweed," Biff said in a soft growl. "And you're gonna listen."

David tried to jerk his arm free, but Biff held on. "I have to go *now!*" he shouted.

"You're not goin' anywhere," Biff laughed.

"Let me go, Bronto Butt," David shouted. He could see the SUV through the screen door. He pulled hard and got himself halfway out the door. One of the agents stepped up to the door. He grasped Biff's arm and pulled the big man outside. Biff lost his grip on David, then turned angrily, but hesitated when he saw the man dressed in black.

"Who the hell are you?" Biff asked.

"Who the hell is he?" Janet repeated, rushing out the door.

The man held up a badge and an ID card. "NSA," the man said quietly. "The boy's coming with us."

"The hell he is," Biff said, "I'm gonna shove his head so far up his butt he'll need a glass belly button to see." He reached again for David, but the agent pulled Biff off balance, then pushed him to the ground.

David ran to the waiting vehicle, carry-on bouncing behind him.

"David! Where are you going."

"D.C.," he shouted over his shoulder."

"What the..."

"He has an appointment with the President, Ma'am," the agent said quietly as he turned and followed David to the vehicle.

Janet stopped and shouted. "The President? The President of *what?*"

David answered without looking back, a single finger raised high in the air. Then he ducked into the back seat and pulled his carry-on after. The agent slammed the door then jumped into the front passenger seat.

The SUV squealed tires and sped off.

The three vehicles arrived at the school within a minute of each other. A U.S. Navy helicopter was idling on the front lawn of the school. Principle Evans was standing at the helicopter's door, yelling at the pilot and waving his arms around a lot. A small crowd of students and teachers had gathered near the entrance, watching the events unfold.

David, Samantha, and Dwight exited their respective vehicles, each followed by one of the NSA agents. One of the men-in-black pushed Evans out of the way, and the six boarded the aircraft. The door was slammed shut, each passenger was handed a headset. The blades began to rotate faster and higher in pitch. The craft rose two feet into the air, paused for a second, then lifted up and off toward the airport.

The six passengers did not talk, but the three high school students were busy looking at their city from the air.

"Your attention, please," the co-pilot said over the headsets, "we will be arriving at Lambert International Airport in seven minutes. We have priority landing clearance. An airport van will meet us and transport you three to your aircraft. Make sure you take all your luggage with you. This bird can fly fast, but it can't catch up with a jet."

Dwight laughed. David and Samantha just looked confused.

The helicopter landed in a relatively deserted area of the airport. A large van awaited their arrival. David managed to thank the pilots, then the three were urged toward the van by their escorts. All six of them piled into the vehicle, which sped away.

After several minutes, they approached a relatively small Gulfstream GIVSP 12-passenger jet modified for use by the United States Navy. The aircraft was outfitted with the U.S.

Navy emblem and painted battleship gray and Angel blue. It sat alone in front of an unmarked hangar. A set of stairs had been wheeled to the jet, awaiting its passengers.

Once again, the youngsters were ushered aboard. This time, the NSA escort remained behind. "Good luck, you three," one of them said.

"Say hello to the President for us," a second added. The three agents rolled the stairs away.

Two Navy enlisted ratings, one male and one female, helped them aboard and stored their luggage. "Please take your seats and fasten seat belts. We will be departing immediately." As three belts clicked, one rating notified the pilots, then both sailors sat and fastened their own belts.

The jet taxied to the adjacent runway and immediately took off and arrowed into the sky. One of the ratings turned around, "Any of you get airsick?"

The three shook their heads. "Actually, I don't know," Dwight said, "this is my first time flying."

"Well, you'll probably be okay. We should have smooth flying all the way to D.C.," the male rating said. "But just in case, you'll find a barf bag in the seatback in front of you. If you need to use it, please don't miss."

Everyone laughed. "Our flight time into the District. is approximately two hours. Sit back and take a deep breath. Once we reach cruising altitude we'll serve some soft drinks and snacks. Relax and enjoy the ride." The sky was clear except for a few distant clouds. With no other passengers, the three felt no embarrassment pressing their heads against the windows, enjoying the view.

"Man, I could get used to this," Dwight said softly.

After consuming sodas and some sandwiches, David visited the back of the plane where he exchanged his school clothes for his dress-up duds and good shoes. After he was finished, Samantha freshened up, followed by Dwight.

About ninety minutes later, Dwight woke David and Samantha. "How can you two nap when there is so much to see out there?"

"Tired. Too much going on," David said. He shook his head to clear the cobwebs. "Where are we landing? Ronald Reagan?"

"Andrews," one of the Navy guys said. "Ladies and gentlemen, please fasten your seat belts. We are on our final approach."

As the Gulfstream touched down and streaked along the eastern most runway, Samantha pointed to the left where Air Force One awaited its next mission. Their aircraft parked near a hangar some distance away from the larger jet. They were met by another large black SUV with two almost identically-dressed men, and one woman, decked out in requisite black suits just like their colleagues back in St. Louis.

"Please take your seats," the woman said, opening the back door. "We will have you at the White House in a few minutes."

This SUV was equipped with blue and red emergency lights as well as a siren. They made good time, avoiding the major gridlocked thoroughfares.

Dwight leaned over and whispered, "I could get used to this, too."

Once at the White House, the three passed through metal detectors, all were physically checked and patted down, photographed, and, probably, x-rayed. The only thing that raised eyebrows was a thumb drive in David's pocket. He explained its contents, and it was handed back to him. They were given clip-on visitor passes. Their black-garbed escort passed the three teens off to internal security and a public-relations flack named Ned.

"How was your flight?" Ned asked.

"Uneventful, but very fast," Samantha said.

"Where can I get me one of them jets?" Dwight asked. "That's the way to travel."

"Yeah, get me one, too," David said quietly. He realized there were a lot of things the three students were finding that they could get used to. All three looked around in wonderment as they strode the halls of the highest office in the land.

Ned led the group not to the Oval Office, but to one of the private residence rooms on the second floor.

"Look at that art," David whispered to Samantha, who nodded. "Not being able to visit a place like this isn't worth the price you paid to remain anonymous."

"It was a hard decision," she replied. "But I was here once before during Grandpa's inauguration."

Seated inside the next room, at an ornate antique dining table, one hand on a coffee cup and the other shuffling between a stack of papers and a tablet, was President Troy Dickson.

Ned knocked softly on the door frame. "Mr. President," he said. The Chief Executive turned and looked. "You have some visitors, Sir."

"Grandpa?" Samantha said softly.

The tall man broke into a large smile. "Sammy, Baby!" he shouted. He put down his coffee and work. "Come here and give me a hug!"

Like a little girl, Samantha ran to her grandfather and threw herself at him.

"My, my, you're getting so big," Dickson said, holding the girl close.

"I'm almost old enough to vote, Grandpa."

He pushed her up and smiled at his granddaughter. "Good! The next election is going to be very close and I need all the help I can get." He chuckled and held Sam at arm's length. He looked into her blue eyes. "It's been way too long," he said softly.

"I know," she said. "Sorry."

Dickson pulled her close and planted a kiss on her forehead. "Don't be, it was a mutual decision. We all agreed. Now introduce me to your friends." The President turned further around to look at the boys.

"Grandfather, this is my friend David and his friend, Dwight."

"I'm pleased to meet you, Mr. President."

"Yeah, what he said," Dwight pointed at David. "This is sooo cool."

"I'm happy to meet you both. We need to talk. Come on over here and have a seat boys" the President said. "All of you sit down. Can I get you guys sodas?"

"I'd love one," Samantha said. The two boys joined in.

Dickson pressed a button and a butler appeared. "Three sodas, please, Martin." Prompted, the teens called out their preferences and the butler disappeared, only to return less than a minute later with a large tray, three cans of cold soda, and glasses with ice. Also on the tray was a silver bowl with salted peanuts.

"Nice," Dwight muttered, holding up the can and turning it in wonder, "Presidential Dr. Pepper."

"I love salted peanuts," the President said, grabbing a handful, "but I can't have too many? Bad for my blood pressure."

"You look very healthy, Grandpa," Samantha said softly. She popped the top of her soda can and filled the glass.

"Now, kids, or should I say lady and gentlemen, let's take a look at what brought you here." The President looked at David. "You did bring your data, right?"

"Oh, yes sir," David said, reaching into a pocket. "It's all here on this thumb drive."

"So we'll need a computer." The President pressed the button below the edge of the table again.

Martin appeared almost instantly. "Sir?"

"Martin, please bring me my laptop."

"At once, Sir."

His return was not "at once" but close. He set the running PC in front of the Chief Executive. David handed over his drive. The file loaded almost at once, which caused David to wonder what kind of processor that beast had. He supposed the President enjoyed the latest and greatest.

"Mr. President, the video itself was the result of scanning thirty individual data sheets derived from the radio signals."

"I see."

"When you press 'start' a slowed-down two-second video will play."

The President watched the file. "That went by fast."

"Yes, Sir." David left his seat and knelt down next to the President. "We'll slow it down some more," he said, his hands working quickly. David didn't seem to notice the raised eyebrows of everyone in the room except the President, who smiled.

"Now, watch carefully. The two triangles stay together until almost the end, then they separate slightly, with the one in back moving down just a bit. Right here," he said, pointing, "see that?"

"Yes, yes, I can see that now. So you think the triangles represent..."

"Two asteroids, traveling in concert. I think this is a warning from the aliens that tells us the second rock is likely to impact the Earth."

David suddenly became aware of where he was, stood, and quickly regained his seat. "Sorry, Sir, I didn't mean to..."

"No problem, Son. You are aware that our military is poised to launch several nuclear-tipped rockets at what they believe is a single asteroid."

"Yes, Sir. And that's the problem. If any of those rockets succeed by hitting the leading asteroid, it will most likely push it back into the second one, altering both their speed and trajectory. Instead of one dinosaur killer hitting us, it's very possible we may have two."

No one spoke for a long moment. The President watched the short video several more times.

"The military has this same data," he said slowly, "but I don't think they reached the same conclusions you have. Last time I spoke with the Chair of the Joint Chiefs, they still hadn't decided what the two triangles represented." He looked at the three students. "Good work, you three."

Ned entered the room. "Sir, we have a phone call for you, someone from NASA. She says she has important new information about the, uh, asteroid."

"She give a name?"

"Uh, Mary Hiddleston, Sir. Shall I put her through? Or do you want me to send her to your science advisor?"

"Go ahead and send her through, Ned. I have a pretty good science advisor right here," he glanced over at David.

"As you wish, Sir." Ned left.

David had just taken the last drink from his soda. When he realized who the President was talking about, he almost sprayed the table. Science advisor? Him?

The President put the call on speakerphone so all of them could listen.

"Dickson here."

"Mr. President? Thank you for taking my call, Sir. I have some critically important news for you. It's about the asteroid."

"Are you calling me, Ms. Hiddleston, to tell me there might, in fact, be two asteroids?"

There was a pause. "Why yes, Mr. President. How did you know?"

Dickson glanced over at the three high school students. "Oh, I have my sources of information."

"You can't let the Air Force launch those missiles. We now have photographic confirmation of two distinct and separate asteroids traveling in tandem, and we..."

"Can you send those photos to me at once?"

"Why yes, Sir. I could do it right now if I had an email address..."

"Try tdickson92@globemail.com. That's an address I used before I got into politics. Never got rid of it. Comes in handy sometimes." He winked at the three teens.

"Coming your way right now, Sir. There's one more thing."

"Yes?"

"We also got photos of the alien spacecraft that's pacing the asteroids. I'll send that over as well."

"So it's real?"

"Indeed, Mr. President. The photos aren't the highest resolution, but there's no longer any doubt."

David almost shouted, but managed to limit his response to a silent fist in the air.

Dickson ~40 Hours before Flyby

After their first meeting, President Dickson had sent the kids off to check into their hotel rooms and get unpacked. They were to meet back at the White House a few hours before flyby. He'd invited the kids to be with him in the Situation Room. In the meantime, they were given escorted tours of the various D.C. sites and museums. It was educational for them, Dickson thought, but also kept them out of his hair for the time being.

After reviewing everyone's opinion in his Cabinet, and listening to various scientists and military experts, Dickson needed some quiet time to decide what needed to be done with the fast-approaching missile launch. General Smithson was a hard-headed officer. He'd been against the launch at first, but he would obey his superior officers. Once he'd made up his mind, it was going to be tough getting him to change.

The President smiled. There were some perks to being the Commander-in-Chief.

Dickson reached for his phone, but before he could make the call, his intercom buzzed. "Sir," his appointment secretary said, "the Speaker of the House is here. She insists on seeing you right away. Shall I have her make an appointment?"

"No, Donna, it's okay. Cancel my next appointment. No, wait. That's the one with Sheikh Raman, isn't it? See if you can push that back an hour and cancel..." he tapped a pen on the table, "...cancel that delegation from Greenpeace. Tell them I'll see them when this crisis is over. Got it?"

"Right, Mr. President. Speaker Valdez is on her way in."

Dickson took a deep breath and stood. He would meet the House Speaker in the Oval Office, sitting opposite her on one of the sofas. Speaker Valdez was a member of the opposition, a leader of the "other" political party, and most likely his opponent in the next election. He had an open-door policy, so the two had met frequently and not always harmoniously. However, as unusual as it was these days, they honestly respected and liked each other.

Dickson stood as the door opened and Valdez was ushered into the room. As was typical of her visits, she eschewed greeting and began speaking immediately. "Troy," she said forcefully, "I've heard on the news that the Air Force is going to try and launch nuclear missiles at the damned asteroid."

"I'm glad to see you, too, Sally," he motioned her to the other sofa and waited until Valdez had seated herself.

"Well?" she said.

"The Air Force is preparing for a multiple missile launch designed to impact the asteroid, and hopefully deflect it away from Earth."

Valdez ran a hand through her medium-length black hair. "You can't let that happen. We've told the American people all along that the asteroid is going to miss the Earth. How can you justify this reckless action under those circumstances?"

"Well," Dickson said, "they are confident that their missiles will impact the asteroid."

"Mr. President, there is no need!"

"I agree with you, in general. There's another reason as well."

"Another reason?"

"Let me tell you about it." He related the discovery that in fact there were two asteroids headed for Earth, and that one of them would, by all evidence, hit the planet with devastating consequences.

"And how do you know this, Mr. President?"

Dickson smiled. "Aliens told us."

Valdez sputtered. "Seriously, Troy."

The President laughed. "I am serious. And we have photographic proof."

"Mr. President, you really believe what you are saying?"

The President nodded, trying to hold back a smile.

"And who convinced you there were aliens involved?"

Dickson opened his mouth but broke into a chuckle. "I'm sorry," he said. "I was told this by a high school student."

Valdez leaned forward, a frown on her face. "Perhaps I should call someone? I think the stress has gotten to you, Sir."

Dickson waved a hand. "I've been toying with you a bit. While the information was told to me by a student, I've had the information validated and confirmed by other science advisors. So, in fact, there *are* two asteroids, and one of them will probably hit the earth. And I agree with you. Shooting at those things with missiles, even if they are successful, isn't the right answer. So I'm going to call off the missile launch."

Valdez sat back and relaxed. "Do you realize, Mr. President, that this is the first time we've agreed on something in the past four months?"

"Really? That long?"

"I've kept track." Both laughed at that.

"Okay, Sally, you got what you wanted. We're canceling the launch. Now get out of my hair. I've got to call General Smithson before he gets antsy and starts shooting off his missiles." He stood and the Speaker stood.

The two shook hands. "How about we do lunch sometime next week," Valdez said.

"I'd love to, Sally. Provided we're all still here."

"There is that, isn't there? Well, you take care, Troy. Mr. President."

Dickson held her hand as he walked the Speaker to the door. He gave the hand a final squeeze and they both smiled. "Say hello to Jan for me."

"Will do," Valdez said.

Dickson hurried back to his desk to call Smithson.

Smithson ~37 Hours before Flyby

O'Brien surveyed his command. There was less than an hour now before the first launch. The countdown had gone flawlessly. His people were ready. He'd trained and drilled them with endless dry runs. The data had been input and verified, and the A.I. routines were online and monitoring all aspects of the launch sequences. They were prepared, and there would be no mistakes.

"Forty minutes to launch sequence begin," Lieutenant Samelson said softly.

"Very well. Listen up!" He called out, "I want everyone awake, alert, and ready for action. No goofing around, no whispering. I want total and absolute attention to duty. Count off by way of acknowledgment, left to right."

The fire control team counted off as ordered. O'Brien nodded in satisfaction. This was a good team.

The door opened and Colonel Meyer entered. "Major, can we talk for a moment?"

"We're very busy, Colonel. We launch in less than an hour."

"Major, it's important."

"What, then? Make it quick." They stepped away from the control center to speak privately.

"I want you to cancel the launch of those missiles."

"I'm sorry, Colonel, you know I can't do that."

"I'm ordering you to suspend operations here."

"Colonel, I understand and appreciate that you outrank me. But you are not in my direct line of command. We will continue countdown until and unless I hear differently from a direct superior officer."

"Major, we have recently acquired more information that makes launching those missiles extremely dangerous."

"I'm sorry, my orders cannot be rescinded without proper authority."

"There's no time to get proper authority," Meyer said forcefully.

O'Brien started to reply but didn't get his words out.

The door opened again and General Smithson entered. "What's going on here?"

Meyer stepped up to Smithson. "General, you've got to stop the launch. We have new information. We think there might be two asteroids. Nuclear explosions will simply push one or both of them into our gravity field. The results could be catastrophic."

"It's a little late to be bringing this to my attention, Colonel, is it not?"

"Sir, we've just received the confirmation. There indeed are two asteroids. And we believe the alien ship is real as well."

"So why are you here speaking with Major O'Brien instead of bringing this information directly to me? You should have contacted me at once."

"Sir, we needed to confirm our findings. A mistake could prove disastrous. And I came here because I didn't know how you would react to the news."

"So you thought you could pull rank on O'Brien, is that it?"

Meyer opened his mouth, but he didn't answer. He shrugged.

"You know, Colonel, you're a lousy soldier, even for an Air Force officer. I'm tired of listening to you..."

Lang and Hiddleston ~37 Hours before Flyby

"So, Mary, you've confirmed our suspicions?"

"Ted, I've got photographic proof. I've spoken to the President, but he was in a meeting and didn't have time to discuss the issue at length. They've got to stop those missile launches. It's exactly the wrong thing to do."

"I agree. Do you think talking to the President again might help?"

"I've left Dickson another urgent message. I just hope he gets it in time."

"The President is also the Commander-in-Chief. The military guys have to listen to him."

"Yes, if they can get the message over there in time. We have less than an hour to get them to abort..."

"Aliens," Lang said softly, "they're real. You know what this means?"

Hiddleston was not impressed. "It's the most important thing that's happened to this planet in a thousand years. But, Ted, it only means something if we manage to survive."

"Yeah," Lang said softly. "Maybe I should try, too. How does one go about calling the President?"

Hiddleston laughed. "Here's the number I use. Go ahead and give it a try. Won't hurt, might help."

Lang scribbled down the number, hung up, then immediately dialed the White House. He didn't have much hope of actually getting Dickson on the line, but he could at least leave a message.

Interestingly, no one answered his call. Instead, he got transferred to voice mail. It was the President's personal private voice mail. Lang was surprised such a thing even existed. "Mr. President," he said, "this is Dr. Ted Lang. I'm an associate working with Mary Hiddleston. I'm calling to urge you to abort the upcoming missile launches. Apparently, there are two asteroids, and an alien spaceship, difficult as that may be to believe. In case you wish to speak with me directly, here is my cell number." He related the digits twice, then hung up. Nothing else to do now but sweat it out and wait.

Smithson ~36 Hours before Flyby

"What are your orders, General?" O'Brien asked. He waited expectantly.

Meyer stepped toward the General. "Sir..."

Smithson turned. "Colonel, I don't have time to deal with you right now. Stand down and be silent."

"But, Sir..."

"That's an order, Colonel." Smithson turned toward O'Brien. "I am in charge, here, Major, do you understand that?"

"Sir! Yes Sir. We will begin launch as ordered in, uh," he glanced at his watch, "seven minutes."

Smithson looked at his fire control officer. The man was sweating, but otherwise in complete control. A picture-perfect image of an officer following orders. Damn, he was proud of O'Brien. Smithson was sorry to disappoint him.

"No, Major," the General said finally. "Please order your team to secure their boards and stand down. And disengage the A.I. protocols."

"*What?*" O'Brien said, his mouth remaining open.

"General!" Meyer shouted.

"Do it, Major. Stand down, now!"

O'Brien half turned toward his fire control center, then turned back. "General. You're sure?"

"That's an order, Major. Do it now."

"Sir!"

Smithson and Meyer watched as O'Brien ordered his officers to secure their boards and abort all launches.

"General!" An aide burst through the door, holding a phone. "It's the President, Sir. He's been calling you but got no answer. He needs to speak with you immediately."

Smithson reached out for the phone. "Mr. President, Sir. General Smithson here."

"I need you to stop the missile launches, General. Immediately."

Smithson didn't answer right away. A tiny smile crossed his lips. "It has already been done, Sir."

"It has? I mean, you have?"

"I ordered it on my own responsibility, Sir. After giving it serious thought, there were just too many variables, too many unanswered questions. And my expert here, Colonel Meyer, feels the same way."

The President took a deep breath. "I'm relieved at your action, General. We've just learned that there are actually two asteroids. Had you successfully impacted one, they both might have altered trajectory just enough to smack the Earth, causing unimaginable destruction."

"Is it possible, Mr. President, that the second asteroid will hit us anyway?"

"My science advisor says there is a very good chance the second rock will hit the Earth. Unless..."

"Yes Sir?"

Rylee ~24 Hours before Flyby

After a week, space station life had become somewhat of a routine. Day and night were useless as indicators of work and rest. Sunrise happened sixteen times every 24 hours.

While awaiting arrival of the massive asteroid, Rylee spent time getting familiar with her camera. She'd brought with her a prototype Fastec HiSpec 7 high-speed digital camera capable of recording 2500 fps at 1280x1024 resolution, in very low-light situations. Rylee was recording her images on a prototype ultra-high-speed 5 TB memory card that would give her 20 minutes of storage with no lag or buffering. A custom-built mount would allow her to affix the camera rigidly to the space station's best viewport in hopes of capturing the asteroid. It wouldn't be easy as it shot past the space station at almost 18-times the velocity of a rifle bullet.

Permission had been given to the ISS commander to reposition the angle of the space station for optimum view of the asteroid's approach.

Rylee's hopes were high that she could capture the asteroid in high resolution so that the images could be slowed, enlarged, and studied back on Earth. Providing, of course, any semblance of civilization on the Earth survived.

"You are going to make history with that thing," the Russian cosmonaut said.

"We hope so."

The Russian nodded. "You will. I have no doubts. You will win, maybe, a Nobel Prize for this, eh?"

Rylee laughed. "If everything goes perfectly, Leonid, a small chance."

"Maybe I will nominate you myself," Leonid said.

As the day for the flyby approached, tension increased. The latest calculations warned that there was a small but calculable possibility that the asteroid, or a fragment from it, might, in fact, impact the ISS.

"Well, it's certainly a quick way to die," ISS Commander Knoblock said.

Leonid snapped his finger. "Like that. Gone. Like hit by a bullet the size of Red Square."

"But I don't think so," Rylee said. "We're too low."

The Russian shrugged and looked out the window.

Then news arrived that stunned them all. There was not one rock headed toward them, but two. And somehow, the Johnson Space Center knew the second asteroid would be coming in at a lower trajectory than the first one.

"How the hell do they know that?" Rylee asked. The question was relayed back to the command center.

Three words came back: "Aliens told us."

"What the hell? Have they gone crazy down there?" Captain Knoblock shook his head.

A survey of news channels piped up to the station confirmed what the command center had said. Apparently, they weren't joking.

"Aliens," Leftenant Carrie Higgins said, shaking her head. "What's next?"

The International Space Station was not a space ship. But it could be moved or re-aligned in cases of necessity. Five hours before predicted arrival of the asteroid, Commander Knoblock would begin the process of turning the space station so that the main window would, hopefully, point in the optimum direction for capturing images of the asteroid(s) as it/they passed.

Rylee mounted her camera and did several test runs, making sure the camera functioned as promised. When she viewed the results, the test images were better than she'd expected. Everything was ready. The crew ate a quick lunch, then it was back to stations.

Cranston ~18 Hours before Flyby

"There's just no way for anyone on Earth to stop either of those asteroids, Mr. President."

"David, we're running out of time. And please, call me Troy until this is all over."

"Yes Sir. Troy, Sir. I believe the second one is going to hit us, unless..."

"Go on."

"Why would the aliens follow that rock all the way here? Why would they send messages to us? I think they're trying to help us, to warn us. When they realize there's nothing we can do, I believe they will take action. They're pacing the asteroids. I don't think it's for their own benefit."

"Let's hope you're right, Mr. Cranston. Otherwise, we're in big trouble. So...what's our next step?"

Mr. Presid... uh, Troy, I have an idea. I think we should send the aliens a message back. They're close enough now that our signal will reach them without much delay."

"Our scientists have already done that, many times, with varying mathematical formulae. There has been no response to date."

"Maybe they've been sending the wrong messages. It has to be mathematical, of course, but maybe they haven't hit on the right formula."

"Okay, son. What would your message consist of?"

"They sent us messages based on prime numbers and the Fibonacci sequence. I think we should send them a message consisting of as much of the value of pi as we have time for."

"And why would we do that?"

"The value of pi describes a basic relationship, and cannot be calculated precisely, it's indeterminate. The numbers just keep going on and on, essentially to infinity. We could still be calculating the exact value of pi when the universe ends. There is only one other thing I know of that doesn't end."

"What's that, Son?"

"Love, Sir. Love. If we send them the value of pi, I think they're intelligent enough to know our meaning. If we send them a message of love and do nothing else, I'm hoping they will realize we don't have the capability of stopping the asteroids. And then, if they can, if it's in their nature to do so, I believe they will try to help us."

The President shook his head. "Son, I'm amazed. You've managed to conflate a mathematical formula and love into a comprehensive message. At least, I hope it's comprehensive. Do you think it will actually work?"

"I don't know, Sir. We're dealing with aliens here, and we don't know much about how their thought processes work, other than what we've received in a few messages. But I don't think it would hurt anything to try. And what other choices do we have?"

"On that point, David, my friend, we totally agree. Now you, Sam, and Dwight follow Ned, here, and get something to eat. I've got a lot of work to do in the next few hours. I'll get that message of yours set up and sent, and I've also got to prepare a response in case one of those rocks actually does hit us."

Ned led the three teenagers out of the room and down a flight of stairs. They were ushered into a rather small eating room near the kitchen. The food arrived quickly, and it was excellent. "I could get used to this!" Dwight said.

"You said that about the jet, too," Sam reminded.

"And the hotel room," David laughed.

"What can I say? I was born to be rich, and probably famous!"

"Well, if we're wrong about the aliens and that asteroid," David said, "we'll all be famously dead."

"That's optimistic," Dwight said, pointing with a spoon. "Now what's for dessert?"

Smithson ~ 17 Hours before Flyby

"Yes, Mr. President. I came to a similar conclusion."

"General, we believe the alien spacecraft may step in and try to assist us. They must have very powerful weapons, weapons far in advance of our own. Let us hope and pray that they choose to use those weapons on our behalf."

"I hadn't thought of that, Mr. President. However, I think it would be prudent to prepare for impact. We've got about eighteen hours before that happens, Sir."

"Less than that. But I agree, General. I'll let you go to do your part while I initiate things here."

An hour later, Major O'Brien was still upset, still pacing over cancellation of the missile launches. He knew that the Russians and the Chinese were very unhappy. Israel was threatening to go ahead and launch its missile anyway, despite new information indicating there were very possibly two asteroids rather than just one. Hitting just one asteroid, the one behind, without affecting the first one, was deemed by the A.I. to be virtually impossible. The best-case scenario of a missile launch at the second asteroid was only 5% better than doing nothing.

O'Brien didn't believe the computer's assessment. He was tempted to go ahead and initiate the launches under his own authority anyway. A successful impact with a nuclear warhead had to have an effect. Everything about this whole setup seemed wrong. What if the Russians, or the Chinese, had convinced the President to abort the launch. Suppose one or both countries had secretly come to the conclusion that the asteroid would hit the Western Hemisphere? We'd be devastated, and they'd be relatively untouched, O'Brien reasoned. Besides that, he'd been humiliated by Smithson's abrupt and rather uncharacteristic change-of-mind. The General must be crazy to listen to an idiot like Colonel Meyer.

His lead fire control officer interrupted O'Brien's dour thoughts. "Major, is it okay if I give our team time to get a bite to eat?"

"Eh? What? Oh, yes, Lieutenant, go ahead, dismiss the team. Our mission has been scrubbed."

"Thank you, sir," the Lieutenant saluted, then turned, clapping her hands and announcing the off-duty status. In just a few minutes, the facility was empty except for the Major.

Half-heartedly, he walked over to the primary fire control console. He lifted the red plastic cover and looked at the button it covered. Push that button and he'd re-activate the entire launch array. He could almost see himself, launching the missiles on his own, saving the day. He'd be the hero, a cinch for promotion. The A.I. could re-calculate the launch sequence in seconds.

"Won't do you any good," a voice said behind him. O'Brien started and whipped around.

"Oh, it's you, Colonel. Why do you say that?"

Meyer shrugged. "Takes at least two, ideally three technicians, for each missile. Besides, it's too late now for everything except the French and English birds."

"But we could launch those two. Help me. Let's do this!"

Meyer shook his head. "I'm not that much of a stickler for military protocol, but I do know how to follow orders."

"Damn the orders. We have to save the world!"

"I believe that might just be possible. The President is making an announcement about that right now."

"About what, exactly?"

"About how he plans to save the world."

"How? How can that, uh, person save the world? That's *our* job!"

"Let's go and find out, shall we. All you need to do is lower that red cover, nice and slow."

O'Brien looked down at the button. He hesitated, then reached out. His finger trembled, hovered, then snapped the cover back down. Then he turned and walked away.

Meyer took a deep breath and relaxed. He led the Major to the door and took one last glance at the operations console.

Once the two had left the fire control center, with the door closed and the lights out, and the room secure, General Smithson stepped out from a shadowed corner. In his right hand was his sidearm. He was tired of holding it, and was overjoyed he hadn't had to use it. It hadn't been fired in ages. He holstered the gun and sighed. His criteria for what made a good officer, and a poor one, had once again been challenged and expanded. That had happened several times within the past five hours. He was getting a little tired of that, too.

Now it was time to go see if the President had his head where the sun don't shine, or if the politician was a genius.

Kylie ~8 Hours before Flyby

"How'd you like to take a trip with me?"

Kylie looked up at her dad. She was lying on her bed, reading a magazine. "Where to, Dad?"

"How about San Diego?"

"What? Are you serious? I'd love it! Warm weather, beaches..."

"And a Navy base that has invited us to listen in on the International Space Station as the asteroid passes by us. We might also be able to speak with Rylee for a minute or two. It's last minute and we might not make it in time. You game?"

"Am I! Let's go. Mom coming, too?"

"Nope. Just us."

They packed quickly, said goodbye to Mom, and ran for the car. An hour later, they were on the road halfway to SeaTac, where Roger Janeway had been able to secure last-minute tickets to Southern California. Both were relaxed and smiling. Traffic on I-5 was heavy, but not clogged.

Kylie was listening to music on her phone. She enjoyed the scenery south of Seattle. She'd only been to the airport a few times, and most of those to pick up relatives. It would be fun to get on a plane and actually go somewhere.

Two lanes over, she saw a red sports car. It almost looked familiar. Then she saw the driver and sat up. She yanked out the earbuds. "Dad?"

"What is it, Kylie?"

"See that red car two lanes over?"

He glanced quickly to his right. "Yeah. Somebody we know?"

"Dad, that's the boy who kidnaped me. That's Chad. That's *him!*"

"Are you sure, Honey?"

"I'm sure! Absolutely!"

Dad slowed down and moved over to the right. They were about five miles from the airport turnoff. He shifted another lane and pulled up behind the red car. "Write down the license plate," he told Kylie. She jotted down the information.

"Here, take my phone and call 9-1-1. When they answer, hand me the phone."

Kylie did as she was told. When the line answered, she handed the phone back to her dad.

"Hello, My name is Roger Janeway. I'm on South-bound I-5 three miles North of the SeaTac exit. We're following a car, license number..." He looked at his daughter, and she held up the paper with the license, which he repeated. "Last week my daughter was kidnaped and raped. She's in the car with me and she recognized the driver of this vehicle as one of the people who assaulted her."

Janeway was told to continue following the other vehicle, but take no action. The State Patrol was half a mile behind and closing fast. Kylie turned and looked out the back window. In less than a minute, she saw flashing lights, then the white State Patrol vehicle pulled ahead and inserted itself between them and the red car.

The driver of the sports car continued on for a while, then slowed and began moving to the right. All three cars pulled off the freeway and stopped. Another State Patrol vehicle pulled up behind the Janeway vehicle.

"Turn off your engine, roll down the window, and drop your keys to the ground," the first cop said via his PA speaker. The window of the red car rolled down, a hand reached out and dropped the keys.

The second officer had exited his vehicle, looked carefully at Kylie and her dad as he passed. He stepped up to the back right side of the sports car, hand on his weapon.

The first cop exited his vehicle and moved to the back left

side of the red car. "Now open the door and step out of your vehicle."

The driver did as he was told. "On your knees, hands on your head," the officer shouted. The other cop moved up to the passenger side and confirmed there were no other occupants in the vehicle. Then he backed up his fellow officer who moved up and cuffed the suspect.

He was placed in the back seat of the first Patrol car. At that moment, an unmarked car pulled up ahead of the rest, its lights flashing. Detectives Carlson and Wheeler stepped from the vehicle.

"We need you to take a close look at the subject," Carlson said to Kylie. "Can you come with me?"

Kylie looked at her dad, who nodded. She got out and was escorted by the detectives to the State Patrol car. Wheeler opened the back door so Kylie could get a good look.

"Well, if it isn't Chad," she said. "How are you doing, Chad? Rape any other teenagers lately?"

Chad looked at her, then looked away.

Chad was given his rights and asked if he wanted to make a statement. "This is a mistake," he said. "I've never seen this girl before. And my name's not Chad."

"You have any identification?"

"Wallet in my back pocket."

Wheeler carefully reached in and extricated the wallet. "So you are Dimitri Korokov?"

"Yes."

"Mr. Korokov, you are under arrest for assault, sexual assault, statutory rape, kidnapping, and about six other counts." While Wheeler continued to interrogate the suspect, Emily Carlson led Kylie back to her own car.

"How did you find him?"

"Total accident. We are on our way to the airport, I saw the car two lanes over."

"Are you willing to make a statement?"

"Now?"

"Now would be great."

"But we're on our way to San Diego, to talk to my sister. She's on the International Space Station. We really don't want to miss our plane."

"Okay. That's cool. Will you be back home within a week?"

"Yeah, sure."

"Good. We'll want you to stop by then and give us a statement. Hopefully, by that time we will be able to identify and locate his associates and get them behind bars before you return. Have a safe flight."

"So we can go?"

"Off with you. And thanks!"

Kylie slid into her seat, clicked the seatbelt. "Can we still make our flight, Dad?"

Roger Janeway laughed. "I am so proud of you, Kylie. You looked right at him and didn't fall apart."

"No chance, Dad. I'm just sorry I didn't have a gun."

"Me, too, for that matter. Let's get out of town before something else happens." He pulled back onto the freeway, then almost immediately exited for the airport.

Kylie had only flown once before. Because of the late purchase, their seats were toward the back of the plane. Kylie had an aisle seat, and Dad had the window. In the middle was a rather large, bald man who overlapped the seats on each side of him.

Kylie adjusted her mask and looked over at her dad. Despite the availability of Covid-19 vaccines, most airlines still required facemasks during the flight. Instead of a small bag of mixed nuts, each passenger got a mask. Refreshments were no longer served on flights of less than four hours.

Once they were in the air, the center seat man offered to switch with Kylee and she readily agreed. The two-and-a-half-hour flight was uneventful, and the plane touched down on the San Diego airport's single runway without incident.

Roger Janeway made a phone call as they were walking from the gate to baggage claim. When they had luggage in hand, a Navy ensign found them and drove them to NAS Halsey Field on North Island. It took almost twice as long to drive there as it would have taken for them to rent a rowboat and paddle over. Kylie opened the car window and fell in love with the San Diego weather. This warm? In April?

At the main base, they were met by Commander Donovan. "Nice to meet you, Sir," he said to Roger Janeway. "We're very proud of your daughter."

"So are we, Commander."

"Come on in, have a seat, relax for a while. The ISS won't be in radio contact for another 45-minutes. You'll have just enough time to say hello before she has to go to work. The asteroid is due to pass by in a little over an hour from now."

"Wow, that's not long at all."

"You have time to introduce me to this ravishing young lady."

Roger laughed. "My other daughter, Kylie."

"Pleased to meet you, Sir."

"The pleasure is all mine," Donovan said, bowing.

They chatted for about 20 minutes, then Commander Donovan moved them into the base control center where they would be able to talk to Rylee for just a few minutes.

"Radio contact secured, Commander," one of the officers shouted.

"Here," Donovan said, "put on these headsets, lower the microphone down in front of your mouth. You won't have long to talk, so say what you have to say quickly."

"Got it," Roger said. He looked at Kylie, adjusted her mike a tiny bit. "You ready?"

"Yep. Can't wait."

Rylee ~30 Minutes before Flyby

Rylee adjusted her headset. Commander Knoblock counted down with his fingers. When he reached one, he pointed at Rylee.

"Hello? Anyone there."

"That you Rylee?"

"Dad! Yes, it's me! How are you?"

"We'll have some news for you when you get back. But right now we're doing fine. There's someone here who wants to say hi to you."

"Okay. Is it Mom?"

"Rylee? It's me, Kylie."

"Kylie? You're in San Diego too?"

"Yep. I came with Dad. We're really proud of you!"

"That doesn't sound like my sister. But thanks."

"We have a lot to talk about, Sis. Can't wait for you to get home."

Roger said, "You get some good pix of that asteroid, you hear?"

"I'll do my best, Dad. Look, I've got to go now. Give Mom my love. Love you, too, Dad. And you, Kylie, love you too."

"Love back at you," Kylie said. "Can't want to see your photos..."

The line went dead. Rylee closed her mouth, then removed the headset.

"Okay, stations everyone," Commander Knoblock said. "We just received a priority one communication. We now have confirmation. We're sure as poop stinks not getting a single asteroid, we're getting two. We may also be seeing an alien spacecraft, so keep your eyes open."

"An alien spacecraft?" Leonid said. "Sounds like they weren't crazy after all."

"Apparently not. Captain Jones told me they now have photos of the craft."

Rylee turned on her camera. Timing of the asteroid's approach was down to the second. Thirty seconds before arrival, she would activate the camera's high-speed shutter.

She checked the aperture, shutter speed, and ISO settings. Battery was fully charged. "Camera ready," she called out.

"Countdown is commencing now," Knoblock said, "we're at minus twenty-one minutes."

After a period of time that arrived much too fast, the Commander's count reached, "Fifty-nine, fifty-eight, fifty-seven..."

When the count reached 30 seconds, Rylee pressed the shutter. The camera commenced making a soft buzzing sound as it recorded 2,500 frames per second.

At ten seconds, she saw a distant flare. At plus one second, a giant flaming rock hurtled past the station and was gone. At plus three seconds, she saw a second giant rock for the barest instant, a flicker of movement toward it, and an explosion. The blast flare was carried past the station in an instant. She kept the camera going. At plus 12 seconds, she saw something flash directly toward her. She ducked as she heard a loud "clang!" followed almost immediately by a reverberating "crack" and there was an object sticking through the top left side of the window. It missed the camera by a couple of inches. She could hear a high-pitched squeal as air leaked out of the microscopic spaces between the glass and the object.

"Holy crap," Commander Knoblock whispered. He flicked on his radio. "Kelly, we need a main replacement window, stat!

Emergency evacuation of this section commences now! Let's move, people, everybody out." In seconds, the Commander and Rylee were the only ones still in the affected area.

A couple of standard-size replacement windows were stored aboard the ISS for exactly these kinds of emergencies. The International Space Station was hit by random debris or micro meteors regularly. It was built to take tiny objects impacting at a lower trajectory. Things moving at a higher speed or larger in size often required external repairs. Luckily, this one could be done from inside the station.

"Okay, Rylee, now you can dismount and remove the camera. Carefully, if you please." The woman did so, first storing the camera in its case, then very carefully disengaging the mount. Kelly showed up with a replacement window. He was already in his spacesuit.

When Knoblock and Janeway were safely out of that section of the station, the airtight doors were closed and sealed, and the air pumped out. Kelly carefully unlatched and removed the damaged window and set it aside. He mounted the replacement, added an expanding sealant, and secured it. The whole process was over in less than half-an-hour. Atmosphere was pumped back into the room and the doors opened.

Within an hour, Knoblock found Rylee and handed her an approximately seven-inch long and four-inch wide chunk of torn, pitted, and slightly curved metal. "That's what almost ended up in your skull," he said softly.

"What kind of metal is this?" Rylee asked, turning the object over.

"Beats me. All I know is it's not radioactive, or not much. It's going back down to Earth with you for analysis and study. To me, it looks like worked metal, part of something."

"You mean, like, maybe part of an explosive shell or maybe a piece of an alien spaceship?"

Knoblock shrugged. "You'll know before me."

"What the hell happened up here?" Kelly asked.

The Commander pointed to Rylee's camera case, "Hopefully that will tell us. The Russians just announced that they had launched a rescue ship half-an-hour before the flyby, just in case. It will be here in a few hours. Rylee, you'll go down with it along with the Leftenant."

"Yes, Sir."

"And, Rylee, you need to promise me one thing."

"Yes, Sir?"

"When they find out what this thing is, you need to let me know. Got it?"

She nodded. They both stared at the chunk of metal again, for a long time.

Cranston ~5 Minutes before Flyby

"We've sent your message five or six times, now, David. No response. The alien ship continues to pace the asteroids." The President shook his head. "They don't do something soon, we're all going to be very sorry."

"What's in the message, Sir?"

"Just as you suggested. We're sending the value of Pi to five-hundred-thousand places, in the same format, speed, and frequencies they used to send their messages. Long enough to hopefully get our intent across, short enough to repeat it several times before...we know."

President Dickson and the three teens were in the White House basement situation room. They stood in front of a giant video screen. The room was filled with military and civilian operatives, most of them on phones or engaged with computer screens. Secret Service officers stood near entrances, silent, and at attention. They seldom had anything to do, regardless of the crisis, but they never looked out-of-place.

"This is an external live feed from the ISS," the President said. "The asteroids will pass by, or collide, in a few seconds."

The live feed showed a flash of yellow light, and the shadow of something here and gone in an instant. Then there was a brilliant white flash and the camera image blanked for a few seconds.

"What was that?" Dwight asked. "Do you think it took out the station?"

"I don't know," David said slowly.

"That image was on high magnification," Dickson said, "Whatever happened, happened quite a few hundred miles from the station."

The ISS camera came back on, but there was nothing to see. In that respect, the crisis had shifted to Earth.

The view switched to a news channel. Marsha Ford was reporting live. "It's over," she said softly. "The asteroid has passed by Earth," she said. "If you were lucky enough, what you saw was a flash of light and possibly an instant of a brilliantly-glowing rock shoot across the sky, west to east, followed by an ear-shattering sonic boom. Windows have broken in numerous areas, but we have received no other reports of significant damage, and the few injuries we've heard about so far have been minor. Some witnesses are saying the asteroid looked close enough to touch." She tilted her head. "I'm being told that we have a slow-motion video of the passing. Take a look..."

A much slowed-down video played next. The same flash of light, a much slower burning rock, tumbling a bit as it passed through the Earth's uppermost atmosphere. Even at a much slower speed, it was gone in an instant.

Chair of the Joint Chiefs was ushered into the situation room. "Mr. President, we have not detected any major impacts on Earth. Apparently, the second asteroid missed us as well."

"What happened to the alien spacecraft?" Samantha asked.

Admiral Ardmore shook her head. "Neither radar nor visual have detected the globe. It has, evidently, disappeared."

"And the second asteroid?"

"No sign of that, either, Mr. President."

"You mean it just flat vanished?" Dickson asked.

"That's impossible," Cranston said, then wished he hadn't. The President glanced at him, then back at the Admiral.

"The boy's right, Sir. It can't have just disappeared. We're investigating that white flash we saw just after the first rock entered our atmosphere."

"Thank you, Admiral. Please remain if you wish."

"Thank you, Sir, but we have much data to review. We'd like to find out exactly what happened to both asteroids and the alien craft, if, indeed, such a craft ever existed." She saluted and exited the room.

The President took a deep breath. "Well, lady and gentlemen, we seem to have survived the crisis. The excitement is over for now. I have arranged transportation to your hotel. Ned will escort you there and provide a small amount of cash for food. Nothing fancy, now. I don't want to get a call from your parents, or the D.C. police for that matter. Enjoy yourselves."

"Thanks, Grandpa."

"You're welcome, Sammy. I'll see the three of you tomorrow afternoon, and we'll go over everything we know. Thanks again, all three of you."

"I'm so happy it's all over and we're still alive," Samantha said, hugging her grandfather.

Ishmael ~1 Hour before Flyby

He went looking for Chet, Dod, and Timmy. He figured they'd be hanging out together as usual. He found them just coming out of the gym.

"Hey, guys! Let's go visit your snake pit. I'll tell you what my dad said when I asked him if we could move."

"Sure. Why not," Chet said. "You just better have the right answer."

"Yeah," Dod chuckled, "you don't want to accidentally fall into that pit, you know."

The four boys walked past the edge of town to the abandoned property. The area was devoid of trees other than those near the abandoned farmhouse, and it was possible to see for miles in every direction. The area was also devoid of witnesses for what Ishmael was about to do.

They stood around the pit, looking at the rattler who seemed to be asleep. The three boys had fed the reptile a rat the day before and refreshed the water.

"Okay, so what'd your dad say?" Chet asked.

Ishmael smiled. "Actually, he didn't say anything. We never talked about it."

Chet frowned. "What are you saying?"

Ishmael opened his coat and grabbed the cigarette lighter. "What I'm saying is you shouldn't have threatened my sister," he hissed. "Any of you, move an inch and I'll blow your asses all the way to Oklahoma."

"Holy crap!" Timmy shouted. "He's got a bomb!"

"Now, Mo-Ham-Head, you just stay calm. Don't you do anything rash."

"Oh, I won't do anything rash, Chet," Ishmael said. "But any of you call me that name again, you're going to jump down in that pit with the snake, or else." He raised the lighter again.

"Okay, sorry," Dod said. "You hear that, Chet? Knock it off with the insults."

"Sure, sure. So, Ishmael, what do we need to do for you not to blow us up?"

"The three of you, have a seat, on the ground. Right next to the pit. Relax. We'll be here for a few minutes." He watched as the three boys sat on the dirt next to the snake pit. Ishmael stood in front of them about four feet away. He kept his finger on the cigarette lighter button.

"Here's how it goes. Me and my family aren't moving anywhere. If you don't like that, the four of us can remove ourselves from the situation with a single push of my thumb."

"Look," Chet said, "you didn't think we were serious about your sister, did you? We would never toss her down there. We wouldn't even toss you down there. It was a *joke!*"

Ishmael held up the lighter, "This is a joke, too. How do you like it when it's played on you instead?" He glanced at his watch. The boys were facing West. It was just about time.

"In fact, I think I'd rather end it all right now than have you morons sneaking around. With you gone, my family could relax and enjoy living here."

"Don't do anything rash," Timmy said. "Think about it." A tear streaked the teen's cheek.

Ishmael raised the lighter. "I have thought about it. Any of you want to pray before we end it all?"

"Don't do this!" Chet shouted. He got to one knee and almost stood.

"Too late." Ishmael glanced at his watch, hesitated a few seconds. Then he heard a distant crack, so he jammed his thumb on the lighter. The boys looked at him, eyes wide in fear. But there was, of course, no explosion.

Chet opened his mouth. The entire sky exploded in bright blinding orange light. Something huge shot past them, roaring west to east. The ground shook, the atmosphere cracked with ear-shattering sonic booms. A giant asteroid shot across the sky, leaving a huge trail of fire and smoke.

"Allah be merciful," Ishmael whispered, but he couldn't even hear his own voice. He faced east, opposite the boys, so he saw the giant rock hurtle across the sky in an instant.

He looked down. The three boys were on the ground, thinking they were dead.

Before Ishmael could smile, and before the orange glow had completely faded from the sky, another burst of brilliance, white this time, followed almost immediately by another loud "crack" flashed out of the heavens. This second explosion also assailed their hearing. But this time, no asteroid flashed across the sky. This time myriad burning streaks filled the atmosphere.

Ishmael stumbled and fell to his knees. He saw one piece hit the Earth several miles East of their location, and he hoped it hadn't struck any inhabited areas. Some of the debris burned up in the atmosphere, but the majority of the broken pieces continued eastward carried by the asteroid's initial terrible velocity. Many small meteor fragments rained down on the earth, most burning up before landfall. A few caused minor damage beyond broken windows. Most of the falling rocks that didn't burn up ended up in the Atlantic Ocean. Some were carried over Europe, falling, burning, with a few impacts.

Ishmael stood, looking down at the terrified boys. He doubted they had even been aware of the approaching asteroids. They were not too keen on current events. They did not have the intelligence or the knowledge to understand what had just happened.

"Beware," Ishmael said loudly, "of what happens when a believer in God prays for deliverance." He took off his vest and tossed it in front of the three boys. Then he walked away, toward home.

The next day, he returned alone with a pole and loop which he used to capture the snake. He took it further down the road and into an unused field where he released it. He went back to the pit and used a shovel to fill the hole with dirt and rocks.

Chet, Dod, and Timmy were not seen for several days afterward. When they did appear, all three avoided Ishmael. Their loud, brash, arrogance was considerably subdued.

What the three thought about the asteroid passing, Ishmael never knew. The boys ignored him and never spoke to him again.

Thereafter, in the weeks that followed, Ishmael made several new friends. One of them was a girl!

Her name was Molly. She was in his Social Studies class. She was thin, with dark brown hair, glasses, and dancing eyes. Molly seemed very curious and had a lot of questions for Ishmael.

"Hi. My name's Molly," she held out her hand.

He grasped the hand timidly. "Call me Ishmael."

Molly giggled. "You hunt any whales lately?" she asked. Her voice was soft, and it sparkled with humor. Ishmael was almost trembling with excitement. She had gotten the reference. Apparently, not everybody in Central Texas was illiterate. Things were looking up.

Lang and Dickson ~ 24 Hours after Flyby

"Dr. Lang, please come in." Ned ushered Lang into a private meeting room in the White House.

"I'm still not sure why I'm here. Nobody's told me why I'm at the White House."

"Yes, well you'll find out soon enough. Have a seat and relax. Someone will be in to see you shortly."

"Okay," Lang said softly after Ned had left, "but don't call me 'Shortly'."

Ted sat on the sofa. His posture was alert and nervous. He'd made that call to the White House before the asteroid approach. He wondered if he were in some kind of trouble. Could someone go to jail for leaving the President a voice mail?

The opposite door opened and a tall gray-haired man sporting a beard entered. "Ted Lang?"

Lang stood and faced the man. "Yes, I'm Lang."

The man approached, hand out, "Pleased to meet you, Ted. I'm Troy Dickson. Have a seat."

Troy Dickson. The name sounded familiar. Wait. *What*? "Mr. President?" Ted said as the two sat down.

"The reason I called you here is that my official science advisor, Dr. John House, recently submitted his resignation. Personal reasons, he said. Now I need a new science advisor. I'm thinking it might be you."

"Me? I..."

"Mary Hiddleston recommended you. I offered the job to her, first, but she thought you'd be a better choice."

"Me? Mr. President, the ink's barely dry on my Doctorate. There's got to be a thousand scientists more qualified than me."

"Hiddleston doesn't think so..."

"Sir, Mary and I have only met in person once. We've done more work by phone, but I can't say I really even know her."

Dickson smiled. "I tend to go with my gut feelings, Ted, Dr. Lang. That tends to upset some of my colleagues, but my track record is pretty good. Mary is the same way, and her gut thinks you're the right one. I think you'll do, if you're willing to take the job."

Lang was silent for a long moment. Then he sighed. "Mr. President, you need to know that I once killed... shot...someone. A boy, high school age. It was an accident, but you need to know it happened."

"Who was the boy? Did you know him?"

"He was my stepdad's son. Mr. Bonner tracked me down to kill me, but ended up sort of adopting me instead."

Dickson barked a laugh. "Well I'll be. There's got to be an interesting story behind that. Can you give me the thumbnail version? I'm kind of pressed for time."

Lang related the entire story, ending up slightly longer than a thumbnail, but the President listened raptly.

"I must say, Ted, that's an extraordinary story. He showed up with a gun and ended up funding your college education?"

"That he did, Sir. And I'm committed to paying it forward like he wanted."

"I've been searching for a way to reward a, uh, friend. Your story gives me just what I needed."

"Glad I could be of help, Mr. President."

"I'll have your background vetted, of course. But you've told me nothing that would dissuade me from changing my offer. How about it?"

Lang stared at the President. "Okay. Well, yes, Sir. I would be honored."

"Good. We'll let the vetting wait for now. I've got some important meetings coming up, and I'll need you to be there. Get ready for some changes, Ted. Things are pretty fast-paced around here."

"Yes, Sir. I've noticed."

Cranston ~ 30 Hours after Flyby

"Come in, David. Have a seat."

"Thank you, Mr. President." David sat on the sofa in the Oval Office. President Dickson sat opposite.

"Where are Sam and Dwight?" David asked.

"I've asked them to wait outside. I wanted to speak to each of you, privately."

"Okay..."

"My...other...science advisor, John House, met with me earlier in the day, just before he resigned. He had assembled all available data on the asteroid passing. We needed to know what happened to the second rock, as well as the alien craft."

"Yes, Sir. Did you learn anything?"

The President sighed. His eyes remained fixed on Cranston. "Son, it's possible we learned too much."

"Huh? I don't get it."

"David, we think your message worked. Let me show you what Dr. House showed me."

They walked over to a large screen which lowered from the ceiling. Dickson pressed a remote button. "This was put together from various sources. It is slowed down by fifty percent," he said. They watched as the asteroid zipped by followed by a brilliant flash as it entered the outer portion of Earth's atmosphere and was gone.

"That was fast," David said. "What happened to the second asteroid?"

"Here is a second video, using ground and space-based radar, radio telescopes, optical telescopes, and sensors aboard the ISS. Then we had to slow it down a hundred-to-one to make any sense of it. Watch."

This time, two asteroids were visible zipping into Earth's upper atmosphere. The one in front burst into a brilliant orange glow, with small pieces flaking off, trailing smoke, then it was gone. The second rock appeared on the screen but for an instant. It suddenly burst into an unmatchable brilliant flare of white light and tiny particles. Afterward, there was nothing.

"What happened?" David asked. "It looks like something blew up the second asteroid."

"Something did," the President said softly.

"Did the Air Force launch their missiles?"

"No, David. That never happened. There's only one possibility. The aliens."

" They used their weapons...?"

Dickson shook his head. "We don't think they ever had weapons powerful enough to deflect the asteroid," he said slowly.

"Then how?"

"Watch again. I'll stop the video about halfway through. I hope...well, just watch."

This time, just before the flash, the video stopped. In the lower right corner appeared a fuzzy, out-of-focus globe. The President advanced the video one frame at a time. As he did, the globe impacted the asteroid. The frame disappeared in a flash of white.

David stood silent for a long moment. "Their ship...it hit the second rock. They didn't use weapons at all. They...they...they used...themselves."

David looked up at the President, his eyes wide.

"That's our best assessment, David. They got your message. They did what they had to do."

"But...but..." David looked at the screen again, and burst into tears.

The President stepped over and gathered the teenager into a hug, and made soothing sounds while the boy sobbed.

Later, Dickson led David back to the sofas, sat next to him, and continued their talk.

"I was hoping," David said sadly, "that we would have a chance to meet them, I wanted to see what they looked like. We had so much to learn from them.."

"I agree. But I think we learned a few things about them, David. A few important things."

David nodded slowly. The President changed the subject.

"Are you planning to attend college next year?"

"Yes, Sir. At least I was." He explained how his mother had thwarted his attempt to secure scholarships and acceptance at an East Coast school.

"That's unfortunate. Perhaps I can help the situation."

"How, Sir?"

"David, as President, I have at my disposal a small discretionary fund that I get to use for whatever purpose I feel is important." He smiled, "The fund is small by D.C. standards, but adequate for my needs. If you will consider one small change to your plans, I am prepared to offer you a free education, all fees, tuition, books, housing, and living expenses paid for up to six years."

"You're kidding, right? Wait...you're *not* kidding?"

"I'm completely serious. I've come to admire you, Mr. Cranston. I think you are a good and kind young man, and extremely intelligent. It's been my privilege to consider you a friend."

David blushed and looked away.

"What's the small change? You want me to switch political parties?"

The President laughed. "No, no, not at all. Vote however you wish. No, my one condition is that you go to school in Southern California rather than here on the East coast."

"California? Why?"

"First of all, there are some really good schools there. Mainly, though, I want you to keep an eye on Samantha for me. She's going to need a friend there, and who better than someone who knows her, uh, little secret. And besides, I think she really likes you."

David managed a smile. "Well, Sir, I like her, too. When I thought she and I were going to be so far apart...I didn't...we couldn't."

"If you accept my offer, Son, you can."

"Yes, Mr. President. Yes, Sir, I accept." He grinned widely.

"I have two small requests."

"Sir?"

"First, I want to program my personal, private number into your phone. If you have any more suggestions, or need advice, or just someone to talk to, I want you to call me. And even if you don't, I want you to check in with me at least once a quarter. Just don't spread that number around. Okay?"

David shook his head in disbelief. "Yes, Mr. President. Thank you, Sir."

"And secondly, I want you to remember a name."

Cranston looked at the President, one eyebrow raised. "I want you to remember the name of Jarad Bonner. Someday, after you've taken your degree and you've become as successful as I think you will be, find some other young student who needs financial help. Pay all of this forward, along with the name. Jarad Bonner. Will you do that for me?"

"Yes, Mr. President. I would be happy to do that."

"Good. See Ned. He'll take care of everything. He'll also give you a bit of history on that boy's name, so you know why. After you talk to Ned, go get packed. We're sending you home. And when you go out, send in your friend, Dwight."

"I...I don't know how to thank you, Mr. President."

"David, I've just spent the last half-hour trying to thank *you*."

Dickson ~31 Hours after Flyby

"Come in, Dwight. Have a seat."

"Thanks, Mr. President."

"My granddaughter tells me that you have hopes of attending medical school."

"That's right, Sir."

"What school do you plan to attend?"

"Well, Sir, that's the problem. My family, we don't have much money, see. So I'm gonna have to find work and save." He looked up, "I've already got enough saved for junior college." He smiled, "Unless I want to, like, you know, eat every day."

"I understand you have a friend who's currently taking pre-med classes."

"Uh, yes, Sir. We talked about being roommates if things worked out. Only, it don't look like things are working out exactly like we planned."

"What if I could help get that plan back on track?"

"I–I don't understand..."

"Mr. James, I think you'll make an awesome physician. I have an acquaintance at a highly-rated medical school in Michigan. I think that is where your friend is attending, is it not?"

"Uh, yeah. That's where he is."

Dickson handed over a sheet of paper. It was a letter on White House letterhead, signed by the President. "You take that to the person it's addressed to. If you agree to spend two years treating the underprivileged in an inner-city area, she will make you a doctor, all educational expenses paid. Will that help?"

Dwight stared silently at the paper for a moment. Then he wiped his eyes. He stared at the letter again, then up at the President. "Yes, Sir. This will help. Yes, yes, it will."

"You'll also have living expenses. I told my new science advisor, Dr. Ted Lang, about you. He has agreed to pay your housing and living expenses with one proviso. Well, actually two."

"Yes Sir?"

"When you've begun your medical practice and have become as successful as we think you're going to be, Dr. Lang wants you to pay it forward; help fund another young man or woman who needs help achieving their dreams. Can you do that?"

"Can I? Mr. President, you can tell Mr. Lang that I will make him proud, yes Sir. What's the second requirement?"

"Lang is calling this the Jarad Bonner Memorial Grant. He wants you to remember that. And when you pay his kindness forward, keep that name on as part of the grant. Does that sound agreeable?

"I would be happy to do that, Mr. President. Thank you, Sir."

"Good. Before you leave, see Ned. He'll enter a number on your phone, a direct line to Dr. Lang. If you ever need help, or anything else, ring him up. Those are his words. Got it?"

This time, Dwight's grin was too wide for his face to hold it. "I got it, Mr. President. I surely got it."

"Good. Now go pack and send in my granddaughter."

Dickson ~32 Hours after Flyby

"Come in, Sammy. Have a seat." Dickson told his granddaughter what he had done for David and Dwight.

"Thank you, Grandfather. You don't know how happy that makes me. I don't have a lot of good, close friends at school. David and Dwight are guys I can count on. I just hope you're not too upset at me for blowing my cover."

"Never, my sweet. But how about you, my child? Mad at me for steering David in your direction?"

Samantha giggled. "Would I be mad for you sending an ice cream cone in my direction? Not at all."

"He's a bit high strung, so you're going to have to teach him to relax a little."

Samantha looked embarrassed, then grinned. "Don't worry, Grandfather, I know a few ways to help him relax. When I get through with him, he'll be the most relaxed boy you've ever seen."

The President laughed. "You also need to help him realize that he's a brilliant young man. He's so focused on using what he knows that he doesn't realize how much he actually does know. And you, young lady. You are no slouch in the brains department either. Remember that."

"I will, Grandfather."

"Good." He stood and gave the girl a hug. "Now go pack. When you get home, say hello to your Mom for me. And tell that Stepfather of yours if he votes against me again in the next election, I'll have his butt audited with a microscope."

They both laughed, and Sam kissed the President on the cheek.

Rylee and Kylie ~3 Days after Flyby

Several days after the asteroids had passed, the Russian craft made an unprecedented landing in California at Edwards Air Force Base, North of Los Angeles at the Western edge of the Mojave Desert. The capsule actually came to rest near North Edwards at just before 8 a.m. It took fifteen minutes for recovery vehicles to reach the craft. By that time, the astronauts had the hatch open and the returnees were strolling around the capsule, enjoying the fresh air, warm sun, and gravity.

Rylee, with her camera and the damaged window, was whisked via helicopter to Vandenberg Air Force Base on the West Coast just north of Lompoc.

The copter landed near the Y-shaped research facility, and she was met by the Base Commander, General Abe Matheson. "Welcome back to Earth, Lieutenant."

Rylee set down her camera case and a backpack and saluted. "Good to be back, Sir."

"Let's get you inside out of the sun where you can freshen up and we can start looking at your goodies."

"Thank you, Sir."

Half-an-hour later, Rylee felt much better, and really clean for the first time in several weeks. She joined an Air Force technician who was downloading her high-speed capture. The window and metal object had been taken to another part of the facility for analysis.

Twenty minutes later, a large group of base officers had gathered at a viewing room. The lights darkened and Rylee's capture was played for the first time.

The initial run was at the full 2500 fps and did not show much. The same flashes Rylee had seen, and a brief view of the asteroids. The second run was at half speed which showed a bit more. The third run at 120 fps had slowed the images enough to see the first asteroid tumbling as it shot past 500 miles from the station, and it flared brighter as it rounded the Earth just before it passed out of the camera's range. The second asteroid was more interesting. A blur came at the asteroid from the lower right. The impact caused the white flash those on the station had noticed. After the flash, the asteroid was broken into rubble. The object that had impacted it was gone. Seven or eight seconds later, a fragment grew and embedded itself in the window.

The lights came on, and the personnel gave Rylee a loud round of applause.

"Good job, Lieutenant," General Matheson said. "I think we're going to get a lot of answers from that footage."

"Thank you, General."

"Come with me, then. I've got a couple of surprises for you." Rylee elevated an eyebrow in question. She followed the General to the other side of the "Y" where the labs were located. He held the door while Rylee entered a large room with a group of people in white lab coats who were bent over something on a table.

They straightened and several saluted as the General and Rylee approached.

"Dr. Carson," the General said to a tall White man with a substantial gray beard, "learn anything yet?"

Carson pointed to the metal object that had been embedded in the station's window. "Very interesting, General. Virginia Moore, here," he pointed to a short, stocky African-American woman, "has analyzed the material. It's like nothing we've seen before. It's definitely manufactured, and absolutely not from Earth."

Moore held up the piece. She spoke with a slight accent, "I would normally categorize this as a form of carbon fiber, but I think it might be more apt to call it a multi-twisted multi-layer graphene, with sub-microscopic properties that I've as yet been unable to quantify."

"So what are you saying, in English, Dr. Moore?"

"General," Moore said, "this is something we've never seen before. We could not duplicate it. Yet, it was created. It is definitely a piece of a larger structure. Of that I am sure."

Matheson looked at Rylee. "That's a highbrow way of saying you were hit with a piece of an alien spaceship."

Rylee was silent but nodded. "I'd reached that conclusion as well. Nice to know I wasn't imagining it." She turned to Moore, "Can I touch it?"

"Go ahead," Moore said, smiling, "you cannot possibly damage it."

The metal was hard, unyielding. It was warm to the touch, but she suspected it was reflected heat from her fingers.

"Watch," Moore said, taking the object from Rylee. She tried to bend the metal with no effect. Then he placed it on the table and gently stroked it and the metal arched a centimeter or perhaps a little less. "Rigid when you need it, and slightly pliable otherwise. Amazing." She looked up at Carson, "We need to know how to make this stuff."

"Come along, Lieutenant," General Matheson said, "let's leave these people to their exploration. There's one more surprise."

The General led Rylee to the building's main entrance. There, waiting, were the other members of her family; Dad, Mom, and Kylie. All three of them surrounded her. She was determined not to cry. Naval officers weren't supposed to cry when in uniform. She almost succeeded.

After greetings, Kylie pulled her outside the building so they could talk privately.

"So what happened? What's this news you and Dad hinted at?"

Kylie shook her head. "You'll need to ask Dad. He can tell you all about it. I just want you to know how happy I am to see you."

"Well, that's a first."

Kylie laughed. "Things have changed since you left."

"You mean you're no longer a twirling sack of..."

Kylie laughed and pulled her sister into a hug.

"You really have changed."

Kylie stopped smiling. "I got myself into some trouble." She held up a hand, "You'll have to talk to Dad about it. But it turned out to be the best thing that could have happened to me. And things are even better, because yesterday I started my period."

"But you have those like, once a month."

"Yeah, but this was an important one."

Rylee opened her mouth.

"You'll have to talk to Dad. But they caught them, all of them. They're all in jail. And I'm going to step up in court and testify at each trial. I'm gonna stare at each one so they know I'm the reason they're going to prison."

"What...?"

"You'll..."

"I know, I know. I'll need to talk to Dad."

Kylie smiled and nodded.

"So when do we get to see your photos?"

"Not sure. Right now they're classified. But I don't think that will last for long."

Kylie said nothing, but she hugged her sister again. Rylee hesitated for a moment before returning the hug. "Welcome home, big sister," Kylie whispered, "I've been gone a long, long time."

Lang and Ford ~4 Days after Flyby

"Dr. Lang, can you tell us exactly what happened when the asteroids passed near Earth?"

"We may never know exactly what happened, Ms. Ford. Once we discovered there were actually two asteroids, things changed. There was a high probability that the second object would dip low enough to be captured by Earth's gravity field."

"But that didn't happen. Why?"

Lang shrugged. "Both asteroids were traveling at a very high rate of speed, in relation to Earth. Our calculations showed that the second object had a good chance of being captured by Earth's gravity field, but fortunately, it did not."

"Why not?"

That shrug again. "As I said, we may never know. What we do know is that upon closest approach, the second asteroid exploded. Some of the smaller pieces actually entered our atmosphere and were burned up. There is a possibility that one or two larger chunks actually impacted our planet, but they weren't big enough to do extensive damage. No major damage at all so far as we have been able to determine. Whatever pieces hit did not impact populated areas."

"Good enough, Doctor. But what caused the second object to explode?"

A third shrug. Ford glanced at her engineer and wondered.

"One possible explanation is that the asteroid had interior gasses that became heated as it passed through our upper atmosphere. As the gasses heated, they expanded, and finally blew the object apart."

"And then there is that brilliant flash," Ford said.

"Yes, there is that flash."

"Do you have an explanation?"

Fourth shrug. "Not at this time."

"What about the alien spacecraft seen near the objects?"

"If there ever was such an object, it has disappeared."

"I've heard reports that the alien craft was responsible for the destruction of the second object."

"I've heard those reports too," Lang said.

"And...?"

"We're looking into it, but so far there is no conclusive data either way."

"Why is it taking so long to assess what happened?" Ford said.

"You have to understand. Those asteroids approached Earth at about 80.5 thousand kilometers per hour, about 50,000 miles per hour. Even attempting to track something at that velocity coming almost directly toward us is a very, very difficult task. I'm sure you understand. We have a mountain of data to assess and study. We'd like to think that data contains the answers we're looking for."

"This is Marsha Ford. I've been talking to Ted Lang, a Professor of Astrophysics and President Dickson's newly

appointed science advisor. Thank you for your time, Dr. Lang."
After a pause, she said, "Okay, let's do the exit."

"Hold on, Marsha," her engineer said, "we've got another report coming in."

"I'll do the exit later, then. Dr. Lang, thank you for speaking with me." She turned away and glared at her engineer. "Okay, what's this report?"

Lang and Rylee ~4 Days after Flyby

After his interview with Ford, Ted Lang entered a meeting room in the White House. Waiting for him was a Navy Lieutenant who had flown in from the West coast. She was currently bent over a large case. "Hello," he said, "I'm Ted Lang, President Dickson's science advisor."

Rylee turned and stood. They stared at each other for a long moment. "Yes, Dr. Lang. I was told to deliver this to you soonest." She turned again to the case and flipped the latches. The locks had already been removed. Inside was a large camera and a piece of metal.

"Thank you," Lang said. They smiled at each other. "I would appreciate it if you could provide me with all the background information regarding the photographic data and the fragment."

"I would be happy to do so, Sir."

"Call me Ted. I'm kind of new at this job." He chuckled. "In reality, I'm kind of new at everything here. So I don't know if it's appropriate, but I'd love it if I could hear your story over dinner this evening."

"I'm sorry, Dr. Lang...Ted. I don't know the customs of D.C. either. So I'm just going to have to rely on my gut instincts."

"You mean...?"

"I'd love to have dinner with you this evening."

Lang smiled.

Cranston ~ 5 Days after Flyby

"Mom! I'm home!" David walked through the door, but didn't see or hear anyone. He looked back to the street and waved at the agents who had dropped him off. They waved back and drove away.

Getting home had taken a bit longer than he expected. President Dickson, acting on advice of his closest advisor, Samantha's grandmother, sent the three teens to Orlando, Florida for a couple of days to visit the theme parks. All three had enjoyed the warm weather and the thrills.

Dwight let everybody know he could get used to enjoying the various entertainment opportunities in Orlando.

David dragged his travel bag down the stairs and unpacked.

Ten minutes later, he heard the front door slam. He ran back up the stairs and saw his mom and blubbo-butt carrying in bags of groceries.

He heard his mom complaining. "Next time you make goo goo eyes at a teenage cheerleader, Biff, I'm going to shove a can of lima bean up your nether regions."

"C'mon, Babe. I'm a guy. I can't help myself."

"Well, well, well," his Mom said as she entered the kitchen, "the wandering moron has reappeared." She set her bag on the kitchen table. "Where in the hell have you been?"

"As I told you, Washington, D.C.," he said, smiling.

Biff said nothing. His glare, however, was intense.

"For what purpose?"

"I was visiting with the President," David said slowly.

"The President of *what?*" Janet shrilled.

"I believe Troy is President of the United States."

"Troy?"

"Troy Dickson. You've heard of him, right?"

"I've heard of him," Biff said. "What an idiot."

"Coming from you, Biff," David said, "that's quite a compliment."

"So, if you're not lying through your teeth, *why* were you talking to the President," Mom asked.

"He needed some advice, so he had Samantha, Dwight, and me over to the White House."

Biff shook his head. "You went there with that queer n..."

"Go ahead," David said, "finish your sentence. My phone is recording everything. You'll be a sensation on social media before dinner time. Go ahead. Say it. I dare you."

Biff replied, using a different word that made David chuckle.

"Oh, and Mom, after I graduate high school, I'll be moving to California."

Janet laughed. "Dream on, Sonny Boy. You haven't got enough money to reach the end of the block."

David smiled. "Well, what I do have is a full scholarship and living expenses paid, Mommy Dear. In two months, I am so out of here."

Janet looked at Biff. "I think he's delusional."

"Don't worry about it, Mom. Delusional or not, I'll soon be gone. Then you can bring in your foster kids to abuse. CPS might have something to say about that, though, after I tell them about your nefarious plan."

Biff chuckled, then glanced quickly at Janet. "You don't even recognize a joke when you hear one, Sewer Brain."

"Uh-huh, right. Just a joke," David said. "I'm off. I'll be back later."

"You're grounded, young man. You forget that?"

"I've suspended it," David said, grabbing his jacket and heading for the door.

"You go out that door, I'm calling the cops. You'll spend the night in juvie..."

"Go ahead, Mom. You call your cops. I'll call my friend Troy. We'll see who carries the biggest bat." He slammed the door on his way out.

Ford ~4 Days after Flyby

"Okay, Tito, what's in this important report you called me about in the middle of a damn interview?"

"Nothing much, Marsha. Just that two boys in Norway a couple of hours ago found some burnt debris. A pretty big piece. Some kind of metal, very slightly curved metal. Preliminary reports indicate it's of an unknown kind of alloy. Scientists there say it resembles a form of twisted bilayer graphene."

"Yeah, well whatever that means."

"What it means, Ms. Ford, is that the metal is probably from the alien spacecraft. It's not from Earth. And there's a 'leaked' video on social media that shows that the second asteroid was hit by the alien ship at a very high velocity."

"So you're saying the only way they could stop the asteroid was to run into it?"

"That seems to be the case."

"So they gave up their lives...to save us?"

"That's up for interpretation, but, yeah, that's the way it looks. We're alive today because of some little green, uh, people."

The line was silent for a long moment.

"Damn," she said sincerely, but very softly. "Okay, I'll get on that story first thing tomorrow, Tito."

"I'd rather you started now. This going to be big."

"Sorry, Boss. It'll still be big tomorrow. I've got two little girls to pick up. Then I'm gonna take them home and hug them, and hug them, and hug them, and hug..." She found herself leaking tears. She hung up, dried her eyes, then called an Uber. She couldn't wait, could not wait. When she got her arms around Ana and Cherise, she was never going to let go. Never, never.

Later that evening, after the girls had been well hugged and had gone to bed, she received another phone call. An unexpected one. "Hey, Honey, it's me. It's Todd."

"Todd! I thought I recognized that voice. How are you?"

"I'm...fine. Look, I'm thinking of coming home."

"That would be great!"

"Yeah. But this time, I'm thinking of hanging around for a while. You know, like, maybe permanently." Ford remained silent, but a smile hung itself on her face.

"I'm not drinking any more."

"I heard."

"Yeah. And I've kind of given up most of that dangerous stuff too." He laughed. "I'm older now. I've been investing in the stock market. Been doing pretty good, too."

"I'm happy to hear that, Todd."

"Honey? Is it okay if I come home? It's kind of lonely out here..."

"You're such a putz, Ford." She was silent again. "Of course you can come home. There are three beautiful girls here who can't wait for you to come home."

"Wait. What? We only have two kids."

"Shut up! What a jerk."

Todd laughed. She loved his laugh. She hadn't realized it, but she was starved for that laugh.

"Thank you, Marsh. Thank you. I had to make sure it was okay. I didn't want to impose."

"Impose? Are you kidding! Not at all. You belong here, this is your home. Honey, you get your butt home as fast as you can. We got a whole boatload of hugs and kisses saved up for you."

"I'm on my way. I'm on my way." He hung up. Marsha had to wipe away tears again.

Dunbar and Ford ~ 6 Days after Flyby

"This is Marsha Ford speaking with Pastor Danny Dunbar, well-known speaker and author of several books on religion and God. Pastor Dunbar, what do you make of the asteroid and alien controversy? Some say the aliens gave their lives to save us. Some say they never existed at all, that we were just lucky. Others contend they directed the asteroids toward Earth, then something went wrong and they were killed attempting to shove one of the rocks into Earth's gravity field. Your thoughts?"

Dunbar smiled. "I firmly believe it's the former, Marsha. I've said this many times before, and discussed it in my new book. Earth is the center of the universe, and it is also the pit of all evil. Only our unique connection with God gives us hope. Every other living being in the universe is a stranger to evil, so the aliens could not have had evil intentions. Satan rebelled against God, and the Light Bearer's revolt in Heaven caused the universe to happen. Earth was created to confine Satan and evil. Humans, men and women, were created to maintain a connection with the Almighty amid that evil until the end of time, when Satan and his evil followers will be called into account, and then purged from the universe. Those few humans who have maintained that connection to God will join with all the other species in the universe who have never known evil. We will join them with the unique advantage of having known evil and overcome it. God will reward us as foot soldiers against that evil, a battle that will close very soon."

"Bold words, Pastor. By destroying the second asteroid, the aliens have sent us a message. Can you define that message in just one sentence?"

"Marsha, I can define it in one word. That word is 'love.' Without knowing us, without ever seeing us, they loved us. So it wasn't just a single message they sent us. It was four: We are not alone in the universe; there is life someplace besides Earth; some of that life is intelligent, and they have confirmed that love is the universal language."

"I have been told by reliable sources that a message consisting of the value of pi, which is essentially an infinite number, was sent to the aliens in hopes they would interpret the string as equivalent to love. Your assessment?"

"It isn't an infinite number, Ms. Ford. It is the relationship of the circumference of a circle to its diameter. Since the universe is globular, the ultimate indisputable value of pi defines the universe. When that final value is reached, there is no longer a need for the universe to exist. God takes over and returns everything to zero. That value defines God, it defines love, and it defines the entire universe. In the beginning, in the end, Alpha and Omega, God is love, 3.14159..."

"That's a lot of answers, Pastor."

"Indeed. You want mathematical proof? There it is: God is love."

Cranston ~14 Days after Flyby

David met his friends at the coffee shop before school. Samantha kissed him when he arrived. Dwight did not.

"You saw the news?" David asked. "They recovered more pieces of the alien spacecraft."

The other two nodded.

"They sacrificed themselves to save us. It breaks me up every time I think about it. It hurts deep in my soul, thinking about what they did."

"They were noble creatures," Dwight said softly.

"I can't help but think I was partially responsible for that. If Earth hadn't sent my message, they might still be alive."

"Yeah, but we wouldn't," Dwight said.

David half smiled, but still looked sad. "Well, yeah, there is that."

Samantha knelt beside David's chair and gave him a silent hug, holding onto him, giving him strength. "They've given us an example to live up to," she said softly.

"I would love to have met them," David said, looking up at the ceiling as if he could see through it, and up, high up into the far reaches of space. "I wonder if they looked like us, or if they looked like something we can't even imagine."

"Someday we'll know," Sam said, standing. "More of them will arrive someday; they'll want to know what happened." She smiled at him, her blue eyes shining. "And I hope you're the one who gets to meet them. You're perfect for the job."

David stood and hugged Samantha, then kissed her.

"Onward and upward, Dudes," Dwight said, "our diplomas are calling to us."

David grinned, still holding Samantha's hand. "Yeah, I guess we got to go do our high school thing. One more month."

The three of them started for the door, then David stopped abruptly and pulled his phone out. He stared at it, not moving.

"David?" Samantha asked.

The device was making noises. Dots, dashes, and spaces, followed by a series of numbers.

3.141592653589793238....

About the Author

Mark West is the fiction-writing pen name for a best-selling non-fiction author. To date, he has written and published:

Inanna and the Giant – An unprecedented look into our world 12,000 years ago, when Inanna, a young woman and member of a primitive hunter-gatherer tribe meets Ogenus, citizen of a city so advanced, its inhabitants were called Giants. Join the adventure as Inanna and Ogenus come together to face an unimaginable threat to their ways of life.

The Last Barbarian – Morak is a Barbarian and proud of it. He live in the desert land of Karan. A chance encounter leads him to the legendary Tome of the Dark Devices which, if he is lucky, will make him rich. His quest doesn't go well, however, as powerful forces are determined to get their hands on the book. Morak is taken from a land of swords and scorcery, and finds himself facing an alien threat that robs him of his homeland. He is The Last Barbarian.

Both of these books are available from Amazon in print or as Kindle e-books. Get your copy today!

Also by MinRef Press:

Majesty Blake in Queen of the Trillis by Rick Lawler
Way to Much Fun by Neil L. Knoblock and Rick Lawler

www.minref.com
minref@gmail.com

If you have read this book, we would appreciate a review on Amazon.com. Thank you!

Made in the USA
Middletown, DE
30 October 2020

23038185R00139